Feral Bonds

Reforming the Paranormal Council

Book Two

Feral Bonds

Reforming the Paranormal Council

Book Two

Written by Sheri Eleese

First Edition November 2020
Second Printing July 2022
ISBN 978-1-7773217-3-4

Cover Design:
SelfPubBookCovers.com/Joetherasakdhi

Table of Contents

Acknowledgements

A big thank you to my awesome readers. Your support and encouragement make this amazing journey a whole lot of fun.

Mom, your continued encouragement, with helpful feedback, is really appreciated. As is your willingness to always answer the phone. Lol. The craziness will probably continue for some time so keep that phone close by. I guarantee I'll be calling.

Jeremy, thanks for the brainstorming session on how to make my idea come together logically. I hope you like how it all turned out.

A special thanks to my husband, Mike, who has been 110% supportive from the first moment he found out what I was up to. While he may not understand why I write what I do, that doesn't deter him in his efforts to spread the word to everyone he knows.

To Lynn, Ashely, and Angela. Thank you again for your enthusiasm in beta testing the manuscript. You provided incredibly helpful feedback, nailing some key elements that really needed to be corrected. I appreciate you making me look good.

Thanks also to all my friends and family who continue to show their support. Hugs to every one of you.

Prologue

The concrete floor bit into his skin when they forced him to his knees and yanked his back.

"Please. I didn't do anything. You have to let me go." He struggled, pulling fruitlessly against the hands holding him captive. He glared at those standing as judge and jury and saw only condemnation in their eyes. "Why are you doing this? It goes against all of our laws."

The one in charge gestured. The guard behind him slammed a fist into his head before he was hauled to his feet and his arms pinned behind his back.

Blinking through the spots clouding his vision, he squinted at the ones before him. "You'll regret treating me this way."

The cold, emotionless voice that responded sent chills up his spine. "We will regret nothing."

"When I get out, my brother will make you pay for what you're doing to me."

"You seem to be under the mistaken belief we will let you go." A gaze filled with revulsion and — was that triumph? — locked on him.

His efforts to escape increased when he realized he would find no mercy in this place.

The detached voice continued, a spark of hate pushing its way past the coldness. "You will never see the light of day again, wolf."

"But I did nothing wrong." His shout fell on deaf ears.

"Take him away," another harsh voice said.

"Stop! You can't do this. This isn't right." His protests echoed around the chamber as he was dragged from the room.

Deep within the bowels of the earth, imprisoned in a long-forgotten cage, a body threw itself unceasingly against rusted iron bars, howling its torment and fury into the never-ending darkness.

Chapter One

Edgar stepped into the room, then froze, wondering if there was any possibility of him backing out without anyone noticing, then winced when the chaotic noise hit his sensitive ears. His gaze landed on Jinx in the center of the room, his tail lashing as he growled and hissed at Roman. The vampire Prince of North America ignored him as he juggled a wriggly screaming baby in one arm and held his laughing mate, Lysander, in the other.

Deciding to take the chance, Edgar began edging backward, stopping with an oof when he bumped into a body behind him.

Roman looked over and smiled. "Edgar. Max. You're just in time. One of you come and take Nico from me." He held out the baby.

Max laughed, pushing his way past Edgar. "Not a chance. Get Edgar to take him."

Edgar stepped sideways along the wall, shaking his head and holding his hands in front of him. "No. No babies. Not even for you, Prince Roman."

"Roman, you promised to talk to them about that." Lysander raised his eyebrow at his mate, who smiled before dropping a quick kiss on his forehead.

"I was just about to do that, beloved." Roman turned to Max and Edgar. "We have decided there is no need to address us formally when we are in our private quarters as we want to set a familial tone in our home. In this space, we are friends and family on a first-name basis."

"If you insist, Prin—" Edgar's eyes darted over to Lysander, who raised an eyebrow. "I mean Roman." This would take some getting used to. There had been far too many changes since Lysander had come around.

Lysander patted Roman's chest. "I'll go heat up Nico's bottle while you can change him." Lysander walked from the room, calling out to Jinx. Taking one last swipe at Roman, the cat strutted from the room, following the promise of food.

Edgar frowned when Roman gazed fondly after his mate. He still didn't understand it. Roman had always been strong and ruthless. Why did he turn into a ball of mush around his mate and let him do whatever he wanted? Edgar was still on the fence about whether this was a change for the better or not. The only thing he knew for sure was that he was busier than ever looking after Roman's business interests. Ever since his mating and fatherhood, Roman had been neglecting the management of his companies. Enough so, that Edgar had needed to take over to keep everything running smoothly.

As Roman went to change Nico, Edgar tilted his head, confusion growing when Roman laid the squalling baby down on some kind of small table with side rails and fastened a strap around his waist. Surely all of that wasn't necessary just to change a baby? It wasn't like Nico was going to fly away.

Roman unfastened the tape and pulled the diaper away. Edgar almost swallowed his tongue as a stream of liquid arced through the air, spraying down the front of Roman's best Armani suit. He choked on his breath and made his eyes as big as possible so that he wouldn't laugh and draw his Prince's ire.

Max, obviously not caring, broke out into loud, booming laughter.

"Nico, why must you do that every time?" Roman shook his head at his son, patting his suit dry with some kind of cloth. "This is not how we treat Armani."

"I told you to put on different clothes. Maybe those jeans I got you." Lysander's voice floated from the kitchen.

Roman shuddered at the word jeans. Grimacing at the mess on his clothes, Roman glared at Max. "Do you mind?"

"No. Not at all." Max grinned, elbowing Edgar. "We're going to stand back here, out of the line of fire, and watch the mighty vampire Prince get bested by a seven-pound tadpole." He snickered.

Edgar quickly turned to face the wall, shoulders twitching as he struggled to control himself. It was a losing battle. He collapsed against the wall, laughing uncontrollably.

"If you are both are quite done, I could use a hand here."

Edgar just pressed his forehead hard against the wall, laughing too hard to speak, and flapped his hand behind him.

"For the love of—" Lysander pushed Roman out of the way, handing him the baby bottle. "Let me finish this." He snorted. "Big scary vampires, my ass. If only your enemies could see the three of you now." He shook his head in disgust. "I have the baby." He pointed at Roman. "You go talk to them."

Roman grinned at his mate, not put out in the slightest by his order.

Edgar leaned against the wall, catching his breath as he studied Lysander. The dynamics of his relationship with Roman was so confusing. He understood intellectually about fated mates. He even realized there was a strong pull and a driving need to care for your mate. What he didn't understand was why Roman doted on Lysander, whose bossy, snarky personality was rather annoying. At least, it was to him.

"Max, Edgar, please have a seat." Roman pointed to the couch as he sat on the loveseat angled next to it.

Sitting, Edgar watched Lysander confidently change the baby. In short order, the Consort was sitting by his mate, the freshly changed baby cradled in his arms grunting and drinking noisily from his bottle. Really noisily, like a starving lion. Edgar leaned forward to see if the baby was turning into some kind of animal. "Is it supposed to be that loud?"

Lysander chuckled. "He's a baby, not an it. And yes, Nico always drinks like it's going to be his last meal. Sometimes it's all I can do to hold onto the bottle." He smiled fondly down at his son. "I'm starting to wonder if he's part bear."

"Or lion," Edgar muttered.

"Is there such a thing as a bear shifter?" Max asked.

Roman shrugged, "Not that I've ever heard. However, that doesn't mean they don't exist. Wolves are not the only shifters in existence. I have met one or two others in the course of my life."

Edgar interrupted, not wanting to waste any more time talking about shifters. "Roman, why did you call us here?"

"Ah Edgar, my ever-efficient assistant. Always wanting to get right to business." Roman smiled at him.

Uh oh. He knew that smile. Edgar braced himself for whatever was coming.

"There are a couple of things we wanted to discuss with the two of you. The first is to let you know we have decided we will not be moving back into the suite at Darkness. We will instead continue to live here at the mansion."

"What?" Edgar exclaimed. "But your coven. Your businesses." He shook his head. "I don't understand. You need to be there to look after everything."

Lysander spoke up. "With our enemies running around free, we have to make sure Nico is well protected. The mansion's safeguards and shielding will do a better job of keeping him safe than living above a club will." Lysander raised his eyebrow at Roman. "Never mind the fact that over a club is not the best place to raise a child."

Roman nodded and smiled down at the baby, running his fingers over Nico's head before gently tapping his nose. "Agreed. It is not the lifestyle he should be introduced to at this young age."

"Or any age," Lysander muttered.

"Who's going to live in the suite then?" Edgar asked.

Roman looked up from the baby. "That brings me to the next item I wanted to discuss. Max, I will need you to take on a greater role in leading the coven. My loyalties are conflicted between my home life and finding the required time to care for our vampires. Both are suffering from my lack of attention. I know I can trust you to take care of the coven on my behalf." Roman arched his eyebrow at Max. "But do not take this to mean I expect you to handle everything on your own. I expect you to come to me for assistance if necessary."

"Of course. I won't let you down."

Roman leaned over, placing his hand on Max's shoulder. "I know you will not. Your loyalty and friendship mean the world to me." He sat back. "Now, in answer to

Edgar's question, I think it would be best if Max stayed in the suite. Once the coven moves back into Darkness, Max should be on hand to look after any situations that arise."

"I'll make arrangements to move in once it's safe for us to do so," Max said.

"Thank you, Max."

Edgar braced himself when Roman turned toward him, a serious expression on his face.

"Edgar, I need you to take on greater responsibility for the business end of things. I know you are more than capable. Sometimes I feel like I only get in your way."

Edgar nodded. That was a true statement. And really, he was already doing that. It was only another sign of Roman's distraction that he hadn't realized it yet.

"I have one further request to make of you. I need your assistance to deal with the captured vampires. They've been under guard in the security holding cell for the last couple of weeks. However, as the situation with the Elders could continue for some time, keeping them there is not a practical long-term solution. Bryan has suggested we make use of the dungeons under the Council building."

Edgar nodded. "That would be a more secure place to hold them."

"I am glad you agree. I need someone I trust to take care of transferring them." Roman looked pointedly at Edgar.

"You're asking me? Has mating with the Consort affected your mind?" He ignored Lysander's snort. "You know I only deal with administrative responsibilities. I do not go on field expeditions." Edgar could tell by the look on Roman's face he was going to insist on this. But that didn't stop him from trying to get out of it. "Surely one of your enforcers would be the better choice to look after transferring the prisoners."

"Edgar." He turned to Lysander. "The more Bryan teaches me about controlling and using my magic, the more my powers evolve. The latest development is that I seem to be gaining powers of premonition."

"Okay, but what does that have to do with me?"

Lysander gave him an apologetic look. "It's telling me you need to be present when the vampires are relocated."

"And as you are one of the few whom I trust implicitly," Roman said, drawing Edgar's attention back to him, "it only makes sense to put you in charge of the transfer."

Edgar squinted at Lysander. "Is this for real or are you just looking for an excuse to get me out of the way?"

"It's like you forget we have a truce," Lysander said, rolling his eyes. "I have no reason to get rid of you. My magic says you need to do this. I don't know why, just that if you aren't there, there will be far-reaching consequences that will bring chaos to the world."

Edgar blinked. That didn't sound good. Not one bit.

* * *

Edgar did a final check of the vampire prisoners, ensuring all of them were securely strapped in the vehicles. The cavalcade of Escalades would depart from the mansion's underground garage as soon as the sun rose, one of the safety measures Roman and Max had insisted on. Between two enforcers and a magic user to every vehicle, spelled manacles the vampires couldn't get out of, and the sun which would prevent them from running on the off chance they did manage to overpower the enforcers, the vampire prisoners had few options for escape.

"Everything looks good to go," Edgar said to Bryan as he opened the door of the last vehicle in line.

"Good job." Bryan smacked the roof of the car. "See you on the other side." He walked down the line and got into the lead vehicle, which began driving up the exit ramp the moment his door closed. As the remaining vehicles fell in behind, Edgar settled in for the long ride across the city.

Shortly after their vehicle got underway, the vampire sitting behind him began kicking his seat and hissing at him.

"You will not hold us prisoner much longer. You will all die when our Master comes for us. You are weak American vampires, who have forgotten your roots. I will laugh when I pull your heart from your chest and eat it slowly in front of your dying eyes."

The rest of the prisoners laughed.

Edgar turned to Bruno, who was driving. "Wasn't this guy one of the first vampires to submit to Roman during the battle at the mansion?" At Bruno's nod, Edgar turned his head to look at the vampire seated behind him. "If you're an example of the strength of your Master, I think we'll be fine. The lot of you didn't present much of a challenge to us in battle."

Edgar turned forward, holding back a smile when a chorus of loud hissing and dark threats came from the prisoners. But when the idiot behind him kicked his seat one time too many, Edgar turned around again and glared over the seat, his long-drawn-out hiss enough to stop him.

He faced forward again, ignoring the angry muttering behind him for the remainder of the ride to the Council grounds. He wasn't worried about a handful of poorly trained and overconfident vampires. No, Edgar was far more worried about why the Consort had been insistent on him taking charge of them.

The rest of the vehicles had parked by the time their Escalade came to a stop in the underground parking garage, all of the enforcers standing by the passenger doors, ready to escort the prisoners to their new home. Edgar exited the SUV, straightening his tie as he waited for Bryan to reach him.

"Edgar, I want you to stay back with everyone while I take a look around to ensure there aren't any nasty surprises waiting for us. The building was secured, so I don't expect there to be any problems, but with the Elders involved it's always best to be sure."

"Sure. We'll wait here until you give us the all clear." Edgar put his hands in his pockets and leaned against the SUV, pretending not to hear the yelling and banging coming from inside the vehicle.

Bryan raised his eyebrow. "Problems?"

"No. Everything's fine here. Go do your thing. I want to get these traitors behind bars as soon as possible." This place gives me the creeps."

Bryan stilled. "Do you sense something?"

Edgar reached out but couldn't find anything to explain what he was feeling. "No. Not really. Except…I can almost sense something, but not quite." He shook his head. "Whatever it was, it's gone now."

"Hmm." Bryan looked around. "Could someone be shielding themselves?"

Edgar shrugged. "Maybe. I can usually tell though."

"Well, keep your eyes sharp while I check everything out. I'll try to be as quick as I can."

Edgar kept one eye on Bryan as he neared the exit and the other on his surroundings. He was still surprised when a ball of fire burst through the exit, knocking the doors from their hinges. He and Bruno ducked when the flames flew over them, hitting the wall behind the vehicles.

"Damn it." Bryan leapt to the side, taking cover behind a support pillar. Who the hell was attacking them? And how had they gotten in? The place had been secured after the mansion fight.

He gestured, erecting a barrier in front of the SUVs to protect them from any further magical attacks, then peered around the pillar, not surprised when he saw Charlotte and Ruth standing where the doors used to be.

"You dare to tread foot on these hallowed grounds, young Galway?" Ruth asked.

Bryan rolled his eyes. The posturing never ended when dealing with the Elders. "I dare that and much more, Ruth. The Council has been abolished. You no longer have permission to be here. Did you not get the memo?" He ducked reflexively when a ball of flame hit the cement pillar he was hiding behind. Idiots. They had to know their attacks couldn't reach him through his personal shields.

"Bryan." Edgar's frantic yell caught his attention. Twisting to look behind him, he saw Edgar and the enforcers engaged in a fight with another group of vampires. Damn it. Where the hell had they come from?

Clancy, the magic user who rode with Edgar, was trying to help them fight off the intruders, but the vampires had closed in too quickly for him to get off a clean shot without hitting any of the enforcers.

Another ball of flame crashed against the wall behind Bryan, his mother and Ruth obviously providing a distraction to keep his focus off of the vehicles. Annoyed, he shot a fireball back at the women, trying to push them back and buy some time. He needed to even the odds as the enforcers were outnumbered. Concentrating his will, he created a wedge of air. Yelling at Clancy to move back, he drove the wedge between Clancy and the enemy vampires, knocking the majority of them away from the vehicles. He quickly adjusted his barrier, creating a dome that surrounded the vehicles, preventing the enemy vampires from closing in on the SUVs again.

The enforcers who had ended up on the wrong side of the shield quickly paired up, standing back-to-back and continued to fight, though they were slowly being overwhelmed by the greater number of opponents facing them.

"Clancy, all magic users are to shield the vehicles. Keep the prisoners secure."

"But Sir. The enforcers," Clancy shouted. "We have to help them."

Bryan ducked another fireball and saw one of Roman's vampires go down under a swarm of enemy vampires. Shit. Roman would kill him if he lost all of his enforcers.

Making quick adjustments to the magical weave of his barrier, he called out. "Clancy, you and the others start picking off the enemy. I've modified the shield to allow your shots to go through." Bryan gave a sigh of relief when enemy vampires started bursting into flames, giving breathing space to the trapped enforcers.

He turned back to the doorway and saw Ruth and Charlotte had used his distraction to close in on his position. He shot another barrage of fire at them, which bounced harmlessly off their personal shields, splashing on the walls and floor behind them.

Clancy's voice rang out behind him. "Sir, they're running away."

"Let them go," he called back. "Make sure nothing else is hiding behind the vehicles and keep those damned prisoners secure."

"I'm on it, sir."

Now that the vampires had been dealt with, it was time to put an end to the stalemate he was in with the women.

Standing, he strengthened his shield, then stepped out from behind the pillar and threw webs of power at the women. He'd been working on a special binding spell with Lysander which would wrap around a shielded magic user, trapping them within their own protective barrier. And while his spell couldn't touch them physically, it could touch their shielding, solidifying against it to prevent them from moving, as well as blocking their magic from getting past it.

He started toward them, then stopped, dumbfounded, when the weaves of his spell slowly slid off Charlotte. A quick glance showed Ruth was firmly ensnared in the magic which had immobilized her, yet Charlotte had somehow managed to escape.

She raised her hand to him, her expression gleeful as she prepared to attack. Without warning, a gust of wind came rushing through the area, sweeping Ruth and Charlotte aside with enough force they flew sideways through the open doorway. There was a loud crash and the distinctive sound of bones breaking.

Any vampires who had been standing on the wrong side of the barrier protecting the vehicles were also caught up in the wind, flying past him to crash into the parking garage wall. Bryan was flattened against the pillar next to him. He strengthened his shield some more as the wind pressed against him, pinning him to the cement column.

When the gale had finally subsided, Bryan moved away from the pillar, stepping into the open area. Frantically he looked around for the source of the magical attack but couldn't see whoever had cast it. Groaning from the injured enforcers had him rushing over to the wall and dropping to his knees, checking to see how badly they were injured.

"Clancy, Edgar, are you guys alright?" Bryan called over his shoulder.

"Yes, sir."

Bryan dropped the barrier protecting the vehicles. "Good. I could use some help over here." Footsteps pounded across the cement floor as the magic users rushed over to assist.

Clancy, slightly out of breath, spoke. "We've got this, sir. Go after them. You can't let them escape."

Nodding, Bryan got up and ran through the doorway, Edgar right on his heels, as they raced after Charlotte and Ruth. Reaching the entrance, he could see blood smears on the wall but no other signs of their quarry. Moving stealthily down the hallway, he heard groaning from one of the rooms ahead of them. Exchanging a glance with Edgar, he crept up to the doorway and ducked his head inside, barely holding back a gasp when he saw Elder Thomas half leaning against the wall, blood pouring from a multitude of wounds. After making sure the room was empty of threats, Bryan crossed over to him, wincing when he saw the ends of broken bones that had pushed through his skin. From the sound of his wet breaths, he didn't think Thomas would last long enough for help to arrive.

Kneeling by his side, Bryan pressed his fingers against his neck, barely able to feel his pulse. He'd been right in his initial assessment. Thomas was dying. And quickly. Needing answers before it was too late, Bryans asked, "What did you hope to accomplish today, Thomas?"

"Your death," Thomas wheezed, then coughed weakly, blood running down his chin. He grinned up at Bryan, blood staining his teeth. "Your time will come. Just like it did for the shifters." He coughed again, a spray of blood hitting Bryan in the chest. Then his eyes rolled back as his body sank in on itself.

"Thomas, what do you mean, the shifters? What did you do to them?" Bryan grabbed him by the shoulders, trying to shake the answer free. But it was too late.

Thomas gasped, then breathed out. He didn't breathe in again.

"Damn it, Thomas." Bryan's hands fell from him as he sat back on his heels. "What the hell did you guys do to the shifters?"

Chapter Two

Edgar stood off to the side, looking on silently, as the enforcers herded the prisoners into the iron-barred cells. Once the vampires were locked in, Bryan checked the wards on the doors, then after nodding to Edgar indicating they were secure, he stepped back.

Edgar moved over to the cells. "Everyone, put your hands through the bars." When none of the prisoners responded, Edgar turned his attention to the vampire who had kicked his seat the entire drive to the building. "Do as you're told or else you'll end up wearing the handcuffs permanently. I personally don't care if your hands rot off but Prince Roman has asked that all courtesies be extended to you." Edgar leaned in, speaking quietly. "But since he's not here, well, you know...." Edgar shrugged.

"Our Master will kill you for your treatment of us."

Edgar snorted. "I highly doubt it. He's probably already upgraded to a better model and forgotten all about you." He stepped back, raising his voice. "This is the last time I'm going to say this, so pay attention. Put your hands through the bars so we can remove the handcuffs." Edgar turned to Clancy. "Anybody who doesn't cooperate in the next sixty seconds, leave their cuffs on. I'm curious to see how long it takes for the magic to eat through their wrists."

Edgar walked over to stand next to Bryan, biting back a grin when the vampires quickly stretched their arms through the bars. When Bryan raised an eyebrow, he shrugged. "He pissed me off."

Bryan nodded. "Works for me." They both waited while Clancy and the other magic users removed the spelled cuffs. "Do we know who the vampires were that jumped us at the Council building? The one you were fighting with seemed familiar."

"What?" Edgar faced Bryan in shock. "How could you not know? Max and I dragged him over to Roman after the mansion battle."

"I was a little busy at the time, if you recall."

"Right." Edgar turned back to see the magic users had almost finished removing the cuffs from the captive vampires. "That was Carlos."

"Carlos! Damn it. I wish I'd known that. I'd have tried harder to stop him from escaping."

"I don't think there was much—"

One of the enforcers interrupted them. "Excuse me, Mage Bryan. Edgar, sir. I found something you should see." He gestured to a spot further down the passage.

Edgar straightened. "What is it, Eric?"

"A prisoner. I really need you both to come look at him." They followed the enforcer down the long row of cells. The conditions worsened the further down the passage they went. Rusted bars and mildew competed with the stench of death and decay. The darkness deepened, requiring Bryan to conjure up a glowing orb to light his way, though the darkness wasn't a problem for Eric and Edgar.

They continued walking long enough that they could no longer hear the other enforcers or the prisoners.

The further they went, the more anxious Edgar got. He was beginning to suspect that whatever they were about to see was the reason Lysander had been insistent on him delivering the prisoners. He became convinced of it when the scent of fresh blood reached his hypersensitive vampire nose and his fangs started to ache.

Eric guided them to the last cell. Standing in front of the rusted bars, the three of them looked down at one of the largest gray shifter wolves Edgar had ever seen.

The wolf was lying on its side, wheezing, its tongue lolling from its mouth. The wolf's fur was blood-encrusted, matted, and patchy in sections where the fur had been completely torn out. The chunks of fur stuck to the red-stained bars of the cell attested to the ferocity of its efforts to escape. Wild, glowing eyes looked at them distrustfully. The wolf's muzzle quivering as a weak growl rumbled from its chest.

Edgar looked closer, hissing when he saw slowly healing welts on the exposed hide. Someone had whipped the wolf severely. Many times over. His heart hurt as he cataloged all of the injuries the wolf had sustained and the gauntness of his body. It had obviously been starved, and was more than likely dehydrated in addition to everything else it had suffered.

How had they missed it when they rounded up everyone in the building weeks ago?

"Dear Goddess," Bryan whispered. "What did those bastards do to him?"

Him? Edgar looked again. Sure enough, the wolf was a male. A very finely developed male. Quite impressive, in fact. Whoa. Edgar shook his head, appalled at himself. Where had that even come from? The size of the wolf's anatomy, even if he was a shifter, should never have registered in his mind. He definitely shouldn't be ogling him.

And he wasn't the only one.

Bryan whistled beside him. "Man, he's quite the big boy."

Edgar hissed, holding onto the bars with a death grip so he didn't attack Bryan. He shook his head again. What was the matter with him?

"Edgar?"

"Give me a minute," Edgar hissed, his teeth fully elongated. In his peripheral vision, he watched Bryan slowly back away from the cell's bars. Good. His agitation decreased the further Bryan moved from the wolf. Finally managing to regain control of himself, he faced Bryan. "Sorry about that. I have no idea what came over me."

Bryan's gaze flicked over Edgar's shoulder, then back to him. "I think I do. If you give it a minute, I'm sure it'll come to you."

Edgar squinted. "What are you talking about?"

"You really don't know?"

"Not a clue. What's going on, Bryan?"

Bryan gave him a look he couldn't interpret, then shook his head. "Let's not worry about it right now. First things first. We need to get him to shift so we can find out why he's here."

"How are we supposed to do that?"

Bryan shrugged. "Maybe you should ask him."

"Me? Why should I ask him to shift?"

"Why not you?"

Edgar stared at him suspiciously. Bryan was definitely hiding something from him. "You think that'll work? If I ask him to shift?"

"It couldn't hurt to try."

Rolling his eyes, Edgar turned back to the cell, surprised to see the wolf pressed up tight against the bars. He jumped back, glaring at Bryan. "You could have warned me he was right there."

Bryan stepped closer. "He's not going to hurt you. Quite the opposite, if I'm not mistaken."

Edgar edged closer to the bars, surprised when the wolf stayed motionless, not even giving him the tiniest growl. Though the way its eyes were locked on him was a bit unnerving. Squatting in front of the wolf, Edgar felt an overwhelming desire to kill everyone involved with imprisoning and hurting his wolf.

As his words replayed in his mind, Edgar started shaking his head. No. Oh no. No, no, no. This couldn't be happening. Not to him. This would ruin everything. Edgar jumped up and bolted from the area, leaving his wolf shifter Bloodmate behind.

Bryan gaped after Edgar as he rushed off, then looked down at the wolf, who was once again lying on the floor, his head resting on his paws and his eyes locked on Edgar who was speeding down the long corridor as if his life depended on it.

"That's not quite how I expected that to go. Sorry about that." Bryan crouched in front of the wolf, cutting off his view of the fleeing vampire. "Could you try shifting so I can talk to you. I need to know why you were put in here before I can let you go." The wolf gave a weak growl. "Whatever the reason was, we'll still try to help you." Bryan stood and looked down the path, but Edgar was no longer in sight. "Besides, you can't talk to your mate until you shift."

Those seemed to be the magic words.

A few moments later, a severely injured naked man lay panting on the ground. Bryan whistled again. The man was as well-endowed as the wolf had been. He snickered at the look he was given when the man slowly started pulling himself to his feet.

"Sorry. Completely inappropriate, I know. But damn, Edgar's a lucky vampire." Bryan helped him up, then checked him over, frowning when his eyes took in all the partially healed wounds riddling his torso.

Bryan turned to the enforcer, who'd been standing quietly off to the side. "Eric, is it?"

"Yes, sir."

"See if you can round up some clothes or a blanket for him. I don't think Edgar would appreciate everyone looking at his naked mate."

"Yes, sir."

"If you can't find anything in the building, there should be something in the vehicles. Bring some water too."

"Right away, sir." Eric took off down the corridor.

Bryan focused on the wolf. "Can you tell me your name and why you're locked in this cell?"

It took a couple of moments before the shifter could work up enough spit to get his words out, his voice raspy from disuse. "Jackson. Jackson Miller."

"Good to meet you, Jackson. I'm Bryan. What can you tell me about why you were put in here?"

Jackson licked cracked lips, then struggled to get words out. "I-I don't kn-know. Nothing makes s-sense."

"Then tell me what you do know."

"I didn't…I w-wasn't…"

Seeing how difficult this was for Jackson, Bryan changed his mind. Answers could wait.

Holding up his hand, he said, "Never mind. Let's get you something to drink and some clothes first. You can tell me why you're here later." He looked him up and down. "Even though I'm sure you're normally a strong wolf, in your current condition, I'll have no problem stopping you if I'm making a mistake by letting you out."

Jackson nodded, then leaned against the bars of his cell, staring down at the floor.

Poor man. Bryan could see anguish in every line of his body. And not from being locked up. Edgar had better have a damn good reason for running away and abandoning his injured mate.

How could he have a wolf shifter for a Bloodmate? What had he ever done to the Goddess for her to punish him like this? His family would never speak to him again if they found out. What about his dreams? He had his future all planned out. And it didn't include a wolf. Why couldn't it have been another vampire? One of good breeding, who would travel the world with him to visit exotic cities and dine at the finest establishments. Someone who would know the difference between Versace and flannel. He needed a mate he could show off to his family, to impress them and rub it in their faces about how well he'd done. A mate who would prove his family had been wrong about him following Roman to America. A mate who was not an unsophisticated redneck wolf. With a wolf for a mate, he'd never be able to show his face back home or be proud to introduce him to any of his friends.

Edgar stopped dead, his inner monologue screeching to a halt. He gasped in shock at his thoughts which sounded a lot like someone he never wanted to be like.

What was he doing? He had a fated mate, a rare gift from the Goddess most vampires never found. A mate who'd been imprisoned and tortured. And instead of putting the wolf's needs first and making sure he was cared for, he'd run, thinking only of himself and how it would affect him. Roman would be so disappointed in him.

Hanging his head, Edgar trudged back the way he'd come, his mind in turmoil as he tried to figure out what he was going to do. Partway down the corridor, he ran into Bryan helping his mate walk along the pathway. He moved to assist, but Bryan waved him off. Edgar opened his mouth to argue but was cut off.

"Not now, Edgar. Let's get Jackson back to the mansion before we get into anything. I'd like the healer to look at him. He's not doing very well. With his shifter abilities, he should be healing quicker than he is."

"Jackson?"

"Yes. If you'd stuck around long enough, you'd know that." Bryan moved past him. Jackson didn't even lift his head as they continued their slow walk down the hall.

Edgar watched his mate being led away, wondering how he was going to fix the mess his moment of idiocy had created.

Jackson couldn't decide if his circumstances had improved or not. Physically they had, but being rejected by his mate might be what finally killed him. He sighed. Between being falsely imprisoned, tortured, and starved, to then finding his mate and being rejected before he'd even had a chance to speak to him, this was turning out to be one of the worst years of his life.

He came out of his thoughts when Bryan reached in front of him and opened the SUV's door. Needing his help to get into the vehicle was hard on Jackson's pride, but he was barely keeping to his feet, so didn't have much choice. Jackson sank thankfully into the soft leather seats that cushioned his aching body. Leaning back and closing his eyes, he tried to ignore his wolf spirit who was unhappy at Jackson for refusing to look at his mate. His wolf half wanted to connect with the vampire and didn't care about Jackson's pride. But Jackson couldn't forget how easily he'd been dismissed as unworthy. Now his mate would have to prove he was worth the effort before Jackson gave him another chance.

However, he couldn't help but listen in avidly to his mate's conversation with Bryan. Jackson relaxed further into his seat when the warm richness of his voice flowed over him, even if it was filled with anger.

"Just get in the car, Edgar. I need to check that there are no breaks in the shield around the building and grounds, then reinforce it before we leave. We don't want to find any more surprise guests the next time we come here."

"Are you going to look for underground tunnels this time? That might be how the vampires got the drop on us."

"Yes. Thank you for bringing that to my attention." The sarcasm in Bryan's words was pretty clear even if Jackson didn't know what they were talking about.

"You missed that before. I just want to make sure you have it covered this time."

"Edgar, I get you're upset but you're taking it out on the wrong person. I suggest you stop poking at him and get in the car before I seal you in with the vampires."

Jackson growled. The magic user had better not touch his mate.

"Fine." The car door opened. "Once you seal the building, will anybody be able to tell that the vampires are being held here?"

"No. The reinforcements I'm putting on the shield will block any kind of intrusion, physical, metaphysical, or psychical. Nobody will be able to get in or sense the vampires imprisoned inside."

"Roman will be pleased to hear that."

Jackson growled again, wondering who this Roman was. The fondness in Edgar's voice when he spoke of him did not make either him or his wolf happy.

"Great. Now get in the car so I can do this and get Jackson to the mansion's healer before he gets any worse."

"Yes, of course." Jackson felt the vehicle shift as Edgar settled in the front seat. "Are you doing okay back there?"

Jackson grunted, pretty much all he was prepared to give at this point.

"I'm sorry, Jackson. I shouldn't have run off like that."

Jackson refused to respond.

He heard Edgar sigh. "All right. I'll wait until you've had a chance to see the healer. Once you've been looked after, I'll try to explain my actions." Jackson could hear him sigh again. "Although I don't think it's going to improve your opinion of me."

Jackson shifted, wincing when pain flared throughout his entire body. He breathed deep, forcing himself to relax. By the third breath, his damaged body had finally had enough. He sank into a deep, healing sleep.

Chapter Three

Edgar stalked into Roman and Lysander's suite. "You." He pointed at Lysander. "You knew. Why didn't you warn me? Do you have any idea of how badly I messed that up? My mate may never forgive me."

Lysander grimaced. "I'm sorry, Edgar. I didn't know the details about what you would find. I just knew you needed to go."

Edgar looked at Roman. "Did you know?"

"I do not know what you are talking about. What happened today?"

"We found a wolf shifter locked in the cells when we were transferring the vampires to the Council dungeons."

"A wolf shifter. Why would they do that?" Lysander asked.

"We don't know. He was too badly injured to answer our questions so we brought him to see the healer first. Once she's done with him we'll be able to talk to him."

"A healer?" Lysander asked, brow furrowed. "But he's a wolf shifter. Why can't he heal himself?"

"The injuries he sustained are too much for his shifter abilities to handle."

"I see." Roman frowned. "Until we know why he was imprisoned, he will have to be put under guard."

"Roman," Edgar licked his lips nervously, "he's also my Bloodmate."

"That is unfortunate. I am truly sorry, Edgar."

"What are you talking about? Why are you sorry for Edgar? This is his mate. A cause for celebration. Why are you looking at me like that?" Lysander's voice got quieter with each successive question. "What's going on, Roman?"

When Roman glanced at him for permission to tell his secrets, Edgar nodded. "Edgar's family is very conservative and strong speciesists. They will never accept a wolf into the family. Or Edgar, for that matter, if he goes through with the mating. Essentially, he has to choose between his mate and his family."

"But he'll die if he doesn't accept his mate. We all know this after what nearly happened to you."

"That would be true if Edgar tried to live separate from his mate. However, if the wolf is prepared to gift Edgar with his blood, they don't actually have to complete their bond. They only need to stay near each other."

Lysander frowned. "That's hardly fair to the wolf."

"Jackson," Edgar said.

"Excuse me?" Lysander looked at him.

"His name is Jackson. And Roman is correct. My family barely accepts me now, especially when I chose to come with Roman to North America instead of staying with them."

"They're mad at you for following Roman?" Lysander's eyes flashed when Edgar nodded. "But he's a vampire Prince. His coven is wealthy. He rules over all of North America and is respected by all other coven leaders. How could they possibly find fault with any of that?"

"It's mostly because he dared to leave England to forge his own path in the Americas. As Roman said, they are very conservative and unforgiving."

Lysander shook his head. "I have no words. Well, I have words, but they're not nice."

Edgar could only imagine.

Lysander pinned him with his gaze. "You need to accept that you're going to lose your family. You have no choice but to mate with the wolf."

Edgar's back stiffened. "You don't have the right to order me around."

"That's not what this is."

"Then what is it?"

"It's a feeling I have. You have to bond with your mate. There's something essential riding on it. Something of life or death importance." Lysander held his hands up, shrugging his shoulders. "Sorry. I wish I could tell you more, but that's all I can figure out. This premonition stuff is pretty new and I'm still learning how to interpret it."

"Mating with Jackson might be a problem."

"How so?"

"I won't be able to bond with him if he doesn't forgive me for rejecting him the moment we met. I panicked when I realized we were Bloodmates and ran. Right now, he doesn't want anything to do with me." Edgar glanced at Roman, who returned his look, understanding in his eyes. Which was a huge relief to Edgar. He hated letting Roman down. "And if I'm being perfectly honest, I don't know if I want to join with him either. He's not what I've always envisioned for myself. Pretty much the opposite, in fact."

"You're going to have to get over it. What you've always wanted might not be what you actually need." Lysander smiled at him. "I think this is one of those times where you have to put your faith in the Goddess. There is more riding on this than just you."

"So you've said." Edgar turned to leave, then stopped. "Is this how it's going to be with you from now on,

Consort?" Edgar wiggled his fingers. "Woo, woo. I have a feeling about something. You must do as I say because lives are at stake."

Lysander snorted. "Probably."

Edgar narrowed his eyes.

Lysander held up his hands, chuckling. "I'm just kidding. I have no idea how it's going to go."

"Uh, huh."

"How about if I promise to only use my powers for good?"

Edgar hmphed. He wouldn't put any money on it. He turned to leave.

"Edgar," Roman said, "stay a bit. We have some documents to go over."

"Yes, Prince."

Edgar held the page out for Roman's signature. "This is the last one."

"Excellent." Roman finished signing with a flourish. "Thank you, Edgar. I don't know how I would ever manage without you."

Edgar smiled, feeling warmth in his cheeks. Even after three hundred years, Roman's approval made him glow, filling the part of him that yearned for acceptance.

They both looked up at the sound of someone knocking on the doorframe.

"Ah, Bryan. Please, join us."

Bryan stalked over to Edgar and leaned on the desk. "Do you mind telling me what you were thinking? How could you reject your mate like that? After everything that man went through. Don't you have a heart under that fancy suit of yours?"

Edgar ignored his questions, even if the accuracy of them stung. His shortcomings were none of Bryan's business. "How's Jackson?"

Bryan snorted. "Oh, now you care. Too bad you weren't worried about that earlier."

"Bryan," Roman interrupted, "you are not aware of all of the facts. Please answer Edgar's question."

"The healer is seeing to him now. I'm not sure how long they had him locked up, but Mrs. Davies said he'd been systematically tortured to the point his shifter healing abilities couldn't keep up anymore."

Edgar felt sick at the idea of Jackson helpless under the cruel hands of the Council. His heart ached when he thought of how badly he, himself, had treated his injured mate. Then he became enraged. Whoever was responsible would pay for every mark on his mate's body.

"What happened in there, Edgar?" Bryan asked in a softer voice. "Why did you reject him and run away?"

Edgar's anger was swept away in the tsunami of guilt that flooded him. He swallowed the lump in his throat, before looking at Bryan, not sure how to explain. Thankfully, Lysander, who was never at a loss for words, jumped in.

"Edgar's family are a bunch of conservative, judgmental, unforgiving pricks. They won't accept Edgar mating with a wolf, so he would have to choose between his family or his mate." Lysander looked at Edgar and shrugged. "The obvious choice is his mate, but since Edgar is also conservative and judgmental, he's going to make it hard on himself first before he finally accepts his fate and makes the correct decision."

Edgar's eyes opened wider with every word Lysander said. "Do you know this from a premonition?"

Lysander rolled his eyes. "No. I know this because I've been living with you for the last while. Do you deny anything I just said?"

Edgar thought about it, then shook his head. "It's possible I might be a bit reserved. It's hard to break away from your upbringing."

Lysander snorted. "Especially when you live and work with another vampire who is just as uptight as you are." He smiled at his mate. "Though I will admit he is getting better at chilling out."

"You are the cause, beloved. You bring joy and laughter into my life."

Edgar wasn't sure if he felt jealous or nauseous at the obvious connection between Roman and his mate. Though now that he'd found his own Bloodmate, he was beginning to understand how compelling the pull was between fated mates. It didn't take much imagination to see how much stronger the connection would be when the bonding was complete.

Bryan looked up to the ceiling, sighing loudly. "So if I'm hearing this correctly, we're going to have more mating drama to deal with. How wonderful."

Lysander reached over and smacked his brother's head. "Shut up, Bryan. One day you'll meet your fated mate. Then you'll be singing a different tune."

Edgar wondered if he was the only one who noticed Bryan flinch at Lysander's words.

Bryan glared at his brother, before rubbing his head and walking over to the window. He stood silent for a moment, staring out onto the grounds, before he said. "Did Edgar tell you we were ambushed when we arrived at the Council building?"

"What?" Lysander said. "No, he didn't say anything." He scowled at Edgar.

"I didn't have a chance to get to that yet. I was more focused on yelling at the Consort for not warning me about Jackson."

"Yes. I can see how that would distract you." Edgar saw Bryan's lip's twitch in the window's reflection.

"Eric reported in and advised me of the attack," Roman said, grief in his voice. "However, Lysander and Max are not yet aware. I will update Max when he is free to join us."

Bryan looked over apologetically. "Roman, I'm sorry about losing Bruno. I didn't anticipate an attack from behind. None of us sensed the vampires when we arrived. Well," he paused, looking at Edgar. "Edgar sensed something off, but couldn't tell what it was. Probably because Mother and Ruth were shielding them."

Roman nodded. "Undoubtedly."

"Please pass my condolences on to the rest of the enforcers," Bryan said.

"Thank you. Bruno was well respected and will be missed.

"I know it won't help, but please let the enforcers know I'm going to figure out where the vampires were hiding and plug up the hole. At the very least, I'll plant traps in it for the next time they want to try that trick."

Lysander's eyebrow lifted. "I like the idea of laying a trap. If we leave the opening for them, we can control how they come at us." He nodded. "Yes, that's what you should do. Lay some sneaky and deadly time-delayed traps. We want to catch as many of them as we can."

Bryan chuckled. "You're getting more devious every day, baby brother."

"I had to grow up eventually."

"I suppose, though I wish it wasn't because of a war with the Elders." Bryan frowned. "Something unusual happened in the middle of the fight with Ruth and Mother. I tried the new binding spell we've been practicing, Sandi. It worked on Ruth, but Mother was somehow able to shake it off. She was setting up to attack when a powerful wind came out of nowhere and knocked Ruth and Mother away. And I mean it completely swept them from the garage. I didn't notice where Thomas was, but he was hit by the wind as well."

"That's strange. What could have caused it?"

Bryan shook his head. "I don't have a clue. I couldn't find where it originated. Unfortunately, in the short time I spent looking for the source, Mother and Ruth managed to get away. Edgar and I found Thomas in one of the rooms. He'd been too badly injured to escape with them and died shortly after we found him. Before he passed, he said we would pay, just like the shifters."

"The shifters? What does that mean?"

"I don't know, but maybe there's something in their records. Speaking of that, now that Jackson is being tended to and I've given my report, I'd like to go back to the Council building and start digging through the documents again. I want to see if there's an explanation for why Jackson was imprisoned."

"Make sure you take either your guards or my enforcers with you. Nobody is to travel alone until we have found and eliminated all of the rebels," Roman instructed.

"I'll do that. I'll also bring along a couple of magic users in case we run into any more surprises. I'll return as soon as I can. Call me when Jackson wakes up if I'm not already back. I want to ask him some questions."

"We will. Be careful, Bryan."

"Always." He turned to leave just as Max was coming through the doorway. Edgar watched as he stiffened before relaxing and nodding at Max.

Max hesitated, his hand raising slowly before dropping. "Bryan. Can I speak to you for a moment?"

"Sorry, Max. I'm just heading out. I'll have to catch up with you later." He walked quickly out of the room without looking back.

Max stared after Bryan with a puzzled look on his face.

How interesting. Edgard turned back and saw Lysander watching him. When he made eye contact, Lysander gave a brief shake of his head. Edgar narrowed his eyes. Lysander rolled his eyes and shook his head again. Hmm. Looks like their resident psychic knew something but didn't want anybody else to know. Fair enough. Edgar had his own issues to deal with. He didn't need to take on anyone else's. Nodding his agreement in their silent conversation, Lysander's smile of thanks was confirmation his suspicions were correct.

* * *

Jackson woke with a start, rolling to his side and curling to protect his ribs from the kicks and blows raining down on him. Gasping for breath from fear and pain, it took him longer than it should have to realize he was alone. And that his tormentors were only phantoms in his mind. He stilled, locked in remembered fear, before he slowly straightened his limbs and forced himself to take deep, calming breaths. He lay quietly, giving his racing heart time to settle, trying to remember a day when waking hadn't been filled with fear and pain.

It had been a very long time.

Once he was fully in control of himself, he sat up and took stock of his surroundings, frowning when he realized he was in a strange bedroom. The mint green walls, light gray carpets, and expensive-looking mahogany furniture didn't belong to anyone he knew either. Worry growing about what new trouble he'd found himself in, Jackson breathed deep to pull in all the smells around him, giving his wolf senses as much information as he could. The strong smell of disinfectant stung his nose, but he could tell that many people had been in and out of his room while he'd been lying there, defenseless.

He started to panic, not knowing how he got here, his wolf rising in response to his fear. Then he recalled being rescued from his prison cell…and meeting his mate. Jackson quickly shut off that train of thought, not ready to deal with his mate's rejection of him just yet.

Slowly getting up, he was surprised to see his body was mostly healed. He'd either been here much longer than he was aware of or they had an exceptional healer. Either way, it was time for him to leave.

Moving quickly to the dresser, he started pawing through the drawers, looking for anything that might fit. As grateful as he was to be rescued, he needed to get back his pack. He'd been out of touch far too long.

The sweatpants he found were pulled up to mid-thigh when an older woman stepped into the room.

"And what do you think you're doing out of bed?"

He froze, except for one hand, which quickly moved to cover his bits. "Umm, getting dressed?"

She snorted. "No, you're not. You march yourself right back into bed. I did not spend all this time and energy healing you, only for you to relapse because you pushed yourself too soon."

"I'm sorry, ma'am, but I have to go."

"The only place you're going is back to bed. Hurry up and do as I say before you take a chill."

"But I feel fine."

"I should hope so. I worked hard for that. Just think of how much better you'll feel with one more day of rest."

"With all due respect, ma'am…"

"What lovely manners you have. Your mother must have taught you well. I'm sure she also taught you that it's not polite to argue with a lady." The woman put her hands on her hips, then pointed to the bed.

Sighing in defeat, he finished pulling on the sweatpants, then did as she told him.

"That's a good young man." She walked over and fluffed his pillows. "I'll have your lunch brought in to you shortly."

The thought of food was enough to wake up his stomach, which started growling loudly. He winced, but the woman only laughed.

"I'll let the kitchen know you're ready. It's only broth for today, I'm afraid, so don't get too excited."

"Broth. That's not nearly enough. I'm starving." He tossed a little whine in his voice, hoping it would help his case.

"I know you're starving, young man, but you need to let your body adjust to having food again. It's been a long time since you've eaten properly and we don't want to cause your stomach any distress." He tried puppy dog eyes on her, but she just laughed. "I bet that works just fine on the girls. It's unfortunate for you I've raised four lads. I know all the tricks you boys like to pull." She smiled, then said with a whisper, "I'll have them add a couple of buns to your soup, but that will have to do."

"Thank you," he whispered back.

She nodded and walked to the door, then called over her shoulder. "Don't even think about getting out of that bed." Jackson quickly pulled his leg back in and straightened out the covers. She shook her head at him. "Stay in bed today, then tomorrow you'll be free to leave." She walked out of the room. A second later, she poked her head back in. "You have some people who want to talk to you. I'll hold them off until you've had a chance to eat, but I suspect that's as long as they'll wait."

She pulled her head back and was gone. Presumably on her way to arrange for his lunch. Broth. His wolf whined, no more looking forward to soup than he was.

Chapter Four

Knocking startled Jackson out of his thoughts. Before he could say anything, the bedroom door opened and three men walked in. He eyed them warily, having a vague recollection of meeting the magic user earlier, but not the two vampires who accompanied him. He looked behind them to the empty doorway, trying to hide his eagerness as he waited for his mate to enter. Then his disappointment when he didn't follow them into the room.

Unsuccessfully, judging by the sympathetic look the magic user gave him.

As the men came to stand next to his bed, Jackson swung his legs out from under the covers to give himself the freedom to run if it became necessary. His wolf was not happy about these strangers towering over him. He kept one eye on the men as he noted his available points of escape. The vampire Bryan had called Max was frowning at him, as if he knew exactly what Jackson was doing. He was the dangerous one, the one Jackson would need to watch closely.

The magic user held out his hand. "I don't know if you remember me, but my name is Bryan. This is Prince Roman," he said, indicating the tall vampire dressed all in black, who exuded a considerable amount of power. "And this is Roman's Second in Command, Max."

Jackson dropped Bryan's hand and nodded to the vampires.

"Mrs. Davies says you're doing much better."

"I am. I wanted to thank you for saving me. From what your healer told me my wolf wouldn't have been able to keep me alive for much longer."

"I'm glad we got there in time. Would you mind if we asked you a few questions?"

"Not at all."

"Can you tell us why you were imprisoned?"

Jackson shook his head. "I really have no idea. I woke up one morning and six men had surrounded my bed. They dragged me in front of the Council, who refused to answer any of my questions. The next thing I knew, I was being beaten and locked in a cell. Nobody would listen when I said I hadn't done anything. They didn't care. They just found me guilty and tossed me into a cage."

The men exchanged puzzled glances.

"Jackson."

He looked at the vampire prince.

"Before we can let you run around freely, we need to know why the Council imprisoned you. I have people who depend on me for their safety. I would be remiss if I did not ensure you were not a threat to their welfare."

"I understand, Prince."

"Roman will do."

"Okay, Roman. But like I said. I don't know why they imprisoned me."

Roman studied Jackson. "Perhaps it would be best if you told us a little about yourself. After that, we can discuss everything that happened in the days before the Council captured you. Perhaps we will find our answers in that."

"Yes, sir. I mean, Roman. If you think it'll help."

"I do."

Jackson adjusted himself more comfortably on the bed. "I'm originally from Denver. My father was the Denver pack's Alpha. He was killed in a freak hunting accident about twenty years ago. My brother, Clint, became Alpha after his death."

Roman interrupted. "What was your father's name?"

"Wyatt, sir. Wyatt Miller."

"I met Alpha Miller many years ago. He was a good man. I am sorry for your loss."

"Thank you, sir. He was a very good man. So is my brother, or at least he was. I think something's happened to him."

"What makes you say that?"

"I've been deployed for the last year. My brother and I had a monthly check-in call, but he missed our last one. I was a bit worried because his behavior had been different during our last couple of calls, so I tried calling back a few times, but couldn't reach him. Fortunately, I was at the end of my contract. I came looking for him the minute I was released from the service. But I didn't make it past New Orleans."

"New Orleans seems a bit off track if your brother is in Denver." Roman looked suspiciously at Jackson, who rushed to explain.

"I had a buddy I was enlisted with who I wanted to check on. He left under a medical separation so I came here to make sure he was doing okay before continuing on to Denver. I spent a couple of days with him and was heading out the next day, but then I was captured."

"Did you tell anybody about your plans?" Bryan asked.

Jackson looked over at him, wondering at the suspicion in his voice, then nodded. "I left a message with one of the

Gammas since I couldn't reach any of the Betas at the Denver pack."

"It seems a bit strange there were no Betas around."

"I thought so too. But Russel, the Gamma I spoke with, said they were working with the young wolves on tracking."

"And you believe him?"

Jackson shrugged. "I guess. I've been gone a long time. I'm not sure how things are done in the pack now."

Bryan nodded. "Okay. Can you tell me what you did that last night in New Orleans?"

Jackson squinted at him. "What does that matter?"

"I'm starting to get an idea of what's going on, but knowing what happened before you were captured will tell me if I'm on the right track or not."

Jackson frowned at Bryan, not sure how anything he'd said so far could explain why he'd been taken prisoner.

"Please just humor me for a minute." Bryan said. "This could be important."

"Okay," Jackson said slowly. "I went to a bar. I can't remember which one, but it was somewhere on Bourbon Street. I met some magic chick. We hooked up, and the next morning, well, you know what happened after that."

"Roman, do you think it was her?"

"I do. It is too convenient and tidy to be merely a coincidence."

"What are you guys talking about?"

"Did you by any chance happen to get the woman's name?" The intensity of Roman's stare was making his wolf twitchy.

"She called herself Jill. She wasn't the most pleasant girl I've ever talked to, but then again, I wasn't there for conversation."

"Well, shit. It was her. Now what?"

"What? What did I say?" Jackson looked at the three men who were frowning at each other. "Seriously, what just happened?"

Roman turned to his Second, ignoring his question. "Max, could you please ask Lysander to bring Nicolas here."

"At once, Roman." He rushed from the room.

Jackson was getting weirded out by their behavior. "Can someone please answer me what's going on?"

Roman and Bryan looked at him. Bryan held up his hand. "If you could just wait for—"

"Am I in trouble for something?"

"No," Bryan said, coming to stand in front of him. "How long do you think you were held captive by the Council?"

"I don't know. Two, three months, if I had to guess. I'm pretty sure it wasn't more than four." Jackson shrugged. "It was kind of hard keeping track of the days."

Bryan looked at him apologetically. Jackson's gut clenched, knowing he wasn't going to like what was said next. "At my best guess, you were in that cell for almost a year."

"A year," Jackson whispered. Then he shook his head. "No. You're wrong. I couldn't have been there a year."

"I don't think I am."

Jackson was going to argue some more, but the look on Bryan's stopped him. He shoved a hand in his hair, then realized it was far longer than it would be after only a few months. But not if it had been a year. So what they were telling him could really be true. His head shot up when the implications of that hit him.

"A year! That means Clint's been missing for more than a year." He started to get up but was blocked by Bryan. "Let me up. I need to find him."

"I'm sorry. I can't let you leave yet."

"You have to. I swear I didn't do anything."

"I believe you. But if you could just answer a few more questions, I'll tell you what I think is going on."

"No. I need to find my brother. Move out of my way."

"Please, Jackson. Just a couple more questions. Then I promise we'll do everything we can to help you find your brother."

Jackson narrowed his eyes, seeing his sincerity. And the fact he wasn't going to let Jackson leave until he'd done what he wanted. A quick glance at Roman showed him the same.

"Fine," he said, settling back on the bed. "But only a couple more questions. Then I'm leaving, with or without your permission." At least, he'd try.

Bryan raised an eyebrow but let his challenge go. Smart man. "Who would take over your pack if something happened to your brother?"

"What kind of a question is that? Why would you even ask that? Do you know what happened to him?" Jackson started to get off of the bed again, but Bryan blocked him, joined this time by Roman.

"Jackson, you need to calm down." Bryan gestured at him with his palms facing outward. "Nobody here means you any harm. I swear. Just please answer the question."

Jackson sat back, studying him. The first sign of betrayal and he was letting his wolf free to wreak havoc on anyone who got in his way. After checking to see that he still had a clear path to the exit, he finally answered Bryan. "If Clint was no longer Alpha, I would be next in line. Our pack is a true Alpha pack, as my father's bloodline is of the original Alpha line. In our pack, the Alpha position always is passed down to each successive son. If the heir has not yet come of age, usually a strong Beta will act as advisor, almost like a regent, until the heir can assume leadership. Why does this matter?"

"Is there anyone to inherit the Alpha position after you?"

"My brother's son. But he's only three, so I would be Alpha and he would follow after me."

"Is there anyone after him? What happens if your family line ends with no Alpha to take over?"

Growing disturbed by the direction of these questions, he eyed Bryan warily before slowly answering. "We are the true Alpha pack in North America and rank highest because of my family's bloodline. All of the rest answer to us. If there was no Alpha to take over, then our pack would be like every other pack, determining the Alpha through Challenge fights."

Bryan and Roman looked at each other again, grim expressions on their faces.

"Okay, I answered your damn questions. Now tell me what's going on."

Roman sighed. "It would appear that you were deliberately targeted. I suspect someone in your pack advised the Council of your whereabouts and they set a trap for you."

"What trap? I don't understand what you're—"

"Roman. Max said you wanted to see me and the baby."

"Beloved. I would like you to meet someone." Roman wrapped his arm around a young magic user holding a baby. Jackson's wolf started going crazy, the power emanating from the magic user making his nerves do much more than twitch.

It took a few moments for Jackson to calm his wolf down. Once he did, he took notice of the child in his arms, frowning when he realized it smelled like a wolf. But not just a wolf. It smelled like family. Close family. He leaned forward and breathed deep, drawing the infant's scent into his lungs. His eyes widened.

"Why does your baby smell like it's mine? How is this possible?"

"What? No. This is my baby. Not yours. You can't have him."

"Zander, beloved. Calm yourself. Nobody is taking young Nicolas away from you."

"But he said the baby was his. He's not. Nico's ours. We saved him. Nobody is touching my son."

Jackson scrambled out of bed, putting his back to the wall when the magic user's hands started glowing.

Suddenly, Bryan was standing between him and the insane man. "Sandi. Stop. He's a victim in this. And he's already been badly abused by the Council. Get yourself under control or you'll have to leave."

"You're not the boss of me, big brother."

"No, but I'm the only one who can stop you. Please listen to me. I think we've just uncovered another one of the Council's plots, but we need everybody to remain calm to get to the bottom of it."

"He's right, my beloved. I promise, nobody is taking our son away." Roman glared fiercely at Jackson, hissing. "Nobody."

Jackson slid further along the wall, searching for the doorway with his peripheral vision. These people were freaking crazy. It was time to get the hell out of here. He relaxed his hold on his man form, releasing his wolf.

"Jackson. Stop. You don't need to run." Bryan watched as the wolf bowled over Max and made a clean escape through the door. "For the love of…damn it, Sandi. I told you he was a victim of the Council. An innocent victim and we're the only one who can keep him safe from them. Except now he doesn't trust us. And you, Roman. What the hell?" Bryan kicked the wall. "You know what he's gone through. Why would you do that?"

Roman at least had the decency to look ashamed. Not his little brother. Lysander got right in his face.

"What's going on? Why is that wolf saying Nico smells like him?"

"Because he's the baby's father."

Lysander gasped. "What? No. He can't be."

"He is."

Lysander punched Bryan in the chest. "You're lying."

"He is speaking the truth, beloved. The Council set Jillian on him. I don't know if she was supposed to get pregnant, but they definitely put her in his path. He was grabbed by them and imprisoned, and has been systematically tortured for months."

"Why would they do that?"

"Because he is of the Alpha line. The last true Alpha line. I suspect they are trying to either extinguish it or to control the remaining heir. If they control the heir, they control all of the North American packs."

Lysander looked horrified, then his face tightened with determination. "He still can't have my baby."

"Sandi, Nico is his son."

"But—"

Bryan held up his hand. "We at least have to talk to him and figure out what's best for Nico. He's from an ancient and powerful line. He is essentially a prince to the shifters. I don't know that it's our right to take him away from his heritage."

"Roman." Lysander turned to him.

"I know, beloved. Trust me. I do not like this any more than you do. But we have a moral obligation to talk to the man to determine our best course of action. Even if that is not what your heart desires."

"I don't want to."

Bryan snorted at the mulish expression on Lysander's face. He laughed when Lysander gave him the finger, but behind the baby's back so that the infant couldn't see it.

Sobering, he spoke. "Roman's right. I know it's not what you want, but we can't steal the baby away from his father. Especially not one of such a powerful lineage."

"But I love Nico. I won't give him up."

"Sandi—"

"No, Bryan." Lysander held the baby closer to his chest. "Nico's my son. Besides, the wolf is probably long gone by now anyway."

Bryan shook his head. "He's not. I have the barrier up. There's no way he can get out, no matter how powerful his wolf is."

* * *

Jackson slowed, moving forward carefully until his nose bumped into the invisible wall. Even that tiny pressure hurt, not having yet recovered from running and crashing into it at full speed earlier. Damn it. Was there no way out of here? He moved along the edges of the boundary searching for an opening. He needed to get away from these insane people.

One moment, they're having a civilized conversation, the next some crazy magic user with glowing hands is threatening him. And why? Because of some pup he knew nothing about. Why would he care about that? Except…if that was really his son, he did

Jackson came to a stop, dropping to his haunches. And they cared too. Enough that they were willing to threaten a strong Alpha. That kind of protectiveness was a good quality to have if you were responsible for a child.

He replayed the conversation in his head, which seemed a lot less threatening now that his wolf wasn't agitated from being trapped in a room. It took a moment for him to realize they hadn't tried to hurt him. They'd just threatened him to make sure he didn't take the baby. Which he wouldn't anyway, since he couldn't look after a kid right now. Not until he located his brother.

Jackson stood, shaking out his fur. He needed to go back and find out what information they had. If they knew something that would help him in his search, he owed it to Clint to give them another chance.

He growled at the invisible barrier. It's not like he could get out anyway.

* * *

"Let me get this straight." Edgar was incensed. "Jackson was deliberately targeted by the Council to get Jillian pregnant and now you're trying to steal his son."

"I am not stealing his son."

"Yes, you are. Jackson didn't know he had a child before, but now he does."

"So what?"

"So what?" Edgar yelled. "You're trying to keep the baby he just found out about. If Jackson wants to take Nico and you don't let him, that is the very definition of stealing his son."

"What am I supposed to do? I love baby Nico. I don't want to give him up."

"I might have a suggestion."

"Jackson." Edgar whipped around. "Are you okay?"

"I'm not going to lie. I've had better years."

"I'm so sorry for everything that's happened to you."

"That's not really your concern, is it? You've made your feelings about me perfectly clear."

Edgar flinched at the direct hit. One he couldn't refute. When he saw Lysander looking at him with pity, he glared back. Nobody was going to pity him. Especially not him. Edgar looked back at Jackson and straightened his shoulders, ready to try to fix what he'd broken when his mate turned from him and faced Lysander.

"Consort, was it?"

Lysander nodded.

"I seem to be in some trouble with the Council. I've already been captured once. I can't take the chance of the baby falling into their hands, especially if he turns out to be an Alpha."

"No, we definitely can't let that happen."

"I also have to find out what happened to my brother and his family. I can't drag an infant into a possible dangerous situation."

"No, you can't." Lysander tilted his head. "What are you saying?"

"I think he should stay with you, where he can be protected. I can't keep him safe out there."

"And after? What then?"

Jackson rubbed a hand over the back of his neck. "I don't really know. I think we'll have to talk about it when the time comes."

Edgar spoke up. "Are you sure? This is your son." Jackson turned tormented eyes on him. Edgar gasped when he realized this was much harder on his mate than he was letting on.

"What other choice do I have? I can't take a baby into pack territory until I know what's happening there. And I definitely can't risk the Council getting their hands on him."

"No." Lysander frowned. "Why would she do that?"

"Why did who do what?"

"Jillian. If the Elders wanted a child of the Alpha line, why would they let Jillian fall into our grasp? She basically turned Nico over to us."

"Jillian came because Charlotte sent her in here." Edgar stopped and considered. "Huh. Maybe the Council wasn't aware she planned on doing that." His eyes widened. "Or maybe she got pregnant because the Elders told her to seduce Jackson. Then she came here because Charlotte wanted her to spy on us. What if she's taking directions from both of them? What if neither of them knows she's working for the other side?"

Roman walked into the room. "Then she is playing a very dangerous game."

"It's possible she's caught in the middle and is doing whatever she's told to in order to keep herself safe." Lysander made a face as though he didn't quite believe what he'd just said.

"Or she is deliberately playing both sides and is loyal only to herself." Edgar thought this was probably the correct explanation. It fit what he knew of her.

Lysander snorted. "You say that like she's a double agent."

"Exactly."

"You're serious?"

"I am."

Bryan came around the corner. "I think Edgar may be right. Jillian is devious enough to have both sides thinking she answers only to them when she's really just looking after her own interests."

"Okay, that's enough of that," Lysander said. "Where are you guys coming from? Neither of you were here a few minutes ago." Lysander looked over his shoulder. "Max, are you hiding back there? You might as well come out and join the party."

Max sheepishly poked his head around the corner. "Sorry, Consort. We didn't want to barge in. Unfortunately, some people were too impatient to wait." He looked pointedly at Roman and Bryan.

Edgar snorted. He'd miss these guys when he went to live with Jackson. Even Lysander. Then what he'd thought hit him. Live with Jackson? Where had that come from? He didn't even know if he was going to mate with him, never mind live with him. Especially not with the pack in the country where he wouldn't be close to the amenities he depended on. The only things he'd find on the pack lands would be dirt and a bunch of uneducated wolves.

His thoughts crashed to a halt again. Damn it. He really was starting to sound just like his mother and grandmother. The thought was terrifying. They were the cruelest, most judgmental vampires he'd ever known. His mate deserved better than that from him.

Speaking of his mate, Edgar looked around for Jackson and found him standing with his back to the wall, watching all of them. Edgar stood and looked at him

Jackson's head was spinning trying to keep up with the conversation. He was following along with some of what they were talking about, but was missing the big picture. And it sounded like he needed to get caught up fast. Especially since he was now one of the main players. And he had a son to protect. A son. That still hadn't sunk in all the way. What was he going to do with a child?

Jackson's head came up when he felt eyes staring at him. Edgar. His mate. Another thing he hadn't had time to process. As if knowing he was thinking about him, Edgar walked over, stopping just in front of him.

"Are you all right?"

"I'm not really sure. I'm caught in the middle of something and I don't know what's going on. Until I understand what the Council is up to, I can't make a plan."

Edgar nodded in agreement. "You're right. A lot has happened recently that you need to be told about. And we should see if Bryan's found out anything in the Council's records. He's been trying to find out what happened to you and looking for information about what the Elders did to the wolves."

"Did to the wolves? What are you talking about?"

"I don't know. It's something one of the Elders said. Why don't you come sit down again and we can both find out?"

As Edgar led the way over to the couch, Jackson realized everyone had stopped their own conversations to listen in on theirs. These guys were pretty intense. In some ways, they reminded him of the boys in his old unit. Especially the way they were a bunch of nosy busybodies.

He smiled to himself. He could work with that.

* * *

The Elder's secret hideaway…

"We need that child."

Charlotte watched Ruth pace the length of the room, rubbing her newly healed arm, her agitation showing in every jerky movement of her body. Being a rebel was taking its toll on her. She wasn't the pompous, composed Elder she'd always presented in Council chambers.

Charlotte was beginning to realize she'd aligned herself with weak-willed pretenders. They weren't the great and powerful magic users they portrayed themselves to be. It was no wonder they made laws to prevent everyone else from gaining power. They wouldn't be able to control anyone otherwise. And now it seemed as though they were also keeping secrets from her.

"What is so important about the child?"

Ruth whipped around. "It doesn't concern you."

"Doesn't it?"

"No. You are here on our sufferance, to do our bidding. Do not think to raise yourself above your actual value to us. You are easily replaced."

There was the arrogance she was used to seeing. Gritting her teeth, Charlotte bit back what she wanted to say, and calmly replied, "Of course not, Elder Ruth. I understand my place."

"Try to remember it. Finding a replacement for you would take time I can ill afford to waste."

"I will, Elder." Charlotte tipped her head, seething at the implied threat. She looked forward to the day she paid Ruth back for the many slights she'd been forced to endure.

"I brought you here to discuss how we are going to get past your son's barrier. You managed it once when we escaped from the estate. Have you figured out how to break through it again so that we can get the child?"

"No. I still haven't found a way past his new shielding. Bryan's barrier has proven to be impenetrable to all of my attempts to breach it." And when she finally did break through, the others would not be coming with her.

"Keep trying. We need that brat." Ruth swept from the room.

Charlotte narrowed her eyes. If the child was that important to the Elders, she would see to it they never got their hands on it.

Chapter Five

Jackson blinked, then turned to Edgar, completely stunned by what he'd just heard. "The law against mating outside of paranormal communities was made up by the Council?"

"Yes. And we've all been blindly following it because we trusted them when they said there were dire consequences for breaking it." Edgar grimaced. "The death penalty they imposed for not obeying it pretty much ensured nobody broke it."

"And it was just so they could keep us weak? To prevent the possibility of power couples who could challenge them?"

Edgar nodded.

"Bastards."

"Yes, they are. And when Roman and the Consort mated and gained their extra abilities, the reasons for the Elders implementing the law became quite clear."

Jackson wiped his hands over his face. "Goddess. How many couples have they doomed by preventing them from bonding with their fated mates? Or outright killing them."

"More than I want to think about," Edgar said.

Jackson leaned back against the couch. "I don't know what to say. What would make them do something so horrible?"

"We haven't discovered any reasons other than them wanting power," Edgar said. "The worst part is knowing we've only scratched the surface of their crimes. After the Elders attacked Roman and Lysander and tried to kill the rest of us, we had no choice but to declare war on them to stop what they were doing."

"I still don't understand what any of this has to do with me. I've been overseas. Why would they go to the effort of setting a trap for me?"

Bryan turned from where he'd been looking out the window while Edgar caught Jackson up on events. "You said you'd lost contact with your brother before you left the service."

Jackson nodded. "He always made it to our calls until he missed the last one that I told you about. After that, I couldn't reach him, no matter what time I tried calling. The day I was heading to Denver, I called the pack again and this time I reached Mary. She told me Clint had vanished a couple of months previously along with his family. That's not like my brother. Clint would never disappear without talking to me."

"I'm surprised the Gamma you spoke with didn't mention it."

Jackson froze. "You're right," he said slowly. "He should have. He also didn't tell me Clint's family is missing." A growl rumbled up his chest. "He must know what happened to them."

"Maybe. Maybe not," Bryan said.

"No," Jackson shook his head. "He has to know. Otherwise he'd have said something."

"Except I found some notes in the Elders files stating your brother was to be eliminated."

"What?"

"They planned to get rid of him but he vanished before the Council could make that happen. Your brother may have realized something was going on and took his family to safety."

That was something his brother would have done. Clint was pretty sharp and had a sense for danger. But still. He hadn't got hold of Jackson to let him know. That told him that something was seriously wrong. "Do you think…is there any chance Clint might be okay?"

Bryan paused before he slowly nodded. "I think so. I didn't find anything saying he'd been killed."

Jackson blew out a breath of relief.

"I, uhm, also found some messages that make me think your father's death wasn't the result of a hunting accident." Bryan looked at him apologetically. "It wasn't concrete proof, but there were enough bits and pieces that I don't have any doubt the Elders were behind it."

"No," he whispered. "That can't be true."

"I'm sorry," Bryan said. "It looks as though they've been working to eliminate your family for decades."

"But why? Why would they do something like that?"

"I'm not sure. The documentation doesn't explain everything, but what information I've been able to piece together indicates they were trying to wipe out your family. Until you." Bryan walked over to stand in front of Jackson. "Correct me if I'm wrong, but from what I understand as the Alpha line, you can control the other packs."

Jackson nodded his head. "We can."

"The Council must have wanted to ensure you weren't a threat to them, so they eliminated your father. Your brother was meant to be next. Then you."

Lysander suddenly gasped, his face going white. "Bryan, if this has been going on for decades, that means Father knew about it." He shook his head. "No. He wouldn't have been involved. There's no way you can make me believe Father would've had any part in killing shifters for power."

"You're right. Father wouldn't have. He was far too honorable." Bryan clenched his fists. "Which is why I don't think his death was an accident either. Not that I can prove it. Yet."

"Why would the Elders be doing these things? The Council wasn't always like this. They couldn't have been."

"They weren't. Father was on the Council for decades before he died. He would never have allowed it."

"Then what?"

Bryan shook his head. "I don't know. Something happened to change them. I just haven't figured out what. But the Elders' records are quite extensive, so I'm sure there's an explanation in there somewhere."

"What if you can't find anything?"

"I will. It's just taking forever to search through everything." Bryan shook his head. "It's really too bad they never caught on to the computer age. Searching through electronic files would be a hell of a lot faster than going through rooms full of documents and scrolls."

Edgar spoke up. "If the Council was trying to kill Jackson's family, why did they lock him up instead of getting rid of him?

"I don't know. It's a complete reversal of their previous plans. I can only speculate that rather than trying to eliminate the Alpha line, they wanted to control it. If they killed your brother, they'd gain control of his son. With him under their power, they'd be able to control all the packs."

Jackson nodded. "But Clint disappeared. And so did his wife and my nephew."

"Which is why I suspect that's why Jillian was put in front of you. You were their next attempt to get their hands on an Alpha wolf child they could control. The only reason I can think of why they kept you alive was if your child didn't have the Alpha gene, they could use you to try again."

"That's crazy. Why go to all this trouble? The packs don't care about any Council business. We just want to be left alone to live our lives in peace."

"I don't know, Jackson. None of this makes any sense. All I can tell you is that before he died, Elder Thomas spoke about something happening to the shifters. We need to find out what they've done. And fix it before it's too late."

Edgar grabbed Jackson's hand, squeezing tight. When Jackson went to pull away, Edgar held on tighter. After a brief moment, Jackson stopped trying to get free, surprised at how grounded his mate's touch made him feel. He squeezed Edgard's hand back. The shy smile he received helped ease some of his worry about Clint and his family

Until a stray thought crossed his mind, sending his heart racing again.

"Wait a minute. Edgar and I are mates. That means our mating is forbidden according to the Council's law."

Bryan nodded. "Yes, which means you're in danger too. After Lysander and Roman mated, the Elder issued a kill order for them. As well as for Max and me for assisting and harboring them. When they find out about you and Edgar, they'll issue another one."

"Don't I already have one on me?" Edgar asked, looking puzzled.

Bryan shook his head. "Not that I could find."

"But that makes no sense. I've been Roman's assistant for over three hundred years. Surely I'm a known associate of his."

"I'm sorry, Edgar. There was no mention of you. Just Roman, Lysander, Max and me."

Jackson watched as Edgar's confusion turned to hurt. He seemed to shrink in on himself, unhappiness radiating from him.

Why did his mate want to be on a kill list?

"Edgar." Roman walked over. "The Council is clearly shortsighted if they do not understand your importance to me. Everyone who matters knows you are a valued friend. You should know your worth to me is much more than that of being my assistant. You and Max are part of my family. Do not let them diminish your value or your belief in yourself."

"No. Of course not," Edgar mumbled, not making eye contact with Roman.

"As Max is my right hand, you are my left. I would sorely miss you if you were not a part of my world."

"I know that." He shrugged. "They probably just think I'm just someone who works for you."

"Instead of realizing how very valuable and highly regarded you are."

Edgar nodded and gave Roman a smile even Jackson could tell was fake.

He looked between Roman and Edgar with a frown. Was being acknowledged as Roman's assistant that important to him? Did Edgar not value himself beyond that? Before he could say anything—even if he had no idea what—Bryan cleared his throat.

"At least with you not being on the Council's kill list and nobody but us knowing about Jackson, you guys can travel freely to the shifter packs. It'll be easier for you to find out what the Council did to them if you don't have to fight the Elders every step of the way."

"What?" Edgar's head snapped over to Bryan. "Travel to the packs? Have you lost your mind?"

Jackson flinched, at his mate's words. He shook his hand free from Edgar's and went to stand by the wall again.

"Jackson, I didn't mean that the way it sounded." Edgar started to get up, but Jackson scowled at him, stopping him in his tracks. Edgar settled back on the couch. "It's nothing against you or the packs. It's just…I'm an office guy. That's where my skills are. I don't go out in the fields or walk through the woods. I like my comforts and the noise and bustle of the city. The thought of being in the country surrounded by all that nature and quietness gives me the creeps." He hesitated as if realizing how that sounded, then said, "No offense, though."

"You're a little too late for that."

Edgar grimaced. "I'm sorry. I didn't mean to insult you." He turned back to Bryan. "I can't imagine why you think I'd volunteer to do such a thing."

"Perhaps so you could be with your mate," Lysander said, raising his eyebrow. "You know, the scowling guy standing behind you."

Jackson saw the light go off.

"Oh. Right," Edgar said slowly.

"It's time for you to talk to Jackson and explain about your family."

Jackson wondered why Edgar's face drained of color. What could possibly be bad enough to cause that kind of reaction?

"I'm serious, Edgar," Lysander said. "Take him somewhere private and do that right now. There's no time to waste."

"Why do you say that?"

"We know something bad is happening to the shifters. We need to find out what. Which means you guys need to get going as soon as possible, no matter how you feel about it."

"Shit."

Jackson could only agree.

Edgar led Jackson down the hall, heading for one of the mansion's meeting rooms.

"Could we talk outside? I've spent too much time locked up over the last few months. My wolf needs to be outdoors, where he can smell the fresh air and feel free, even though we're trapped inside a giant magical bubble."

"Of course." Edgar took the next left, heading toward a side exit.

"And just where do you think you're going, young man? I believe you were instructed to stay in bed today."

Jackson jerked to a stop.

Edgar turned to look behind them. The household healer, Mrs. Davies, stood there scowling at them with her hands planted on her hips.

"Um, ma'am, well, you see, I just…" Jackson stopped, obviously stumped.

She snorted, shaking her head. "Uh, huh. And don't you think I don't know about a wolf running through the house earlier.

"Sorry, ma'am. I wasn't able to control it. Things kind of happened and he needed to run."

"I heard." Mrs. Davies looked Jackson over carefully. "Well, you don't appear to have done yourself any harm." She pointed her finger. "I want you to take it easy for the rest of today. If you're headed outside, find a quiet place to relax. Some fresh evening air will do you the world of good." She turned to Edgar, pointing her finger at him. "You will not upset him further. Do you understand me?"

Edgar shook his head. "No, ma'am, I mean, yes, ma'am, uhm…." Edgar stopped, not sure what the correct response was.

She chuckled. "It's fine. I know what you mean. You boys run along now."

"Yes, ma'am." They bolted down the hall, followed by Mrs. Davies' laughter.

Edgar walked slowly to the center of the garden, seating himself on one of the benches that encircled the fountain. He was dreading this conversation so he had no problem waiting patiently as Jackson wandered around the area, checking out the various statues and flowering bushes that filled the space.

Edgar leaned back, looking up at the night's sky as he contemplated how much the upcoming conversation was going to change his life. Or even worse, if it didn't.

Eventually, Jackson made his way over to the bench Edgar was using and sat beside him, keeping his gaze on the fountain.

"Why did you reject my wolf?"

Edgar chuckled weakly. "You don't hold your punches any, do you? You just get right to the point with the hard questions."

Jackson shrugged. "I'm a rip the Band-Aid off kind of guy."

Edgar nodded. Ready or not, his mate deserved an explanation for his behavior. "Okay. I guess the best way to start is by explaining about my family and the expectations they have." Edgar paused, wondering if there was any way to show his family in a better light, but really, they were horrible people. There was no getting around that.

He shifted on the bench. "What you need to understand about my family is that they have never been satisfied with their standing among the vampire classes. They've always believed they deserved more and have done whatever they felt was necessary to raise themselves above others in our society. Over the centuries, they managed to offend and alienate most of the great houses. And even though they made numerous enemies along the way, that never gave them pause."

Edgar stood and walked over to the fountain, staring blindly into its depths as he started speaking again. "They were very close to the Crown at one point and relished being able to wield the power that relationship gave them over the other families."

"Close to the Crown how? Through you?"

Edgar shook his head and looked over at Jackson. "My aunt was part of the Queen's inner circle. She was the best friend of Roman's sister-in-law, his older brother Nico's wife." Edgar looked back into the water, sighing. "Even though she was supposed to be her friend, Claire was jealous of the Queen, wanting King Nico for herself. The day came when her jealousy overtook her common sense and she stabbed the Queen in the chest, killing her instantly."

"What the hell?"

"The worst part is that she ended up killing the King as well. I don't mean literally. Roman was the one who actually had to kill him when he went mad because of his Bloodmate's death. But it was Claire's actions in killing his wife that set them on a path where there was no other outcome."

"That's terrible," Jackson whispered. "I don't mean to offend, but how is it that Roman allows you near his mate?"

"Because Roman is the most honorable and logical man I know." Edgar laughed ruefully. "That was a horrendous time in our history. Roman had no choice but to destroy the maddened creature his dearly-loved brother and King had turned into. After he'd completed that dreadful task, he executed Claire. My entire family was banished from Court and threatened upon pain of death from ever returning."

Edgar walked over to sit next to Jackson on the bench again and sighed. "The other families used that opportunity to pay my family back for all the harm that had been done to them over the centuries. There was no way to defend against so many enemies, especially when they didn't have the support of the Crown, so my family ran off to the countryside where they quickly became forgotten. It stayed like that for around five hundred years. Every century, on the anniversary of our banishment, my grandmother would send a family member to make a peaceful overture to Roman, testing to see if his anger had lessened. Her messengers were always returned to her, minus their heads. On the sixth century marker, she sent me."

Jackson gasped. "What?"

Edgar nodded. "I was my father's fourth son. Expendable since I was not in a position to make an advantageous match." Edgar snickered. "Not that my older brothers had any better chance of it. Don't forget, we were confined to the country, our names mostly forgotten except by our worst enemies. My grandmother refused to acknowledge that fact and always planned for the day we would return to court."

"So she sent her grandson to his death? What the hell kind of grandmother does something like that?"

Edgar smiled sadly. "Mine. She never accepted our banishment as a just punishment for the crimes of our family. Her hubris always led her to believe our family would one day be welcomed back to court with open arms, all of our past wrongs forgiven."

"She obviously knows nothing about Roman. Even if I only met him, I know he wouldn't forgive that easily."

"No. He really wouldn't."

Jackson looked at him. "You still have your head. Why didn't Roman didn't kill you like the other messengers?"

"A very fortunate series of events." Edgar shook his head with a laugh. "Even though Roman ruled over the Court after his brother's death, he never assumed the title of King. That had been his brother's position so he was unwilling to take it on. He looked after the people and made rulings, but only ever as a Prince. Many of the higher placed houses took that as an act of disrespect to the throne when it was anything but. Roman never felt worthy enough to assume the mantle of King as he never forgave himself for killing his brother. The great houses chafed under the rule of only a Prince, so were conspiring to overthrow him." Edgar sighed. "None of them were any better than my family. All of that plotting and intrigue to climb higher than their neighbor and none of it mattered in the end."

"Why? What happened?"

"First, let me tell you why I'm still alive," Edgar said. He leaned back, looking up at the stars. "I was about two days away from Court, waiting out the day in a hotel that caters to vampires when I chanced to overhear a conversation where they were planning to assassinate Roman. I was loyal to the Crown, so I finished the rest of my journey as quickly as possible and threw myself on the mercy of the Prince, begging for an audience. Roman knew exactly who I was and couldn't believe I'd actually handed myself over. He asked if I had come to plead for clemency. I told him no, that my family hadn't changed and he should never allow them near his Court. That confused him, enough so that gave me the opportunity to ask if I could speak to him in private. Obviously, he refused. But when I suggested he have me wrapped in chains and surrounded by his guards so he would be safe while I told him why I'd come, he was curious enough to know what I had to say to allow it."

"You really allowed yourself to be tied up? He could have just killed you and there would have been nothing you could do to stop it," Jackson said.

Edgar chuckled. "The moment I showed up at Court, I was under a death sentence, so I had nothing to lose. Besides, I couldn't let anything happen to Roman and needed to tell him about those conspiring to kill him. Being chained up was a small price to pay to be able to speak to him away from the eyes and ears of his Court. I had no idea how many of his enemies were in attendance and didn't want to let them know their plot was about to be exposed."

Edgar got up and went to sit on the edge of the fountain, facing Jackson. He leaned over, elbows on his thighs, and clasped his hands between his legs. "Roman was so intrigued by the fact I would put myself completely at his mercy that he granted my request and met with me in private without the chains. I was then able to advise him of the plot to assassinate him. Little did I know, Roman was already aware of it and had taken measures to deal with the traitors. But my willingness to put myself at risk to warn him went a long way towards establishing my credibility with Roman. Once I allowed him to read into my soul to confirm my intentions, he allowed me to stay with him."

"Read into your soul?" Jackson sounded confused. "What do you mean by that?"

Edgar's lips curled in a small smile as he remembered that time. "Roman was around seven hundred years old at that point. As a vampire ages, their inherent abilities grow stronger. Roman's powers of perception are very strong. He can't actually read minds but he can pick up on intentions. Enough to see I meant him no harm. It was a great relief to me as you can imagine. I didn't want to lose my head because my grandmother thought I was expendable."

"No, I guess not. What happened then?"

"He allowed me to stay in Court. As I had proven my loyalty, I soon worked my way into a position as his Personal Assistant. He even allowed my family back to Court, because really, they were no worse than any of the other families that were constantly plotting and maneuvering for position. Surprisingly, my grandmother even found value in me, what with me being in a position of power and having the ear of the Prince," Edgar said bitterly.

"I hope you told her to go to hell," Jackson muttered.

Edgar shook his head. "How could I? She's the Matriarch of the family. If I turned my back on her, I would lose them all. But with everyone being back at Court and me suddenly having value, she immediately began looking for a favorable match for me." Edgar shook his head. "Sadly, my family hadn't learned anything during the time we'd been banished. If anything, they became worse. Secluded for those centuries, they'd nursed their hatred, becoming extremely conservative and intolerant of anything or anyone that didn't meet their exacting standards. Their hunger for power also grew exponentially. Instead of being thankful for being accepted back to Court, they went in the other direction, wanting to pay back anyone who'd slighted them over the years. There were numerous suspicious deaths that I know would have led back to my grandmother if anybody had cared enough to pursue them. I tried to distance myself from them as much as possible, but my being close to Roman was an advantage over the other families they weren't willing to relinquish. Until Roman changed the rules." Edgar started laughing, remembering the shock and outrage of the Court.

"What did he do?" Jackson was wide-eyed, hanging on to Edgar's every word.

"Roman decided he'd had enough of the games and backstabbing of the Court. He turned the throne over to his uncle and gathered the vampires most loyal to him and brought us all to America. I can still hear the screams of my family when I chose to go with him. All of that time and effort spent getting close to the Prince and then he ups and leaves. The Court was in shambles, with the most deceitful families staying behind. The ones who left with Roman were the younger generation of vampires who were sick of the intrigue and wanted a chance at a different life, to live among the humans and create a more liberal and caring society." Edgar shook his head again. "My family has never forgiven me for leaving with Roman. He became less in their eyes the moment he gave away his throne. Me leaving with him was perceived as being a traitor to my family and tarnishing their supposedly good name."

Edgar sighed and looked up at Jackson, dreading this next part. He spoke softly, "Me being mated to a shifter would be the worst possible crime in their eyes. They're speciesist, along with being super conservative and intolerant. Any chance I have of ever seeing or speaking with them again, as slight as it currently is, will be gone completely if I mate with anyone other than a vampire. Being matched with a wolf would be an insult to the family name that could not be overlooked. Or forgiven. When we first met, I panicked at the thought of never seeing my parents or siblings again. You didn't deserve that reaction. I can't apologize enough for treating you like that."

"I understand. That must have been hard for you."

Edgar looked down at his hands. "I need to be completely honest with you, Jackson. I had certain expectations of who I would mate with when the time came. They would, of course, be a vampire from a good family, one who had powerful connections. We would both have similar interests and enjoy traveling to exotic locations and dining in world-famous establishments." He sighed, taking a moment to say goodbye to his long-held dream. "I didn't anticipate bonding with a wolf shifter from the country who I would have nothing in common with. I don't know how mating with you would work. It would take a great deal of adjustment on my part and giving up my dreams of the life I had always imagined for myself."

"I wouldn't worry about it, Edgar. I wouldn't have you on a bet."

Edgar's head snapped up, surprised at the bite in Jackson's voice.

Jackson stood. "I would never force my mate to give up his dreams. Nor would I want to subject myself to a lifetime of misery in trying to meet your expectations and failing. I think it would be best if I took my unsophisticated, country bred, wolf-shifting self as far away from you as possible." Jackson bared his teeth and snarled, startling Edgar further. "Just know that I don't want to put up with your snobbish, prissy, judgmental, vampire ass either. As difficult as it might be for you to believe, I also have standards and expectations. You, mate, fall very short of them." He turned and stomped off, leaving Edgar wondering what he'd said to provoke such a reaction

Jackson had never been so insulted in his life. As if Edgar was the one who had to settle. How dare he treat Jackson as though he was inferior? He knew nothing about him yet had judged him because he wasn't from the city and dared to be a shifter and not a well-bred vampire. Screw him. He didn't need a mate that badly. What he needed to do was leave here and look for his brother.

Jackson stomped through the house toward the room he'd been staying in. Before he could go anywhere, he needed a change of clothes and someone who would let him through the shields. Once that was accomplished, he wasn't going to stay in this place with that stuck-up, snotty, uptight vampire one minute longer than necessary.

Walking down a long hallway, his anger finally got the better of him. Needing to release some of his fury before he went back and strangled his mate, he drove his fist through the wall., barely stopping long enough to pull his hand free from the plaster before continuing to his room. Seething as he stormed down the passageway, he didn't slow to acknowledge Lysander when he passed him or notice him staring after Jackson with his mouth hanging open.

Chapter Six

Edgar stared into the fountain, wondering where he'd gone wrong. The conversation had been going well. Jackson hadn't even blamed Edgar for his family's shortcomings. Yet something had set him off.

"What did you do?"

He jerked, turning to Lysander. "What?"

"That's what I asked you. What did you do to Jackson?"

"Nothing." Edgar frowned. "At least, I don't think I did."

"Nothing doesn't cause a man to drive his fist through the wall. What did you say to him?"

Edgar's mouth dropped open. "He punched the wall?"

"Yes. Luckily, I was able to get someone to come fix it immediately so nobody has to explain to Bryan why there's a hole in the wall. But something you said made him angry enough to hit it in the first place. What was it?"

Edgar shrugged. "I have no idea. We were talking about my family and he seemed fine. He actually reacted much better than I expected. I don't know what made him so upset."

"You only told him about your family? That's it?"

"Yes. Oh. I also mentioned that I'd always thought my mate would be a vampire with common interests. But that shouldn't have made him mad."

Lysander dropped his face into his hand. "Edgar, what exactly did you say?"

"Just that I'd always dreamed of having a vampire mate from a good family. That I didn't anticipate bonding with a wolf from the country. That I would have to adjust my expectations and give up my dreams, and…oh." Edgar paused, his eyes going wide. "That doesn't sound quite the way I meant it to."

"I should hope not. What did you actually mean to say to him?"

"Just that I didn't know how it would work with him as a mate. That he wasn't what I'd always wanted." Edgar stopped again. "That doesn't sound any better. No wonder he got mad."

"For crying out loud. Are you trying to drive Jackson away? Do you want him to find someone else?"

Edgar's teeth dropped. "Nobody had better touch him. He's mine."

Lysander crossed his arms and arched his eyebrow. "Is that so?"

About to say yes, Edgar paused, then shook his head. "Not at the moment, no." He ran a hand down his tie, brushing off non-existent lint. "I really wanted a well-bred vampire. Someone to rub in my family's face about how well I'd done. I wanted them to choke on their words about what a failure I was."

"And that's more important than accepting the gift the Goddess gave you?"

"No, but…"

Lysander came over and grabbed him by the shoulders, shaking him lightly. "Did you miss the part when I told you it was vital for you two to bond? That the very existence of the shifters is at stake. Did I somehow not make that clear to you?"

"No. I heard you. But I'm not going to do something just because you tell me I have to. I can make my own decisions on who I mate."

"Are you kidding me with this? Do you even hear yourself? Edgar, you're not a child. Stop acting like one."

"I'm not a ch—"

Lysander shoved him back. "The fate of the entire shifter race depends on you mating and bonding with Jackson. You need to get over yourself and figure out how to make him forgive you. This is bigger than you. We don't have time for your snotty little attitude."

Edgar glared at Lysander, wondering how much trouble he would be in if he kicked him in the shins.

Lysander glared back, silently daring him. "As your Consort, I'm ordering you to fix this right now."

"That's a misuse of your position."

"Maybe. But you fixing things with Jackson is too important, so I'll do whatever I have to to make it happen."

Knowing he was beaten, Edgar muttered a sullen, "Yes, Consort." He wrenched his shoulders from Lysander's hold, then stomped into the house in search of his runaway mate.

Now where would you go if you were an angry wolf? Edgar had been searching for the last thirty minutes— racing up and down the halls, running flat-out with his vampire speed—and hadn't found Jackson yet. Granted the house was huge, but surely, he should have come across him by now.

Coming to a stop at the end of another hallway, he felt like smacking himself as the obvious hit him. Jackson was a wolf. He wouldn't be inside the house. He would be outside on the grounds somewhere. Knowing how angry Jackson was, he was probably trying to find a way off the property. Which meant there was really only one place he could be. Edgar headed for the guardhouse at the main entrance.

* * *

"I'm sorry sir. I'm only following the Consort's orders. He said I wasn't to let you out."

Jackson growled, just about done with these people. "I don't care what the Consort said. I don't answer to him. Open this gate right now."

"I'm sorry, sir. You may not answer to the Consort, but I do. Even if I did open the gate, it wouldn't help. The Consort's brother has the area sealed off with a magical barrier. Nobody can cross over without Mage Bryan or the Consort allowing them passage through it."

"Jackson," Edgar called out. "I need to talk to you." He ran up to him and grabbed hold of his arm.

Ignoring him, Jackson growled at the guard. "Open it now, before I get angry."

"Please, sir. My hands are tied. I can't let you out."

Snarling at the guard was the wrong tactic. He took one look at Jackson's face, went ghost white, then bolted for the guardhouse, locking the door behind him.

"Jackson. Please listen."

Growling at the gate that barred his way to freedom, Jackson shook off Edgar's hold and turned to go back to the house. If Bryan was the person who could let him out, then Bryan was the one he needed to find.

A blur went racing past him, then cut sharply in front. Only his quick wolf reflexes prevented him from running Edgar down. He dodged past him and continued toward the mansion.

"Fine. If you won't stop and talk to me, you can listen as you run away. I'm sorry. I didn't mean to hurt you with the things I said."

Which wasn't at all the same thing as being sorry for saying them in the first place. Or that he didn't mean.

Jackson rushed through the front door of the mansion and started randomly opening doors and looking inside rooms. He needed to find Bryan quickly.

"I really am sorry. I didn't mean what I said, it just came out wrong. That isn't how I really feel. Would you please just stop and talk to me?"

He rounded on Edgar. "Why? You've made it abundantly clear what you think of me. That I'm less because I'm a wolf. That I'm not what you're looking for. Why worry now about my feelings? I don't care what you think anymore, Edgar. Go look for your perfect, city vampire who will make you happy. I'm done with this."

Or he wanted to be done with this. Inside of him, Jackson's wolf was whining. He didn't want their mate to find someone else. He wanted Edgar. But Jackson only wanted Edgar if he wanted them back, which wasn't the case.

"Jackson. I don't think less of you. I just needed a moment to realign the direction I've always thought my life would go. It doesn't mean I don't want you…"

Jackson stopped him with a look. "Doesn't it? Because that's not how I remember it. But don't worry. I can take a hint. There's no need for you to force yourself to be with me. My wolf and I will be just fine without you."

"The rest of the shifter race won't unless we can work out our mating."

"What are you talking about?"

Edgar stepped toward him, putting a hand on his chest, apology in his eyes. Refusing to let that affect him, Jackson took a step back. Edgar's hand fell from his chest. Sighing, Edgar spoke. "The Consort said that we needed to work out our differences and bond the way fate intended. If we don't, the shifter race would suffer."

"How would he know this?"

"I guess he's developing powers of premonition and can see things. He told me it was necessary for us to bond to save the shifter race."

"And that's the reason you're chasing after me? Forget it." Jackson turned, heading for the next room and looking inside. Still no Bryan. Damn it. Where was that man?

"Jackson, no. That's not the only reason. The Goddess would not make a mistake in matching us. I know I've treated you horribly and you deserve better than that."

Jackson snorted. "You would think so, wouldn't you? Where I come from, we rejoice when we meet our fated mate. We don't treat them like trash or look at them with disgust." Jackson would not feel bad for his words, no matter how distressed Edgar was now looking.

"You're absolutely right. I've been so focused on what I was giving up that I never thought about what I was gaining."

"And what, exactly, is that?"

"I don't know yet. I'll need to get to know you better before I can answer that. In fact, we both need time to get to know each other because I'm not really the kind of person I've been showing to you. At least, not all the way," Edgar said ruefully as he took his hand. "Can you perhaps give me another chance? To see if there's any hope we can get along? I'm asking for both our sakes, because we deserve it, not just because of what the Consort said."

Jackson stared into Edgar's eyes as he considered his options. On one hand was his wolf, who was whining, pushing for him to get closer to their mate. On the other was the way Edgar had discarded him when they first met. But…was he willing to give up his chance to bond with his True-mate because his feelings were hurt? Could he trust Edgar enough to bond with him, knowing the risk to himself and his wolf? No, he couldn't. He didn't know the vampire well enough to know for sure, which told him what he needed to do.

He stepped up to Edgar until their chests pressed together. "If I bond with you and then you reject me, my wolf and I will die. It's not a chance I can take right now. I need to know you better before I'd be willing to take that kind of risk. So far, I'm not impressed. You're going to have to convince me you're worth it."

Edgar nodded. "I understand."

Jackson blew out a breath. "I'll give you time to prove whether or not we can trust you or if we have something we can work toward. My wolf and I deserve the opportunity."

"Thank you. Just so you know, once we bond, I won't be able to feed from another, so I will also die if you and your wolf reject me." Edgar stepped back, putting a small amount of space between them. "I also agree that it's best we take the time to get to know one another better before we take that final step." He held out his hand to Jackson.

After giving the vampire one last look, gauging his sincerity, Jackson shook it, agreeing to the terms.

"Finally."

They both turned to see the Consort standing behind them.

"I thought you two would never get this sorted out. Now come with me. We need to plan your trip. You leave at midnight." He turned and headed down the corridor.

Jackson looked at Edgar. "Is he always this bossy?"

Edgar sighed. "You have no idea." He headed down the hallway.

Jackson hurried to catch up. Walking beside Edgar as they followed the Consort, he hoped he didn't come to regret his decision to stay.

* * *

Jackson reclined in one of the most comfortable chairs he'd ever sat on in his life. He'd say one thing about the people in the mansion, they had great taste in furniture. He looked around the, well, he supposed it was an office; but it looked more like a den. Colorful pictures hung on every wall, overstuffed couches and chairs were placed around the room, creating numerous conversation areas. There was a crib to one side of the desk and a daybed with suspiciously messed up pillows on the other. His eyes stopped on a fantastically lifelike charcoal sketch of a hissing cat. It was hanging on the wall in a lighted alcove, located in a space behind the daybed. As amazing as the sketch was, it was a peculiar thing to see hanging in the office of a vampire. As he wondered at the significance behind it, the object of the drawing sauntered into the room, jumped up on the daybed, then posed like one of the great majestic cats of Egypt. As he stared at it, the cat returned his look with unblinking eyes. Jackson shivered, the feline's intense scrutiny was making his wolf nervous.

Jackson looked away from the cat when Roman entered the room. He pressed his lips together to keep from laughing when the cat hissed and growled at Roman, then swiped at him with its claws when he moved past it. The picture having a place of honor in Roman's office made even less sense.

"Thank you for coming, gentlemen. My mate will be along shortly. He is putting Nico down for his nap." Roman set his phone on the desk then came over to Jackson. "I owe you an apology. The Consort and I were both out of line in our reactions to you over Nico. I tend to react quickly and violently whenever those I love are threatened. Even though you did nothing to warrant it, I nonetheless reacted to the fear of losing my son. Please accept my apology."

Jackson stood, and offered his hand. "Of course. I understand. However, we will eventually have to talk about Nico after I find out what's happened to my brother and this Council matter is dealt with."

"Agreed. However, that time is not today."

"No, not today, but we will discuss it when we can." Jackson pushed his point, not willing to back down from the powerful vampire Prince.

Roman nodded. "We will. All of us will decide what is best for Nico's future." He gave Jackson a pointed look, as though to make sure he'd picked up on the all in his statement.

Jackson nodded his understanding. Roman gave his hand a quick squeeze, then went and sat behind the desk. He smiled to himself, pleased at knowing Nico would be looked after by such fierce protectors. The baby would be safe and well protected at the mansion.

While they waited on the Consort, he took the time to covertly study the other men in the room. Edgar sat in the chair next to his, sneaking glances his way every few minutes. Jackson's wolf preened, excited by Edgar's apparent fascination with them. Bryan spent his time looking out the window with a grim expression on his face. Roman's Second, Max, stood at attention near the desk, watching the rest of them, though Jackson noted his eyes seemed to linger on Bryan more often than not. Jackson's eyes flicked over to Roman, who was watching him with an unnerving intensity. He held his gaze to show he wasn't intimidated by the ancient vampire. The Prince tipped his head respectfully to him, one predator acknowledging another.

The Consort breezed in through the doorway, his appearance instantly charging the room with energy. After taking a quick look around, he smiled. "Good. It looks like we're all here." He went behind the desk and sat on Roman's lap, giving him a quick kiss. It looked like an unconscious move, something he did so often it had become second nature and expected.

Jackson glanced over at Edgar, wondering if they'd ever achieve that much familiarity with each other. The way they were going, he highly doubted it.

Lysander exchanged a private look with Roman, then turned to face the room. "Okay, let's get started. We have no time to waste. Bryan, I need you to call Nick and have him pick out two of his strongest magic users."

"Why do you need Nick's men?"

"They need to meet up with Edgar and Jackson when they get to Denver."

"Why don't we just send a couple of our magic users with them?"

"We are, but they're going to need the extra support when they get to Denver. Call Nick and tell him to have his men ready for Jackson's call."

"Okay, but he's going to want to know why."

"Because I saw something that makes me think Denver is where Edgar and Jackson are going to run into the greatest danger."

"What kind of danger?" Bryan asked, frowning at him.

"I don't know for sure. I know you're doubtful of these feelings I'm suddenly getting, but I'm going to trust what my gut is telling me and act accordingly. Please call Nick.

Edgar and Jackson are leaving at midnight, so he needs to have his men ready to go in four days.

"Um, Consort," Jackson raised his hand partway. "I'm not sure if you realize it, but it's only about twenty hours from New Orleans to Denver."

"Yes, I know. However, you need to stop in Dallas on your way and deal with the Alpha there. There is a chance you might run into a couple of other delays so I'm guessing it will take you about four days to get to Denver."

It was Jackson's turn to frown. How did the Consort know these things? Or was he just making it up? He stared at him, not sure if he believed in this premonition stuff. The Consort held his gaze. Long enough for Jackson to become suspicious about the Consort's ability to read minds. He blew out a relieved breath when his attention finally moved to Edgar.

"Edgar, you'll probably be the one to make these next arrangements. You need to get two of Roman's vampire equipped SUVs prepared for an extended trip. Bryan can give you the names of two magic users you need to take with you. Roman, can you please pick three of your best enforcers to go as well." He paused and looked down. "There's something I'm forgetting." He snapped his fingers. "Right. Max, I need you to equip both vehicles with as much firepower as they can carry. The vampires will need weapons for any fighting that happens during the day when they can't leave the vehicles."

By this time, Jackson's head was spinning with the orders the Consort was barking out like a four-star General. Who was this guy? He seemed much too young to be in charge like this.

"Who on earth will be attacking them, beloved?"

"I'm not sure, but the vampires will be vulnerable during the day. I want them armed so they can properly defend themselves."

"Beloved, our vampires have survived a long time using their own skills. You don't need to coddle them so much."

"I don't care how long they've survived or how good at fighting they are. I will do whatever I feel is necessary to keep everyone safe so they all come back home to us."

"Then it shall be as you ask. I want them returned safely to us as well. Edgar, Max, do whatever my mate tells you."

"Yes, Roman."

"Make sure you take satellite phones too," Lysander said.

"Why on earth do we need those? Denver is a large city. I'm fairly certain regular cell phone service is available." Edgar crossed his arms, glaring at the Consort.

"You'll need them because you and Jackson will be spending a great deal of time traveling through the mountains towards Montana."

"No. I will not be going into the mountains," Edgar argued.

The Consort nodded. "Yes, you will. I need you and Jackson to work your way north and check on as many of the alpine packs as you can."

"Why? What's in the mountains?"

The Consort frowned. "I'm not exactly sure. The magic is telling me that you and Jackson need to go north." He looked up, his piercing stare causing the first tendrils of alarm to fill Jackson. "And quickly, Edgar. You need to get there as fast as you can."

Edgar's eyes widened. He glanced over at Jackson, who nodded, then back to the Consort. "Okay, if it's that important. We'll do as you say."

Lysander blinked, then smiled, his eyes friendly and warm again. Jackson shivered. "Thank you. Do you have any other questions?"

Jackson shook his head. His orders were clear. He was ready to go.

Edgar's brow creased in thought before he asked. "What exactly am I supposed to wear in the mountains?"

Jackson stared at him, at a loss for words. That was his big concern? Then he began to laugh, looking forward to seeing how his prissy mate dealt with being in the wilderness."

86

Chapter Seven

Jackson glanced over when Edgar shifted in his seat and began running his hands up and down his dress pants.

"Try to relax. The wolves will be able to smell your anxiety. If you go in there like this, they'll consider you prey and treat you accordingly. When you're at the pack, you need to show that you're strong, a predator just like they are. That's the only way they'll respect you."

"I know that. I've just never done anything like this before. I'm not sure what'll be expected of me when we get there."

"Pay attention and let me lead the conversation. If you have any questions, save them until we're alone. You cannot, under any circumstances, show weakness in a wolf pack."

Edgar gulped. Jackson could smell when his agitation increased. He sighed as he looked at his mate. This was going to go so bad. Edgar was dressed as if he was going to spend the day at the office—wearing a fancy suit and tie—instead of taking a trip through the country to check on the wolf packs. His mate was going to quickly realize his mistake in not listening to Jackson on what to wear. He'd be lucky if the wolves only laughed at him.

Fortunately, the Consort had understood what was required and had handed him a suitcase he'd packed for Edgar, along with a wink. His mate would appreciate the more suitable clothing when they hit the mountains. Once he'd finished complaining about them, that is. Jackson was looking forward to the hissy fit Edgar was going to throw when he got a look at the jeans and Henley's the Consort had packed for him.

Looking out the window as the night gave way to dawn, he saw with relief they were finally nearing the outskirts of Dallas. He'd spent the entire trip worried about what was happening with the pack, so was anxious to get started dealing with whatever the problem was. He just wished they'd been able to get there sooner, because as fast as they'd driven, they hadn't managed to beat the sun. Whatever they found when they reached the Dallas pack lands, he was only going to have the two magic users with him as the vampires would need to stay in vehicles.

Seeing the turn coming up, Jackson leaned forward and touched the magic user who was driving on the shoulder. "You want to take the next right. The pack lands are near the lake."

"We're not going into Dallas?" Edgar asked.

"No," Jackson said, leaning back and turning his head to Edgar. "It's called the Dallas pack but they don't actually live in the city. Wolves try to find spaces where they can let their animals run free, establishing packs around natural lakes and protected forests. It's the only way to survive as humans take over the world, turning the landscape into concrete."

"Oh. I never thought about it before. That makes sense."

"Edgar," Jackson looked at him seriously. "Could you please keep an open mind when you meet the packs? Try to see the beauty in the areas the wolves live and imagine the possibilities that staying in the city doesn't provide. If we decide to complete our bond, we'll have to live with the pack. I am of the Alpha line and have a responsibility to the wolf shifters. I can't live in the city with you, so you would have to come with me."

Jackson stared at this mate, his heart sinking when he saw the panicked denial cross Edgar's face. He sighed and closed his eyes, done with the conversation. It was hard to keep in mind he'd promised to give Edgar time to adjust when he reacted like that.

"Sir, I believe we have arrived." Jackson lifted his head to see a wolf escort running alongside the vehicles.

"Drive slowly down this road until you come to the packhouse. I want everyone to stay in the vehicle until I see what we're dealing with." He turned to Edgar. "You and the vampires need to stay in the vehicles. The sun will be up any moment. I don't want you to get caught outside."

"Obviously." Edgar sniffed, looking pointedly out the window. Jackson ignored him, not having the patience to deal with his pouting.

Jackson leaned forward and looked out the windshield as they made their way up the long drive, then squinted, wondering if his eyes were deceiving him. As the SUV neared the packhouse, he began growling in anger when he realized exactly what was happening.

"What are they doing?" Edgar screamed. "Stop the car."

"Edgar, wait." Jackson grabbed for him, missing his arm by inches when Edgar bolted from the vehicle. He threw open his door, chasing after his foolhardy mate.

"Stop. What are you doing? Get away from them."

Jackson raced up beside Edgar, who was standing in front of a pyre with his arms stretched wide to prevent three men with torches from lighting it. He helped block the men from getting any closer, then glanced over his shoulders at the terrified people tied to posts.

"Best get out of the way, son, or you'll be joining them," a man drawled as he stepped off the packhouse porch and joined with the men holding the torches. He sniffed the air, then glared at Edgar. "Though seeing as you're a vampire, I suspect you'll be going up in flames momentarily." He looked pointedly at the brightening sky, smiling viciously when Edgar hissed at him.

Jackson glared at the Alpha, then nudged his mate. "You need to get back to the car."

"I'll be fine for a few more minutes. We have to save these people."

The Alpha laughed. "There will be no saving them. They will die with the morning sun." He glared at Edgar. "Just like you will." He pointed to two of his men. "Grab the troublemaker and throw him on there with the rest."

Jackson's wolf went on high alert as he bared his teeth, his growl louder. "The first person who lays a hand on him dies."

"And who are you, boy, to threaten my men?"

"Jackson Miller from the Denver pack. Perhaps you've heard of my family?" Based on how the Alpha's face paled, he had indeed heard of the Millers. Allowing his wolf to show in his eyes. Jackson asked, "What is going on here?"

"They're being punished."

"You're going to burn them to death. This is far beyond punishment. What could they possibly have done to warrant that?" Edgar asked, stepping in front of Jackson, who grabbed him before he could get too close to the men with the torches. He didn't trust any of them to be smart enough to not set fire to his mate.

"I don't answer to you, boy."

Jackson pushed Edgar behind him and took a step forward. "But you do answer to me. As Alpha, you should be protecting your wolves, not killing them. Tell me why you're doing this."

The Alpha scowled at him. Jackson pushed with his Alpha power, which the weaker Alpha had no chance of standing up against. Paling, he took a step back, then recovered. Glaring at Jackson, he spat on the ground near his feet. Jackson let the insult go, more concerned with saving the wolves. "They were having unnatural relations. I won't abide with that kind of behavior in my pack."

"Unnatural relations?" Jackson tilted his head having no idea what he could be talking about. "What kind of unnatural relations?"

The Alpha sneered. "Boys with boys, women with women, two men and a woman. It's not right. I won't have that in my pack."

"We're wolves. We don't worry about things like gender or the number of partners. It's all about instinct and attraction, what the animal half wants. You should know this."

"It's unnatural," the Alpha yelled.

"If you were in touch with your wolf, you'd know there's nothing unnatural about it. You not liking it is not justification for the death sentence you intend to impose. If you don't want to see it, walk away and ignore it."

"I can't ignore what happens in my own pack. I'm in charge here, not you." He spat on the ground, again narrowly missing Jackson's boot. One more time doing that, and Jackson couldn't continue to overlook the insult. "These unnatural relations may be fine where you come from, but here in my pack, it's against the rules and punishable by death."

Jackson looked at the pyre. There were at least fifteen shifters tied up, maybe more. "Why are you going to kill so many wolves? You can't possibly have that many who broke your so-called rule at the same time?"

"Anybody who is a known associate or helped hide the lawbreaker suffers the same punishment. They have all earned their fate. As their Alpha, this is my right."

"Jackson," Edgar spoke up behind him, "there are children in there."

Jackson bared his teeth, his voice low and dangerous. "You're burning children? How dare you harm an innocent?"

"We need to stop the contamination from spreading. They are born from the filth that plagues this pack, so they will die with them. I will purge this pack and make everyone clean again."

Jackson kicked off his boots and started unbuttoning his shirt. "Edgar, try to get the children free, then get back to the vehicles. You three," he pointed at the men with torches, "put those down and cut everyone loose or you'll be the next to die after your Alpha."

"Don't listen to him. They must be punished." The Alpha rushed one of the men, ripping the torch from his hands and throwing it high in the air. "They will burn today. All of them. You can't stop it now." He started laughing maniacally as the torch slowly arced, then fell toward the pyre.

Edgar leaped into the air, missing the falling torch by inches. The burning brand landed on the mountain of dried wood, which immediately caught on fire. Edgar rushed after it, jumping and landing on top of the torch, screaming as his body snuffed it out and smothered the fire before it had a chance to spread.

The smell of his mate's burning flesh and the sounds of his screams was too much for Jackson's wolf, who took control and forced the shift, shredding his clothing. In seconds, his large gray wolf form stood in place of the man. Jackson shook out his fur, then charged the Alpha, taking him to the ground.

The Alpha began his shift, but by then, Jackson was already tearing out his throat, showing no mercy for the crazed man.

He rose from his kill, circling it once, then left the body lying in the dust, its blood soaking into the ground as he raced toward his mate who was moaning weakly atop the pyre. He howled when he saw the rising sun's morning light slowly climbing the side of the woodpile, its deadly rays nearing Edgar's hand. Leaping up beside him, Jackson forced his wolf down and shifted back to human form, then grabbed Edgar and ran for the closest vehicle. The door opened as he reached it, allowing him to dive inside.

Jackson laid Edgar on the seat and pushed the tattered remains of his shirt to the side. His breath caught when he saw the extent of the damage to Edgar's torso. Furrows had been burned into his skin, charred black at the edges. On his left side, sections of his ribs gleamed whitely, a stark contrast to the reddened and blackened flesh around them. With the roaring of his own heartbeat drowning out all sound, he didn't at first hear the high-pitched whine Edgar was making, but once he did, the sound scraped raw every nerve Jackson had.

"Sir. Sir, you must listen to me."

Jackson dragged his eyes off his critically injured mate to the vampire leaning over the front seat trying to get his attention.

"What?"

"You need to give him blood."

"What?" Jackson asked again, in confusion.

"You must give him your blood. It will help him heal the damage. His injuries are too expensive to mend on their own."

"My blood?"

"You're his Bloodmate, are you not?"

"Yes," Jackson said slowly, still not understanding.

"Then it must be you who provides him blood. He can't take it from anybody else. But hurry."

Jackson reached for Edgar, then paused. Looking at the vampire, he asked, "Will giving him my blood create a bond between us?"

The vampire's brow wrinkled as he squinted at Jackson. "You just said you were Bloodmates. Don't you already have a bond?"

"We're mates, but we haven't agreed to bond yet. Will feeding him cause a connection to form?"

"More than likely."

"I'm not sure—"

"The alternative is that he'll die, after suffering agonizing pain. You must decide which one you can live with." Giving Jackson a look that dared him to make the wrong choice, the vampire turned around in his seat.

Jackson stared at the back of his head, then down at Edgar, realizing there really was only one choice. He needed to do what was best for his mate. They could deal with any consequences later.

Jackson flicked out a claw. Swiping it across his wrist, he let the blood pour into Edgar's mouth.

* * *

Edgar sat up with a start, his breath coming fast from panic. Patting his chest, he stared down at the mostly healed marks. His memory of the excruciating pain from the fire was fresh in his mind. He could still feel the flames burning through him. He ran his hand down his chest again, needing a moment to understand the pain was only in his mind and that his body was not engulfed in an inferno. Someone had obviously healed him.

He fell back to the bed and closed his eyes, trying to figure out what happened. The last thing he remembered was throwing his body on the flames so the children wouldn't burn. He had a vague recollection of Jackson carrying him somewhere, but nothing after that. Lying there, he became aware of a faint pulsing in his mind, as if sharing the space with another presence. Poking at it mentally, he realized it was Jackson.

He bolted upright. "Oh, shit. Jackson. What did you do?"

"Not quite the response I was expecting, but I probably should have known better."

Edgar's head spun toward the door, where his mate was leaning against the doorframe. "Jackson, I'm so sorry. I didn't intend to force you into a bond with me."

Jackson frowned, tilting his head. "You're sorry I was forced to bond with you? I thought for sure you'd be mad I forced you into a bond with me."

"Of course I'm not mad at you. I put you in a position where you had no choice. But we'd agreed to wait before we took this step. I'm so sorry that option was taken away from you."

"It's not your fault. You were so badly injured we didn't think you'd be able to heal on your own. I made the decision to give you my blood to save you. I'm not sorry I did it and I'd do it again if I had to.

Edgar swallowed the lump in his throat. "Thank you for saving me."

"It's what any mate would do." He paused, giving Edgar a strange look. "I don't imagine this is going to be easy just because we're now bonded."

"Probably not," Edgar sighed. "It's a good thing we have long lives. We'll need that time to work it out."

Jackson snorted. "Hopefully not all of it."

A laugh escaped Edgar before he sobered. "Did you find out why the Alpha was trying to burn everyone to death?"

Jackson pushed off the doorframe and walked over to sit in the chair by the bed. "I spoke with a couple of the Beta wolves, who incidentally were also on that pyre."

Edgar's eyes widened. "Why?"

"They tried to stop him so were sentenced to death with the rest. All of the other men were too afraid to speak up as they didn't want to be next."

"I imagine not. What a terrifying threat to have to live under."

"Yes. According to Betas, the Alpha had been leading their pack for about fifty years. He'd always been a bit conservative and old-fashioned in his thinking but not enough to give them any trouble. But that changed. In the last year, he began to get angry at supposed infractions, punishing anyone who broke his rules, which became more unreasonable by the day. It finally reached the point where everyone was afraid to say or do anything as he would strike out, killing for the slightest reason."

Edgar narrowed his eyes. "Doesn't that seem a little strange to you? That kind of behavior can't be normal."

"It isn't. Anger like that would usually be a sign of his wolf going feral. That happens sometimes with old age, but this Alpha was relatively young. His Betas couldn't find anything to explain his escalating temper and rage. When it reached the point where he was attacking the pack members, a couple of Betas challenged him for control, but his madness made him stronger, almost impossible to kill. The remaining few Betas instead tried to help the at-risk wolves to escape to save their lives. They managed to get a few of them to safety but were caught by the Alpha while assisting this last group. That's when we showed up."

Edgar paled, a thought crossing his mind. "Dear Goddess. The Consort was right. If we'd waited any longer, all those people would have died. The children would have died." Edgar covered his face, stunned by how close it had been.

"I know. It was fortunate we got here when we did."

Edgar dropped his hands from his face and nodded. "And that you were strong enough to kill him."

"About that. I'm not sure how much you understand about how wolf pack Alphas are determined."

He looked at Jackson, a horrible suspicion crossing his mind. "Pretend I know nothing."

"Okay." Jackson clasped his hands and looked at the floor. "There are a few ways wolves can become Alphas. It can pass down from father to son, like my home pack in Denver, or it can be earned through a challenge match."

"Okay, and…."

"Or it can happen if you kill the current Alpha."

"What are you saying?"

Jackson looked up at him. "Since I killed the Dallas Alpha to save his people, I'm now Alpha of this pack." He winced at whatever he saw on Edgar's face.

"You can't be Alpha here. You're already Alpha of the Denver pack."

"I know," Jackson said miserably. "It's a problem. I can't be Alpha of both. In fact, I can't be Alpha of either one of them until we figure out where my brother is and what the Council has done to the shifters."

Edgar gasped. "Could the Council be responsible for what happened to this Alpha?"

Jackson froze, then shook his head. "I don't know, Edgar. It's possible that's why he went mad. But what could they do to cause an Alpha to get so angry he'd turn on his pack?"

"I'm not sure. But I think we should call Roman to let him know what happened."

"Good idea. Maybe they'll have some idea of what happened."

"Or it'll give Bryan something to search for in the Elders' files." Edgar hesitated, then asked, "What're you going to do with the pack?"

"I put two of the Betas in charge. But that's only a temporary measure. Without an Alpha in place, the pack is at risk for takeover. Any lone wolf Alpha or second son could challenge the Betas for control of the pack. That means a fight to the death, which is not something either of the Betas can win. They're just not strong enough to take on an Alpha."

"We can't let that happen to them."

"No. But I can't stay here. At least, not now."

Edgar nodded. "Perhaps we'll think of something on way to Denver. Speaking of Denver, when do we leave here?"

Jackson smiled at him and stood. "We were waiting for you to wake up, sleeping beauty. We can leave whenever you're ready."

Edgar bounced off the bed, only a slight twinge in his chest reminding him of the horrific injuries he'd sustained. "I'm ready now. I think I've had enough of this place. I can call Roman from the car." He looked around the room, not seeing his suitcase. "Where are my clothes?"

Jackson grabbed a suitcase Edgar didn't recognize from under the bed, then started laughing as he walked out of the room.

Edgar stared after him, having no idea why that was so funny.

Chapter Eight

Meeting in Roman's office…

"You're sure Edgar's okay?" Lysander asked after Roman hung up the phone.

"He said he was fine. Jackson was able to heal the worst of the damage."

"That's a relief, though it might have created another problem. If Jackson healed him, that means they've partially bonded. I know they both wanted to wait until they knew each other better." Lysander frowned. "While part of me is relieved they've bonded, they need to fully accept each other to get the Goddess' blessing. I hope Edgar doesn't get too stubborn about that."

Roman pulled him into his arms. "I have no doubt they will sort it out. If we could get past your stubbornness to work out our differences, I feel confident Jackson can get around Edgar."

Lysander glared up at him, not sure how offended he should be. Roman's lip twitched. Realizing he was being teased, no matter how much truth was behind it, he snickered. "You make a good point." He leaned up to kiss Roman.

An unconvincing cough broke the moment.

He turned to glare at his brother, including Max who was standing next to Bryan. "Do you mind?"

"Not really. I have more questions for Roman."

"Please, go ahead, Bryan," Roman said, sitting in his chair, pulling Lysander down with him.

Bryan paced around the office. "Edgar said the Alpha's anger was escalating and they could find no explanation for it?"

"Correct. Jackson spoke with the pack while Edgar was healing. They said the Alpha had grown angrier and more intolerant over the last year. They were unable to find a cause."

"And nobody else experienced this unexplained anger themselves?"

"No. I do not believe so."

"That's not good."

"Do you think the same thing is happening to the other packs," Lysander asked.

Bryan blinked, then looked at him. "It probably is. Damn it! What the hell did the Elders do?" He made like he was going to punch the window.

"Bryan! Don't."

Bryan froze, his clenched fist almost touching the glass.

Lysander climbed off of Roman's lap and went to him. "Are you okay?"

Bryan closed his eyes and took a deep breath. Opening them, he nodded. "I'm fine. I think not being able to find any answers is making me tense."

"Are you sure?"

Bryan nodded again. "Like I said, I'm under a lot of stress these days."

Lysander saw his eyes flick over to Max, which explained a lot. "All right. Have you taken too much on? Is there any way we can help?"

He shook his head. "I'll be fine. Let's just carry on. We need to figure out what's going on." Bryan looked over at Roman. "Are you positive it was just the Alpha who was affected?"

"That is what Edgar said. However, they have only been to one pack. He is going to phone again when they get to Denver to let us know what they find."

"Okay. I'll go back to the Council building to see if I can find anything in the records related to Alphas. Please let me know when you hear from them." He strode from the room.

Max stared after him. Bryan stumbled, as though feeling his gaze, then kept going.

Lysander sighed, hoping Bryan dealt with that soon. For both their sakes.

"Beloved, are you picking up any hints about this?"

Lysander shook his head. "No. The only thing I'm getting is that Edgar and Jackson need to hurry."

* * *

Jackson glanced over at Edgar, who was pulling at his neckline again. He chuckled at how uncomfortable Edgar looked in the jeans and Henley. He fidgeted the same way Jackson did when he had to wear a suit and tie.

"Stop laughing at me."

Jackson tried to look contrite, but judging by the glare he received didn't think he pulled it off. Giving it up as a lost cause, he started chuckling. "I'm sorry. I just don't think I've ever seen anyone wear jeans and act like they were being tortured. Most people find them comfortable."

"Well, I'm not most people."

"I'm coming to realize that about you."

"Just what is that supposed to mean?"

Jackson smiled as Edgar glared at him. "Not where your mind is going." Jackson shrugged. "We've really not had a chance to see the best of each other to this point. I'll admit I was surprised by how quick you responded to save the wolves."

"There were children there. Of course, I tried to save them."

"That's not what I meant. I was talking about how you jumped in to help them with no thought of the danger to yourself. You have no idea how much I respect you for that. And as much as I'd rather you not put yourself in danger like that again, thank you for saving them."

Edgar's cheeks pinked up. "Oh. Well, yes, you're welcome."

Jackson felt warmth stirring in his chest. Shyness looked good on his mate. He tentatively reached out a hand to touch Edgar's cheek but dropped it when the driver interrupted them.

"Sirs, we'll be reaching the Amarillo pack in about fifteen minutes."

"Thank you, Eric," Edgar said.

Damn, Jackson berated himself. Not once had he thought to ask their driver's name. Or anyone else's. His mate had him off balance enough that he was forgetting the manners his mother had drummed into him.

"Eric."

"Yes, sir?"

"When we reach our destination, would you please take me around to meet the rest of our escort. I apologize for not introducing myself to everyone sooner."

"No worries, sir. You've had a lot going on. It would be my pleasure to bring you around to everyone." Eric looked pleased by his request. Glancing sideways at Edgar, he was surprised to see a proud look on his face too before he caught his eye. At which point, Edgar made a point of looking out the window, showing his disinterest. Jackson chuckled at his prickly mate. Inside, his wolf perked up, happy that they'd pleased their mate. The warmth in his chest grew.

* * *

Pulling up to the packhouse, Jackson was dismayed at how desolate the place was. He couldn't see any signs of the pack who should be here and the only sound he could hear was the banging of the screen door as it swung in the wind. With his hand on the door handle, he exchanged a glance with Edgar, seeing the same worry he was feeling in his mate's eyes. Sucking in a breath, Jackson opened the door and climbed out of the SUV.

Jackson kept an eye on the packhouse, becoming more concerned when nobody came out to greet them. Wolves were notoriously difficult to surprise. There should have been someone waiting for them long before they reached the center of their territory. Where was everyone?

"Jackson," Edgar asked quietly, coming to stand next to him. "How many wolves are supposed to live here?"

"It's a small pack consisting of two brothers and their families. Last I'd heard, the children were grown, so perhaps twelve to fifteen people. Why? What do you sense?"

"I can only hear one heartbeat. There's nobody else here."

"That makes no sense. Why would they all leave?"

Edgar started to speak, then hesitated.

"What is it?" Jackson asked.

"I don't think they left. I can smell a lot of blood," Edgar paused again before whispering, "and death."

"Damn it. I hope you're wrong about that."

"Me too."

Jackson could tell by his voice that Edgar knew he wasn't mistaken. Dreading what they would find, Jackson headed toward the packhouse, Edgar keeping pace with him. He startled Jackson when he grabbed his hand, the contact sending tingles shooting up his arm. Jackson reflexively squeezed his hand, his heart giving a bump when Edgar squeezed back. Together they reached the main entrance. Opening the screen door, Jackson saw that the inner door stood ajar. He exchanged a grim look with Edgar before gently pushing it open.

"Oh, no." Edgar's soft cry echoed through the house. Jackson pulled away and walked into the den, cursing at seeing the bodies strewn across the floor, covered with flies.

"What happened to them?" Edgar asked.

Jackson knelt down next to one of the women, brushing the flies from her face before gently closing her eyes. Her torn throat told the story of her last minutes. Checking on the other bodies, he saw they too had gone down fighting but inevitably lost to a superior wolf's strength. Studying the men, he realized the Alpha wasn't lying among the bodies.

"We need to find the Alpha. His body isn't here."

"Tell me he didn't do this to his own family."

"I don't want to think it's possible, but everyone died from injuries caused by a wolf, so…"

"Then it was probably him. Damn it. What's going on?"

"I don't know." Jackson stood, his anger growing at whoever killed them. "Edgar, I'm not disrespecting your strength, but please stay behind me while we search. I don't want my wolf distracted worrying about you instead of staying vigilant. The Alpha could be anywhere. I'd rather not be taken by surprise."

Edgar glared at him, then the anger drained from his eyes. "Fine. But we'll be talking about a vampire's fighting strength once we're back on the road."

Jackson nodded his head. "All right, but for now, please let me lead the search."

They made their way carefully through the house, checking in every room. They found two more women, their bloody, wolf-mangled bodies jammed in the space between the wall and the bed. Jackson and Edgar carefully lifted them out and brought them down to lay with the others. Jackson's wolf howled in mourning for the dead wolves, Jackson grieving with him.

After clearing the rest of the house, Jackson led the way outside and headed toward the barn. Pulling the door open, he saw the animals hadn't fared any better than the shifters inside the packhouse. Jackson grimaced at the smell, swatting the buzzing flies away from his face.

"Why would anyone do this?" Edgar asked.

"I don't know. A natural wolf will only kill for food or to defend their territory. A shifter would have to be completely insane to destroy this many domestic animals in such a senseless manner. If it was the Alpha who did this, his wolf has to be completely feral. There's no other explanation."

"He's in here, Jackson. I can hear his heartbeat," Edgar whispered.

Nodding, Jackson stared down the length of the barn, his stomach twisting. He started walking slowly down the row, searching in each of the stalls. He came to a stop when he heard rustling coming from the far end of the barn. He turned to Edgar. "Please wait here."

"Jackson, I'm not a weakling. I can defend myself."

"I know you're not, but please do as I ask." Jackson's heart clenched at the thought of Edgar rushing into more danger.

"This one time." Edgar crossed his arms, fuming, but stayed put.

Jackson reached out a hand and gently touched his cheek, startling his mate. "Thank you," he said quietly.

Edgar's face softened, the frown dropping away. He nodded at Jackson.

Any relief he felt knowing that his mate would be safe was overshadowed by his dread of what he might find. Senses on high alert, Jackson walked the remaining distance, pausing a moment before pulling open the door of the last stall. Growling, he bared his teeth at the Alpha crouched in the dirty hay. When he growled back, Jackson allowed his wolf to rise, showing him who the more dominant Alpha was. Stepping into the stall, he pulled the door closed behind him and he walked over to him, taking note of the blood that streaked his body. His hands were crimson with dried blood that cracked when they flexed, with more thickly caked around his mouth, and eyes filled with wildness and anger. No, not anger. Rage. Enough rage that the Alpha was pushing against Jackson's dominance, who could barely control him.

"Why did you kill them?"

The crazed Alpha crouching at his feet bared his teeth, then sprang at him. Jackson, ready for an attack, had his large hand around his neck before he could get close. Holding him at arm's length, he shook him and asked again, "Why?"

The Alpha growled, his clawed hands swiping through the air, trying to slash Jackson's face, as his legs kicked wildly. Unable to get past Jackson's longer reach, the Alpha grabbed onto his arm, digging in with his claws down to the bone.

Gritting his teeth against the pain, Jackson shook him again. "Stop it." He pushed harder with his Alpha powers, baring his teeth and growling fiercely at the man, trying to subdue his wolf. The Alpha continued fighting against his hold, so Jackson squeezed his neck tighter. Then some more.

Running out of air, the Alpha stopped fighting him, hanging limp in his grip.

"Now answer my question," Jackson said again, his voice filled with the fury of his wolf.

"She burned my dinner."

"What?" Jackson asked, horrified. Dear Goddess, no. He couldn't have heard that right. The Alpha couldn't have killed his family over something trivial like that.

"I said she burned my dinner. Stupid bitch had one job and screwed it up, so I fixed her. Oh yeah, I fixed her good."

"And the rest. Why did you kill them?" Jackson asked, already building shields around his heart as he prepared for what he had to do. There was only one way this could end now.

"They tried to stop me. I showed them who's boss around here. Ain't nobody gonna get in my way again."

"No," Jackson said sorrowfully. "No, they're not." With a quick move, he snapped the feral wolf's neck, putting him out of his misery. There was no chance of saving the Alpha, not after that. Jackson closed his eyes for a moment, grieving for the lost wolf.

Setting him down gently on the ground, he turned to the stall door and cursed when he saw Edgar, who hadn't stayed back like he'd asked him to do. He shoved open the stall door and strode angrily past him.

"Jackson, wait."

Turning quickly, he yelled, "Why don't you listen to me? Why?"

"Jackson…"

"No. I asked for one thing from you. One thing, Edgar. And you completely ignored my wishes." Jackson spun around, and stomped down the aisle, intent on finding a hose to clean off the blood covering him. "Go away. I don't want to talk to you right now."

A moment later, he had his arms full as his mate hugged him tightly.

"I'm sorry they all died, Jackson. I'm so sorry this is being left for you to handle."

Jackson put his trembling hands on his shoulders to push him away, but Edgar squeezed him harder, holding on tightly. Jackson stood stiffly, his body shaking in rage, before his anger finally let go, grief taking its place. Sobbing, he bent over Edgar, and grabbed fistfuls of the back of his shirt. He gave in to his anguish, letting Edgar support his weight while he cried out his sorrow, pain, and horror at so many senseless deaths.

His mate's gentle voice whispered sorry over and over again while his arms held Jackson's trembling body.

Jackson eventually raised his head. Wiping the wetness off his face with his shoulders, he rested his cheek on Edgar's hair, grateful his mate hadn't allowed Jackson to push him away. Especially, since Edgar's strong arms were the only thing holding Jackson together. He breathed deeply, letting his mate's scent soothe both him and his wolf.

Edgar whispered to him. "I wish you hadn't had to deal with that. I'm sorry I couldn't have done more to help."

"There's nothing to be sorry about." Jackson shifted, pressing his forehead to Edgar's. "As Alpha, it's my responsibility to take care of the packs."

"I know. I just wish there was more I could do to help you."

"This is enough."

They stood silently in the middle of the barn for a few more moments, holding each other close, before Jackson finally pulled away. He cupped Edgar's cheek, stroking softly with his thumb. "Thank you for being here. I'm sorry I yelled at you."

Edgar grabbed his hand, pressing it firmly to his face. "It's fine. I should have done as you asked, but I'm glad I was here for you." He reached up and brushed some residual dampness from under Jackson's eye.

Smiling his thanks, Jackson grabbed Edgar's hand, pulling him to the entrance. "Let's get out of here. There's nothing more we can do." They walked toward the house. Jackson breathed in the fresh, clean air, trying to remove the smell of death from his nose.

"Are we just going to leave the bodies here? What about their families?"

"They have no other family. This was all of them" Sadness and anger started to build again. He quickly pushed it aside, locking it up. There were more pressing issues to deal with right now. "We'll bury the shifters behind the packhouse. Please gather everyone to help. Tell them to grab shovels. There should be some in the barn."

"What about the Alpha?"

"We'll bury him with his family. Whatever happened here, wasn't his fault. Something else was in control. If he'd been able to come back from the madness, knowing what he'd done to his family would have broken him. Killing him was the only mercy I could give him." Jackson clenched his fists as the anger started to rise again. "He should be put to rest alongside his family."

"All right. I'll let the others know where to find him." Edgar looked over his shoulder. "What should we do about the animals? That's a lot of digging if we need to bury them."

Jackson glanced over at the barn before shaking his head. "We're not going to bury them. We'll have to torch the barn with the animals inside. If nothing else, it will help keep predators away. Hurry and get everyone organized, Edgar. We need to get this all done before daybreak."

Edgar nodded, running off to do as he asked.

Looking around at the devastation of the Amarillo pack lands, Jackson prayed this was the last time they came across a situation like this. Goddess help them all if this wasn't an isolated incident.

* * *

Edgar was keeping a close eye on his mate, worried about his emotional state. Jackson had been stewing in silence since leaving the burning wreckage of the Amarillo pack. Realizing they couldn't go to Denver until Jackson had time to come to terms with everything, Edgar leaned forward to speak with the driver. "Eric, find the nearest hotel that caters to vampires. We're going to wait out the day before we meet up with the Denver pack."

"No," Jackson contradicted, "we go there now."

Ignoring him, Edgar addressed the magic user in the front passenger seat. "Clancy, call the other car. Let them know we're stopping for the day. Tell everyone to be on their guard. I don't want any surprises while we're stopped."

"Yes, sir. I'm calling right now."

Nodding, Edgar sat back in his seat. Feeling the side of his face burning, he turned to Jackson. "You can stop glaring at me. We're going to wait out the day. You need time to process what happened back there, and I need to change into something more comfortable. When we meet up with the Denver pack, we'll be going in at full strength. There will be no more heading into dangerous situations during the day where we're trapped in the car like what happened in Dallas. Not again."

Edgar figured he'd won that round when Jackson's lip curled up, showing a fang before he turned back to the window. It was a silent ride to the hotel even as Jackson held tightly to the hand Edgar had slipped into his.

* * *

Edgar nodded, pacing as he spoke on the phone. "Yes, Roman. It was completely over the top rage from the Alpha that made him kill his pack and destroy everything else. The magic users looked around but didn't find anything that could've caused his madness. Bryan needs to keep searching in the Council records. There has to be something in them to explain what's happening to the packs."

He listened as Roman spoke. "He is. Okay, that's good. I might be wrong about this since we've only seen two packs so far, but have him look for something that only affects Alpha wolves." He listened for a moment. "Jackson? He's good. I mean, not good in that he's obviously upset about what happened to the Amarillo pack. And the fact that he's had to destroy two feral Alphas so far on this trip. But otherwise, he's doing as well as can be expected. I don't see any signs of irrational anger, but I'll keep a close eye on him." He nodded again. "Of course. I'll tell you immediately if anything changes. Let the Consort know we're heading out to see the Denver pack once it gets dark. I'll call back when we're done there."

Disconnecting the call, Edgar walked over to the mirror, straightening his tie and brushing off non-existent lint from his sleeves. He'd found his suitcase tucked in the back corner of the storage compartment of their SUV. Not sure why it had been shoved back there, he'd hauled it out, ignoring the snickers around him and glaring at everyone as he carried the bag to his room. However, feeling more like himself, he was willing to forgive them for messing with him and forcing him to wear denim. He shuddered, recalling the feel of the stiff fabric touching his skin.

Someone started banging on his door. Taking a wild guess who it could be, he walked over to check the peephole. Sighing, he let Jackson in.

Jackson stomped into the room. Apparently, the Alpha was still angry at Edgar for ignoring his orders. Too bad. Edgar would do whatever he felt was best for his mate, whether he agreed with him or not. He walked over to the bed and put the last couple of items in his suitcase before zipping it up.

"What are you wearing?" Jackson stopped in front of Edgar and tugged on his tie. "Did you learn nothing after what happened at the Dallas pack?"

Edgar leaned back, pulling his tie free. Adjusting it, he responded. "I highly doubt we will find another pyre I need to throw myself on top of."

"No. But that doesn't mean we won't be running into trouble. We're visiting a wolf pack, not going into a board meeting. There may be fighting when we get there. In fact, if we have to deal with Russell, I can almost guarantee it. You need to dress accordingly."

"I'm going to wear the suit." Edgar crossed his arms over his chest, challenging the growly Alpha.

"Why? Why is it so important for you to wear a suit, that you would put it before your own safety?"

Edgar paused, not sure how much he wanted to say. He looked into Jackson's eyes, which were filled with confused frustration. He sighed, looking down. This was his mate. He needed to be honest with him. The only way Jackson could learn who he truly was, at his core, was if he shared what drove him, even his deeply buried insecurities.

Taking a deep breath, Edgar whispered, "I need to wear the suit because it makes me feel confident. When I wear it, I'm reminded of how important I am to Roman and how much he trusts and depends on me. It makes me feel stronger. I need that extra support when I'm heading into new situations where I don't know what I will be facing."

Jackson stepped up to him again, gently cupping his face. "What about your own strength, Edgar. Where is that?"

He frowned. "I don't understand."

"You're more than just Roman's assistant; as important as that is to you. What about your strength?"

"I don't have any on my own," Edgar said quietly, looking away in shame.

"Look at me."

Edgar lifted his eyes, his heart speeding up when Jackson smiled fondly at him.

"You do have your own strength. That wasn't Roman's assistant who jumped onto a burning torch to protect children from harm. That was all you. You're much stronger than you give yourself credit for. You just need to believe in yourself more." Jackson stepped back, fingertips lingering on his cheek before dropping. "Wear the suit if you think it will help, but know that I see you. Just you, Edgar, not Roman's assistant." He turned and walked out of the room, calling back over his shoulder. "We're leaving in five minutes." Then he was gone.

Edgar looked after him, touching his cheek, his heart so high in his throat he couldn't have spoken a word…even if he'd known what to say.

Chapter Nine

Jackson glanced over at his mate as the SUV came to a stop in front of the Denver packhouse. He'd been silent the entire drive; however, Jackson had been counting how many times he'd touched his cheek. Twelve. He smiled inwardly at the effect he was having on his vampire.

Hoping what he said next didn't erase all the ground he'd made, Jackson turned to his mate. "I know you won't stay in the vehicle, but I need you to follow my lead and do whatever I tell you without hesitation."

"Okay. But—"

"And I'd really like it if you didn't put yourself in danger this time. It distresses my wolf."

Edgar glared at him. "It's not like I ask for trouble."

"I realize that."

"I don't go around looking for fights."

"I know that too. But could you try to stay out of trouble anyway." His skin burned from the ferocity of his mate's scowl.

Edgar leaned in until Jackson could feel his breath on his face. "You seem to forget I'm a vampire. I grew up fighting things much worse than a crazy Alpha. If it comes down to a fight, my claws are longer, my teeth are sharper, and I will always be faster than any wolf. Including you."

Pulling away, Edgar got out of the vehicle, then adjusted his jacket and tie. Leaning down, he raised an eyebrow at Jackson. "Are you coming?"

Jackson grinned at his feisty mate. It seemed you could take the vampire out of the office, but he still wore his best suit to a pack fight, ready to kick ass. This was going to be a very interesting visit.

Jackson got out of the SUV and joined Edgar at the front of the vehicle. Grabbing his hand, he began walking toward the packhouse, his belly filled with nerves. It was time to see if they could find any clues to his brother's disappearance.

Jackson came to an abrupt stop when the door opened and a large Gamma, who should not be in his brother's house, stepped out onto the porch.

"Well, well, well. If it isn't little Jackie Miller, home from war."

"Russel." Jackson growled his name. "What are you doing in Clint's house?"

"Well, Jackie, I don't rightly know that this is Clint's house anymore, what with him just taking off like he did."

"Excuse me?" Surely Russel wasn't trying to make him think Clint had abandoned their home.

"Oh. I thought I mentioned that to you?" Russel's attempt to look innocent fooled no one.

"You know you didn't." Good thing Mary had.

"How 'bout that." He scratched his chin, then shrugged. "Well, whatever. Clint, his missus, and their brat all disappeared one night, leaving the pack without an Alpha. Someone had to step up and look after things. You should be thanking me for taking over while you were off playing soldier." Russel clunked down the stairs, stopping in front of Jackson. "Since I was the only one willing to take responsibility for this pack, I claimed the packhouse as mine. Nobody was using it anyway."

"The packhouse is my family home and not something you can just take over. You need to gather your shit and get out of it immediately."

"Who's going to make me? You and that prissy little vampire holding your hand?" Russel looked Jackson up and down with a sneer. "I don't think you're man enough to make me. Give me a call when you've grown up." Completely disregarding his danger, he turned his back on Jackson and headed back up the stairs.

Jackson gently disengaged his hand from Edgar's. "Stay back and let me handle him." When Edgar looked like he was going to argue, he said, "I need you to listen to me this time. This is pack business. I'm the Alpha, so this is my responsibility to handle. You'll undermine my authority and make me look weak if you try to interfere."

"Okay," Edgar whispered and stepped back.

Jackson turned back to Russel, who was watching them from the porch.

"Get everything settled with the little woman?"

"Russel, it seems you've forgotten I'm from the Alpha line. Let me remind you what that means." Jackson moved closer as he pushed out with his Alpha power.

Russel's eyes widened in surprise. He started fighting against it so Jackson pushed harder. Russel tried to resist but a Gamma had no chance of standing up to an Alpha. Especially not one as powerful as Jackson. Against his will, with hatred burning in his eyes, Russel slowly tilted his head, baring his neck.

Jackson growled at him. "Get on your knees and show proper respect to me as your Alpha."

Russel snarled and struggled harder, fighting against his order.

"Now, Russel."

Dropping heavily to his knees, Russel tilted his head further. Jackson walked up the steps and placed his hand on Russel's neck, his claws pressing against his skin. "Tell me what happened to my brother."

Speaking through gritted teeth, Russel said, "Exactly what I said, Alpha. They were here one night and gone the following morning. Nobody saw or heard anything to explain where they went."

Jackson studied him. He smelled no deceit, but Russel's words felt unfinished. He was holding something back. Jackson flexed his fingers, claws denting but not breaking through the skin on Russel's neck. "What else, Russel?"

"That's it. I swear."

"You would lie to your Alpha? I'm already pissed at you for invading my family home. Do you really think it's wise to push me?"

Russel glared at him. Jackson bared a fang in warning. "Fine," Russel spat out. "Your brother left you a note. I burned it."

Narrowing his eyes, Jackson asked, "What did it say?"

"I didn't read it."

That was a lie. He didn't even need to use his wolf senses to know that. Crouching in front of Russel, Jackson leaned in and sniffed along his neck, his fingers flexing again, this time breaking the skin. Trickles of blood started flowing.

Jackson whispered in Russel's ear. "You know I can smell your lies. Why would you even try?"

"Because I hate you and I hate your family. All of you think you're so much better than the rest of us. Making us submit to you just because you were born with some lucky gene. You have no right to treat us this way."

"I don't want everyone submitting to me. Just you, Russel. And as an Alpha, I do have that right. Lucky gene or not."

"You're a fucking bastard. I'll get—"

Jackson leaned on his Alpha power, cutting him off. Letting it infuse his voice, he growled, "What did the note say?"

Russel tried to pull away but Jackson dug his fingers in deeper. Blood flowed faster. Russel's body shook as he kept trying to resist. Jackson let his wolf rise, his vision going yellow. Russel jerked, then collapsed in on himself, all resistance gone as he finally submitted. He hissed and leaned away when Jackson pulled his hand back.

"Tell me."

Keeping his eyes downward, Russell said, "The note said he was taking away his family for their safety. That he would call you when he could. That's it."

"Why did he feel his family was in danger, Russel? What did you do to them?"

"Nothing. This has nothing to do with me."

The truth this time. Nodding, Jackson stood. "Russel, you have one hour to gather all of your belongings. And I mean all of them. That you would dare to challenge me means you can't be trusted around the rest of the pack members, so you are banished from the Denver pack."

Surprised eyes shot to his. "You can't banish me."

"I can."

"But—"

"No buts. I'm going to let you live, Russel, even though you don't deserve it. I don't want my first visit to the pack in years to be filled with blood. But be warned. If you even think about working against me or go near anyone from this pack, you'll meet me in the Challenge Circle." Jackson bared his teeth at the fuming Gamma. "You and I both know how that will end. Take the gift of life I'm giving you and get the hell out of my territory."

Jackson glanced around as he waited for Russel to stand, realizing they'd drawn a large crowd. Most of the faces looked pleased with Russel's punishment, though a few were frowning. He made sure to take note of those wolves and their scents.

Watching closely in case Russel tried something stupid, Jackson made his way back to Edgar, who seemed to have gained two friends. Raising his eyebrows at the men, he asked, "Who are you?"

"Sorry we're late, Alpha," the man on the right said. "Our clan leader, Nick, told us to meet you here today. Luckily, we got here just in time for the show." He held out his hand. "I'm Bill. This is Ted."

"Bill and Ted? Really?" Edgar snickered. "Are you on an excellent adventure, Bill?"

Bill rolled his eyes. "Like I haven't heard that before. I'm William Sparks and this is Theodore Smith."

Edgar tilted his head as he shook Bill's hand. "Why did you say—" He motioned his finger between Bill and Ted.

Bill grinned. "Because I lost a bet. For the next month, I have to introduce us as Bill and Ted to anyone new we meet."

Edgar's laughter helped soothe Jackson's agitated wolf. He held out his hand. "Pleased to meet you, Bill. You as well, Ted. Did Nick tell you why you were sent to us?"

"No. He only told us we needed to meet up with you and join you on your journey." Bill shrugged. "There was some talk about going to the mountains and needing to hurry, so I suggest we finish up here and get on our way."

Jackson nodded. That sounded like a great idea to him. Movement caught his attention. Looking sideways, he spotted Russel in a whispered conversation with a couple of the wolves he'd previously noted. He crossed his arms and stared at them, making sure they were aware of his regard. When they glanced his way, Jackson lifted his lip, baring his fang. They got the message and quickly scattered. Yelling out, he said, "You have fifty-five minutes left, Russel. If I see you in my territory after that, I'll tear out your throat."

"Fuck you, Alpha. I'm going." Russel roughly pushed his way through the crowd as he headed in the direction of his house.

Jackson just knew that asshole was going to become a problem. Sighing, he turned back to his mate and the magic users.

"I need to go inside to see if he did anything to my family's home."

"I'm going in with you." Edgar grabbed his hand, daring him to argue.

Jackson squeezed his fingers, not about to refuse the support his mate was giving him. He had a feeling he'd need it once they went inside.

Edgar stood with Jackson in the middle of the wreckage, all that was left of the packhouse's family room. Both of them had been shocked into silence, unable to comprehend the deliberate and malicious vandalism that had laid waste to the once beautiful home. Garbage, moldy food, and bodily smears stained all the surfaces. Holes had been punched in the walls. The paneling on one side had an end table shoved in it, the broken remains hanging a few feet above the floor. Shattered glass from picture frames covered the carpet, and the pictures themselves had been torn into pieces and flung around the room like confetti. And the smell. Dear Goddess, the smell was horrific. Edgar's eyes had begun watering the moment they'd stepped in the room from the noxious fumes.

Bill called out as he came down the stairs. "Alpha Jackson. It's about the same on the upper floors. We didn't find any bodies, but it smells like there may have been one at some point." He walked over, stopping in front of Edgar and Jackson. "We can take care of cleaning up in here. There's no need to put yourself through that. You'd be better off talking to your pack to find out what's been happening while your brother's been gone."

Jackson nodded, looking lost. "You're right." But he didn't make any move to leave.

"It's okay, Alpha," Bill said quietly. "Don't worry about anything in here. We'll have it all put back to normal by the time you're done with the pack. Trust me."

The timing might be inappropriate, but Edgar was so relieved Jackson wouldn't have to deal with cleaning and repairing his family's destroyed home that he couldn't help himself.

"That sounds like a most excellent idea," he said, biting his lip, then snorted at the glare Bill leveled on him,

"Good one." His dry tone said otherwise. "Now take the Alpha and get out of here so we can get started." He shooed them away.

Edgar, eager to escape from the toxic wasteland, tightened his grip on Jackson's hand and dragged him out the front door.

"Did you see what he did to my home? To my family's pictures? All of our history, all of the love and pride that my parents had in their home, that my brother and sister-in-law have. It's there in every piece of furniture, every memento, every bit of hand carving my father did, the growth marks on the walls, everywhere, Edgar. And he just destroyed it. Like it was worthless."

"I know. I'm so sorry."

Jackson began growling and started heading in the direction Russel had gone earlier. "Let's go find that bastard? I've changed my mind. There will be no mercy for him. Once I get my hands on him, I'll do the same thing to him that he did to my home."

"Jackson," Edgar said, planting his heels to try to slow him down. "I know you're upset. And you have every right to feel that way. But you might want to calm down. I think you're scaring the children."

That stopped Jackson in his tracks. He looked around, his eyes widening when he saw the pack members surrounding them.

"Alpha, are you here to stay now?"

"Mary?" Jackson turned toward the voice, smiling when a female shifter stepped through the crowd and came to stand in front of them.

"Alpha, you remembered."

"Of course. How are you?" Jackson looked around. "I don't see Simon. Where is he?"

"Oh, Alpha." Her eyes filled with tears. "He disappeared the same night as your brother. I have no idea what happened to them. We looked everywhere, but they vanished without a trace."

"Is anybody else missing?"

"Yes," she nodded. "My brother Simon, Alpha Clint, his Betas, Mark and Steve, and Edith's boy, Eddie. They all vanished at the same time."

Jackson's hand jerked in his when he heard the names. Edgar quickly looked at him, but Jackson was focused on Mary, nothing on his face giving away what had caused that reaction.

"And none of them said anything before they left?" Jackson asked.

"No, I mean, yes, Simon left a note at Ma's house. He said he had to leave for the family's safety."

Edgar exchanged looks with Jackson. That was the same as Clint's note. What was going on?

"Did anything happen before the men disappeared?"

Mary hesitated, eyeing Jackson warily. "I don't wish to speak ill of the missing...."

"It's okay, Mary. You can tell me anything." Jackson let go of Edgar's hand and took hers, leading her to the side away from the others. "You have nothing to fear from me."

Edgar watched from a few feet away, impressed in spite of himself by the compassion Jackson was showing her. He was seeing yet another side of his mate, a softer, more caring side. Watching as he calmed Mary, Edgar knew Jackson would make a fantastic Alpha. Strong and ruthless when necessary, yet kind and gentle when his pack needed that from him. Being an Alpha is what he'd been born for. Jackson needed his pack as much as his pack needed and depended on him. Edgar had no right to take that away from him. He sighed, knowing what that meant for his future.

Looking up at Jackson, Mary took a deep breath, then released it. "All right, Alpha. I'll tell you what I know. Before Alpha Clint disappeared, he wasn't himself. There were times when he became irrational, yelling at pack members for no reason." She rested her hand on Jackson's chest. "You know that's not like him."

"I do. Clint was always the patient one."

"Exactly. He's always calm. Firm, but kind and respectful. He ruled over us fairly. At least, he used to. But he changed, Alpha. He became filled with anger. I saw him actually punch out one of the Betas for bumping into him."

Edgar's eyes widened. Oh shit. It sounded like Clint had been afflicted.

"And he, he…" She leaned closed, whispering under her breath, though Edgar had no trouble hearing what she said. "He raised his hand to the Alpha mate."

Jackson sucked in a breath. "He hit Beth?"

Mary shook her head. "No. He caught himself in time. But it was a close thing, Alpha. And she was holding their son."

Jackson closed his eyes and swallowed. Blowing out a breath, he opened them and said, "Thank you for being brave enough to tell me, Mary. I'm sorry it's been so difficult for everyone lately."

"Does that mean you'll be staying?"

Jackson glanced at Edgar, his eyes filled with anguish. He turned back to Mary and shook his head. "I wish I could, but I can't right now. We have to check on the other packs to make sure they're okay. I'm also trying to find Clint."

"I understand." Mary bit her lip, then asked, "And Simon? My brother. Will you look for him too?"

Jackson nodded. "We'll look for everyone who's missing." He gestured Edgar forward. "I'd like you to meet my mate, Edgar."

"Your mate?" She eyeballed Edgar, then gave him a brief smile before turning back to Jackson. "Congratulations on your mating."

"Thank you. I need to show him something. While I'm doing that, could you please let everyone know that if they need to speak to me, it will have to be today. Otherwise, they'll have to wait until we're finished with our mission and can return."

"I'll let everyone know. I'll set up times so you can see as many of them as possible before you have to go."

"Thank you, Mary. I appreciate you handling that. We'll be leaving before first light, so try to fit in as many as you can. But hold the first meeting off for a couple of hours, so I can show my mate around the pack lands."

"Yes, Alpha. You go spend time with your mate and leave everything with me. I'll have everyone organized by the time you get back."

"Excellent. I'll see you in a couple of hours then." Jackson pulled on Edgar's hand, dragging him off. He waved at Mary over his shoulder, wondering where his mate was taking him.

Jackson was heartbroken. His home was destroyed, no, not just destroyed, defiled. Clint and his family were missing, and others in his pack were missing. The only thing holding him together right now was Edgar's grip on his hand. Without that tether to keep him grounded, he wasn't sure what he would have done.

It had been a spur of the moment decision to take Edgar to his secret place on the pack lands but his instincts told him sharing this part of himself was an important step in building their future together.

They walked for about thirty minutes until they reached the edge of the pack lands, then Jackson led Edgar through the trees and down a ridge, ending up alongside the creek. Once there, Jackson stopped, breathing deep, hoping the fresh air of early evening would cleanse the smell of what had been done to his home from where it was stuck in his nostrils. He tilted his head back, eyes closed, letting the glow of the moon shine on his face as he listened to the nighttime sounds of the forest, all of it underscored by the burbling of the creek in front of him.

Slowly, he felt the tension leach out of his body.

"It's beautiful out here," Edgar whispered, as though not wanting to break the spell.

"It is," Jackson said, tightening his grip on Edgar's hand. Even though he wasn't ready to leave, they were pressed for time, so he started walking again. They traveled along the edge of the creek for a bit, then Jackson led the way up an embankment, walking until they made their way to his secret spot, a small glade, tightly enclosed by the trees. His thinking boulder sat in the center of his private place, surrounded by a field of blue wildflowers. He led Edgar over to the boulder and showed him the best spot to lay down. Settling next to his mate, he looked to the clear skies above and the stars shining brightly above them.

Edgar rubbed his face against his shoulder. "This is amazing. Thank you for bringing me here."

"I wanted you to see that there is beauty in the mountains, just like there is in the city. We may not be as sophisticated as you're used to, but there are good people in this pack. People with homes and families, who love and want to be loved in return. People who care about others. Do you think you could give us a chance? I would love to show you all the amazing things my world has to offer?" Jackson held his breath, waiting for Edgar's response.

After a moment, Edgar whispered, "Yes. I can do that." He tilted his head to look up at Jackson. "I'm sorry for how I've been acting about being out here. I have no excuse for being such an ass about it."

Jackson nudged him. "You weren't all the time."

"No, but I may have been more influenced by my grandmother's thinking than I realized. I think I'd like the chance to see the world through your eyes and not hers."

Jackson smiled, holding his hand and squeezing tight. "I can't wait for you to see the parts I love best."

"How about starting with this one. What makes this place special to you?"

"It was my secret place to escape to when I wanted to get away from the pressures of being the youngest in the Alpha line. When you have a strong and respected father, followed by a stronger, overachieving brother, sometimes the expectations become too much to handle. Once I found this spot, I would run here when I needed a break. Something about the energy in this place pulled all the negative feelings out, recharging me. It always healed my soul when I spent time here, making it easier to deal with everything when I returned home."

"Did your brother know about it?"

Jackson shrugged, jostling Edgar. "He never said so, but I'm pretty sure he did. It wouldn't be like him to let me disappear for hours on end and not know where I was. Either way, he kept it to himself and let me have the time I needed to regroup."

Edgar sighed. "He sounds like he's an amazing big brother."

Jackson appreciated the fact that Edgar spoke about his brother in the present tense. He knew Clint was out there somewhere, waiting for him to find him. "He's a fantastic brother. I have to find him."

"I know." Edgar shifted closer, pressing his side against Jackson's.

They lay quietly together, breathing in the sweet perfume of the wildflowers and watching the stars twinkle in the cool night air.

"Jackson, something bothered you about the men Mary said were missing. What was it?"

"All the men Mary mentioned are the strongest wolves in the pack. The two Betas are almost as strong as an Alpha. In another pack, they probably would be the Alpha. It just seems strange to me that all of the strongest wolves would disappear at the same time. Especially since it would leave the pack vulnerable to an asshole like Russel." Jackson turned his head to look at this mate. "Something is happening to the Alphas. I'm not sure if Clint left on his own or was forced to leave. But I'm getting more worried about Clint with every day that passes."

"It's too bad we don't have his note. It might have contained an explanation for what's going on."

"I know. I could kill Russel for that alone."

"Maybe that wasn't the only one he left. Did you guys have any secret hiding places? You know, some kind of place where you could leave notes for each other or anything?"

Jackson shook his head. "No. Most of Clint's time was spent training to be an Alpha. We didn't play together like that. The closest thing I have to a secret hiding place is here." He froze.

"Jackson," Edgar said slowly, "would he have left you something here?"

"If he'd been able to, he just might have. Help me look."

Jackson started crawling over the rock, sticking his hand into every nook and cranny, Edgar beside him doing the same.

Thirty minutes later, Jackson finally gave up. "It's no use. I've checked it over three times. There's nothing here." He slumped beside Edgar, dejection in every line of his body. "I was sure he would have hidden a message in my secret place if he could have. It felt right," he said, tapping his chest over his heart.

"I'm so sorry," Edgar said.

"You've nothing to be sorry for." Jackson sighed. "We may as well go back. If I know Mary, there'll be wolves lined up waiting to speak to the Alpha by now."

Edgar felt bad for getting Jackson's hopes up. It just seemed logical for Clint to leave a message for Jackson in this place if he wanted to be sure he'd get it. Taking one last look around this beautiful haven of Jackson's, something out of place caught his eye. Casually standing up, he walked over to get a better look, wanting to check it out before getting Jackson's hopes up again. Huh, this flower was red. In the moonlit night, the blue field of wildflowers took on a silvery gray color, but this particular flower had looked black until he got close enough to see it was red.

But maybe it wasn't the only one. Edgar looked around again just to be sure, but yes, it was the only red flower in the entire area.

"Jackson, does a red flower have any significance to you?"

"What?"

"Can you come over here? I want you to look at something."

"What's up?"

Edgar pointed. "It's the only red flower in the entire place."

Jackson fell to his knees, gently stroking the red petals. "This is Beth's favorite flower." He looked up. "Beth is Clint's mate. He always searched for a bouquet of these flowers for her on her birthday." Jackson started digging in the soil at the base of the flower. He stopped, then grinned up at Edgar. "There's something here."

Edgar breathed a sigh of relief when Jackson pulled out a plastic-wrapped bundle.

Jackson looked at the package, his hands shaking. "It's Clint's writing. This is from my brother. He left me a message."

Jackson jumped up, grabbing Edgar to him tightly. "Thank you. Thank you so much."

Edgar wrapped his arms around Jackson, grinning up at him. Moments later, Jackson's mouth descended, covering his. That first kiss, full of joy and gratitude, swiftly changed from celebratory to carnal. Hands framed his face, tilting his head just so as Jackson's tongue pressed against his lips for entrance. Opening, Edgar gasped at his first taste of his mate as their tongues curled around each other. His fangs dropped, the sharp edge catching on Jackson's lip. He groaned at the richness of his mate's blood, the power Jackson carried in his veins making him feel drunk after only a sip.

Moans filled the night air as they feasted, tongues thrusting back and forth, their hunger for each other growing as fangs caught on tender skin, releasing miniscule droplets of blood, the small wounds healing almost as soon as they were made.

Becoming aware of the passing of time, Edgar eventually pulled back, pressing soft kisses to Jackson's lips before dropping his forehead to his chest. "We need to get back. You have to meet with your pack so we can be on our way before dawn."

"I know," Jackson rasped, the arms around his waist tightening. "But we're going to finish this when we have more time."

Edgar's heart gave a thump. He tipped his head up. "We are?"

Jackson smiled and kissed the end of his nose. "We are. How does that sound to you?"

Edgar, feeling uncharacteristically shy, whispered, "That sounds good. Really good."

Jackson's smile spread across his face. "So it's agreed then. The first chance we get, we'll finish our bonding properly."

Edgar nodded. sighing as he looked around the glade before turning back to Jackson. "I wish we didn't have to leave so soon. This would be an amazing place to complete it."

"It would. It's a very special place. Mating with you here would make it even more so."

Edgar's heart thumped again. It was going to explode if Jackson didn't stop being so sweet. Clearing his throat, he said, "We could wait until we came back, but it might be a long time. I don't really want to put it off that long. Your wolf must be getting impatient too."

Jackson barked out a laugh. "You have no idea how impatient my wolf is to get on with it. He doesn't understand why we're making him wait."

Edgar grinned. "Well, he's going to have to live with it a bit longer until we can find somewhere private. I have a feeling our bonding will be quite explosive when we finally get to it."

"Is that right?"

"Oh yes," Edgar purred. "We should also make sure we have plenty of time just in case we have to practice a couple of times to get it right."

Jackson laughed again and pulled him close.

Edgar laid his head on Jackson's chest and held him tight, stealing a last moment with his mate before they had to return and face the world.

Chapter Ten

While Jackson spoke with his pack members outside, Edgar explored the packhouse, staring around in amazement at what Bill and the magic users had managed to achieve in such a short period of time. The entire place had been returned back to its original condition. Or, if not original, as close as was possible. All the holes in the walls and furniture had been repaired, the air smelled like fresh mint and sage, and everything sparkled with cleanliness. They'd even been able to restore the photographs of Jackson's family.

Edgar walked over to the wall to take a closer look. There were tiny hairline cracks where the pieces had been put back together, but they were hardly noticeable. He moved to the center of the room and closed his eyes, then breathed in. The energy of the packhouse felt light and welcoming. It was absolutely perfect, and ready for Clint and his family when they came home. "This is amazing."

"Thank you," Bill replied, walking up to him. "It took a bit of effort, but I'm pleased we were able to get his place looking like it should. The Alpha didn't deserve to have his legacy destroyed in such a fashion. That Gamma is a real piece of work." Bill looked at Edgar, his expression serious. "I think Alpha Jackson may have made a mistake in letting him live"

"Why do you say that?"

"A lot of the destruction we found seemed personal. Like it was done by someone full of rage. And there were hateful messages written on the walls to the Miller family. But the ones that concern me the most were the messages to Alpha Jackson. Those were particularly vile." He glanced at Edgar. "And written in blood."

Edgar studied Bill, who regarded him soberly. "What kind of messages?"

Bill shook his head. "You don't need to know. Just trust me that they were bad. If you ever come across that wolf again, kill him before he can act. I'm convinced the Alpha kicking him out of the pack will have pushed him over the edge. I have no doubt he will attack, and probably from the shadows. Assholes like him are always cowards, so watch your back and be ready to eliminate the threat before he can strike."

"Thanks for letting me know. I'll make sure I pass your warning on to Jackson."

"Good."

His mind churning with Bill's warning, Edgar walked over to the window and saw that the crowd around Jackson had thinned considerably. Seeing the sky growing lighter, he realized they would need to get going shortly. He turned to Bill. "I'm going to see if Jackson is ready to leave. Can you shield the packhouse so nobody other than the Miller family can get in again? I want it kept safe for Jackson and his brother."

"Absolutely. We'll do that right now, sir."

Edgar nodded his thanks, then went outside to check on his mate. Jackson looked even more settled than he had when they'd returned from his secret glade. Spending time with his wolf pack seemed to have eased a lot of the anger and hurt he'd still been carrying.

Jackson looked up when Edgar came up to him.

"We need to get going soon. Are you almost done?"

Jackson nodded. "Yes. I just need to have a quick word with Mary then I'll meet you at the vehicles."

Edgar grabbed his arm and pulled him away from the few pack members left. Speaking as quietly as he could, he asked, "Did Russel leave?"

"Yes. He was gone before we got back from the glade."

"Good. Bill says he really hates you. He's worried Russel will try to kill you the first chance he gets, so you need to be prepared to act first. You can't trust him near you even if you're the stronger wolf, Jackson."

Jackson nodded. "Okay. Thank Bill for the warning." He glanced over his shoulder at the house, frowning at the magic users standing four abreast in front of the building.

"It's okay. I asked them to shield the packhouse to prevent anyone else from getting in until your brother comes home."

"Thanks for thinking of that."

Edgar smiled at him. "No problem. You'll be so happy when you see how it looks. They did an amazing job inside. You'd never guess how damaged it was before."

"I'll have to take your word for it. I don't know if I can face going inside again right now. I may never get that rank smell out of my nose, never mind the memory that's stuck in my head." He leaned down and kissed Edgar's forehead. "Thanks again for making sure my brother's home is protected. It relieves my heart to know Clint will have a safe place to bring his family home to."

Edgar's face warmed as pleasure washed over him. "Whatever I can do to help. You finish with Mary. I'll make sure everyone is ready to go and call Roman with an update." Edgar stood on his tiptoes, planting a quick kiss on Jackson's lips, pleased at the surprise in Jackson's eyes at the first kiss Edgar had initiated. Edgar decided then and there he would do that more often. He would enjoy keeping the strong Alpha on his toes.

Jackson got in the vehicle, relieved that his pack would be in good hands while he looked for his brother. Mary and a couple of the less powerful Betas had agreed to look after everyone until Clint came back. And he would. Jackson had no doubts about that. He patted his pocket to make sure Clint's message was still safe. He hadn't had time to read it yet, but he knew in his heart it would help him find his brother.

"Salt Lake City?" Edgar said. "Are you sure? Do you know how much time that will add to our trip? You said we needed to hurry to get to the mountains."

Jackson listened in on Edgar's conversation with the Consort, his wolf hearing allowing him to listen in on the discussion.

"I know it'll add extra time, but you need to go to Salt Lake. You can head north from there and check in on all the mountain packs on your way. This is important Edgar. I wouldn't ask otherwise."

Edgar gave Jackson a look. When he shrugged, Edgar shook his head and said, "Fine. We'll go to Salt Lake. But only because you haven't been wrong yet…except possibly about Denver. It wasn't as bad as you led us to believe."

"Sorry, Edgar. You're not finished with Denver yet. Keep Bill and Ted close. You'll need them."

Jackson grunted. Denver would get worse?

Edgar's eyes widened. "That doesn't sound good. What do you know?"

"Nothing for sure. Just keep them close."

"Okay, we will. Wait a minute. How do you know their names? Are your powers growing that strong already?"

The Consort laughed. *"No. Nick told us who he was sending to you."*

"Good. The thought of you suddenly knowing everything is a little scary.

"For me too. Could you imagine the noise in my head? It's busy enough with Roman in there."

Edgar snorted. "We're heading out now. I'll let you know what we find in Salt Lake."

"Stay safe."

As soon as Edgar ended the call, Jackson leaned forward. "Eric, head toward Salt Lake City."

"Yes, Alpha Jackson."

* * *

Jackson was startled awake when Edgar elbowed him in the side. "What? What's wrong?"

Edgar snickered. "Nothing. We're stopping for gas. I thought you might want to grab a coffee or something. You were up all night and we'll be reaching the pack in Grand Junction soon."

Jackson rubbed his hands over his face, trying to wake his foggy brain. The last few days had been short on sleep and long on drama. It was starting to take its toll. Unfortunately, if the Consort was to be believed, it was only going to get worse from here on out. He needed to stay sharp.

"Okay, thanks. That's a good idea. I'll be right back." Jackson stopped short of opening the door. "Did you need anything?"

"Well, I, um, do need something to eat."

"Okay," Jackson said slowly, still not understanding why Edgar was being timid. "What can I grab for you?"

Edgar just looked at him. Jackson shrugged, clueless. Edgar rolled his eyes, lifted his lip, and pointed to his fang. Lightbulbs went off. "Right. Sorry. This is new to me. Let me get some things, and I can take care of that when we get back on the road."

Edgar looked toward the front of the vehicle. Eric snorted and rolled up the privacy panel. Jackson frowned, not understanding what was going on.

Edgar shook his head. "I have so much to teach you about vampires. Go get your coffee. I'll give you a crash course when you return."

"Okay. Umm, yeah, so, I'll be right back. Yes, going now." Jackson started backing out of the vehicle, bumping his head. He smiled uncertainly at Edgar as he climbed out, then closed the door. Rubbing his head as he walked into the convenience store, Jackson had no idea why he felt so nervous.

Twenty minutes later, Jackson fell back against his seat, panting. "Holy shit. Is it always like that?" He looked down, grimacing at the mess he'd made in his jeans, then reached for the napkins a smug Edgar handed him. Then did a double take at how much more vibrant he looked. Jackson hadn't realized Edgar needed to feed. But seeing the difference in his skin color and the brightness of his eyes, he now knew how a healthy, well-fed, Edgar should look. It was good to have a benchmark so he'd know when Edgar needed to feed in the future.

"No, not always. Though my understanding from Roman is that joining with your Bloodmate is an earth-shattering experience. In his and the Consort's case, it really did shake the world. I don't think it will be that overdramatic when we bond."

Jackson frowned, not understanding what he was talking about, then realized Edgar was answering his question.

"Oh. So you're saying it was that, uhm, powerful of an experience because we're mates?"

"Partly. Generally speaking, the bite of a vampire is either one of extreme pleasure or excruciating pain. It all depends on the intent of the vampire. But being my Bloodmate did seem to intensify things."

"I'll say," Jackson chuckled. "I'm glad you chose the pleasure option though. Remind me to never get you angry before feeding you."

"You don't have to worry. As my Bloodmate, your happiness means more than any anger I may feel. You are safe with me, Alpha. Always."

"You, too," Jackson said before an anxious look crossed his face.

"What is it?"

Jackson touched his pocket. "I've been too scared about what I might find, so I've been letting everything distract me. I think it's time to read my brother's letter."

Edgar grabbed his hand. "It'll be okay. Whatever your brother tells you, we'll do everything we can to bring him and his family home safely."

Jackson nodded. "I know. I don't know why I'm so nervous to read it."

"Because it could change everything." Edgar squeezed his hand again before letting go. "Just remember. We're all here for you."

"Thanks." Jackson raised his hand, cupping Edgar's cheek. "I'm really glad you're with me."

Edgar smiled shyly. "Me too. I'm going to work on some correspondence for Roman and give you as much privacy as I can."

Smiling his thanks at Edgar's thoughtfulness, Jackson pulled the packet from his pocket. Hands trembling in excitement and no small amount of fear, he broke open the waterproof package and pulled out two sheets of paper.

Hey baby brother. If you're reading this, then I've finally succumbed to the madness that's infected me and have either gone into exile, been imprisoned, or I'm dead. And before you ask why I left, it was the only way to keep our pack safe. But more importantly, it was the only way to protect Beth and Daniel.

Over the last few weeks, I've been filled with anger, losing my temper and yelling at everyone, and getting violent. One day, for no reason, I punched one of my Betas. The final straw was when I almost hit Beth for spilling some water. My sweet Beth, who is my life, and in my rage, I wanted to hurt her. As I'm writing this, I still do. Something is wrong with me. I need to get away from everyone before I seriously hurt someone.

Don't worry about my Alpha Mate. I've already sent Beth and Daniel away, as far from me as they can go. I think she's staying with one of her school friends but I made her promise not to tell me where she went.

Today is one of my more lucid days, so I thought to check in with the Betas to see if they were experiencing the same anger. Mark and Steve, my two strongest, said they were also angrier than usual but nothing they couldn't control. They did tell me that when they were performing tasks as Betas, ones specific to that position, that their anger went away. There is an answer in that. I'm counting on you, brother, to figure out it is.

To keep the pack safe, I'm going to take the strongest Betas with me so that if they also succumb to this madness, they won't be able to harm anyone. But between you and me, the real reason I'm taking them is that they're the only ones who have a chance of putting me down if it becomes necessary.

Baby brother, the day will come when they'll have no choice but to kill me. You need to find out what's causing this rage inside of me before then. I hate to put this burden on you, but I'm hoping that since you've been out of the country you haven't been afflicted by it.

Please hurry, little brother, as I fear more lives than mine are at stake. Whatever happens, I know you'll do your best to find out what's going on. I could always count on you when I needed you.

In the event you don't find the answer in time to save me, always remember I'm proud of you and that I love you. I couldn't have asked for a better brother or friend.

Clint

Jackson brushed the moisture from his eyes. No pressure, huh. Just save the world. Typical of his older brother to think he could do anything. This time, he had no choice if he was going to save Clint's life. He handed the pages to Edgar, then looked blindly out of his window as he tried to regain his composure. He had to keep it together if he was going to have any chance of finding the answers they needed.

Edgar gasped, then put the letter down. "Oh, shit. Jackson. I'm so sorry." His slim hand closed around Jackson's. "Your brother is amazingly strong to fight through his madness to save your pack. You should be so proud of him. He must be an exceptional Alpha."

"He really is," Jackson said, sniffing to clear his sinuses. "Call Roman and let him know what Clint said. The more information they have, the more they'll be able to help us."

"Okay. If you're sure you don't mind." Edgar gave his hand a squeeze. "We're almost at our next stop. I'll call while I'm waiting in the vehicle."

Jackson nodded. Nothing more was said until they arrived in the territory of the Grand Junction pack.

* * *

"Alpha Jackson, we're here."

Edgar raised his head from his tablet, where he was dealing with some of Roman's correspondence. Looking out the window, he saw they'd arrived at a pocket of buildings. He frowned, pressing his face to the glass.

"I don't see anyone. How many wolves are supposed to live here?"

"I think around twenty-five or so." Jackson's head pushed next to his, a growl rumbling up his chest. "There should be some kind of activity. It's the middle of the day."

Edgar kept looking out the window, reaching with his vampire senses, but couldn't find any life signs. "I don't think anyone's here."

"Me either," Jackson whispered as he kissed Edgar's head. "I still have to check."

"I know."

"Here, take this."

A gun was pressed into Edgar's hand. He looked at Jackson, his eyebrow raised. "What's this for?"

"The Consort said there would be times when firepower was needed. You can't leave the vehicle, so I want you to use the gun if there's any sign of trouble." He folded Edgar's fingers over the grip. "If anyone or anything comes at you, don't waste time asking questions. Just shoot. Do you understand?"

"Yes." Edgar set the gun on his lap. "Be careful."

"Always." Jackson opened the door. "Stay safe."

A moment later, Edgar was alone in the car with Eric. He lifted up the gun, flipping it over and poking at it. "Do you know which part is the safety? I'm supposed to take that off first, right?"

Eric choked, then held out his hand for the weapon.

Edgar looked out the window to where Jackson had gone, then set the gun in Eric's hand. It was probably safer for everyone if he didn't try to use it. Jackson would understand.

* * *

Edgar looked up from his phone when Jackson got back in the vehicle, his stomach sinking when he got a look at his mate's face. Whatever Jackson had found, it hadn't been good.

"What did you find??"

"Nothing. There's nobody here. We saw signs of fighting and lots of blood, but no bodies." He scrubbed his face then reached for Edgar's hand. "We did find a burial plot with freshly turned dirt, so someone buried them. That gives me hope some of the pack was able to escape."

"Did you find any tracks?"

Jackson shook his head. "No. But maybe the Salt Lake Alpha will know something."

"Let's hope."

* * *

The Council Building, NOLA…

Bryan stared at the Council building as he finished his call with Roman. "It sounds like it's definitely targeting the Alpha wolves. I'll focus my search on anything related to them." He shook his head as he listened. "No. I'm not sure how long it'll take. It's like looking for a needle in a haystack. It would help if I knew what name they hid their plans under. Tell Edgar and Jackson to keep their ears open for that kind of thing." Bryan listened, grunting. "Of, course. The minute I find something, I'll call. I don't want anything to happen to Jackson either."

He ended the call and frowned at the Council building. There was a strange disturbance in his shield. It appeared solid and he could find no breaks in it, but something was definitely pinging off it.

He opened his car door and slid out, carefully pushing it closed with a soft click. As he moved to the front of the vehicle, he scanned the area but didn't see anyone. But he could feel a presence that shouldn't be there.

His senses on high alert, he boosted his personal shield and walked toward the front entrance. He'd just placed his hand on the door handle when his mother rounded the side of the building, a fireball hovering over her palm.

He dropped his hand and took a couple of steps back, giving himself room to maneuver. "Mother. What a surprise to find you here. I've been looking for you."

"I heard. Such a shame about the midwife."

Bryan gritted his teeth in anger. "Why did you have to kill her? She was an innocent and no threat to you."

"There are no innocents in this game we're playing."

"We're not playing a game. We just want the right to live our own lives without interference."

"It's much too late for that. You either play or you die."

"It doesn't have to be that way."

"Doesn't it?" The hardness in her eyes was worrisome. He was used to her being cold, but this was next level.

"No, Mother. It doesn't." He kept his face neutral, not wanting her to know how alarmed he was by her words and demeanor. "You shouldn't be here. How did you get past my shield?"

"As if I would tell you." She stepped closer, looking around him. "Just you today? How very foolish of you, Bryan. That will make my job much easier."

"And what job is that?" He tightened his shields, hoping she couldn't get past them again. As she came closer to him, her necklace slipped from the vee of her shirt. The sun's rays reflected off the pendant, drawing his attention. He squinted. There was something unusual about it. The sun's light hit it again. He jerked back in surprise when the center jewel seemed to wink at him. He took a step closer to get a better look, but his mother speaking brought his eyes back to her.

"I'm going to destroy these records you're spending so much time researching. It wouldn't do for you to find anything that would help you."

Bryan frowned. How did she know what he was doing? Was someone spying on them for her? Then he pushed that aside to deal with later. His priority right now was to stop his mother from getting near the records. And the easiest way would be to rile her up. Fury always made her careless. That it also made her more dangerous was a risk he was going to have to take.

"When did you become the Elders' Bitch, Mother? I thought you wanted to defeat them, not become their servant and do their dirty work."

"I'm not their bitch," Charlotte gritted out.

"Are you sure? Because it looks like that to me. But they must not value you very much if they're willing to send you against me. Everyone knows I'm more powerful than you."

"You are not more powerful than me. Not even close. You have no idea the power I can rain down on you."

Bryan forced himself to laugh. "I'm not worried about your pathetic power, Mother. You don't stand a chance against me and we both know it."

"You little bastard. You'll pay for mocking me."

Bryan was ready when she flung the fireball at him, quickly releasing his new binding webs. They wrapped around her body, trapping her arms to her sides. He started walking toward her then stopped, watching in shock as they slid down her torso, landing on the ground around her feet. Her next fireball crashing against his shield barely caught his attention as he stared at the weaves of his spell as they faded into nothing. "How did you do that?"

"I've always been stronger than you, Bryan." She raised her hand.

Bryan braced and sent more power to his shields, sure she was going to double up her attack. He was taken by surprise when she breached his shield, knocking him down with a wave of air. As he tumbled down the sidewalk, pushed along by a wall of air, he tried to figure out how she'd managed to bypass his shield again. By the time he was able to regain his feet, she was gone.

Chapter Eleven

Back at the mansion…

Lysander was incensed that their mother had attacked Bryan again. "She hit you with air? And your magic didn't affect her? How is she doing this?"

Bryan shrugged. "I don't know."

"Effective immediately, no one is to go anywhere alone," Roman said. "Everyone must have an enforcer and a magic user with them if they have to leave the property."

Lysander nodded in agreement. "Good idea, Roman. We can't have anybody being caught by themselves without backup. That means you too, Bryan. If something happens to you, we're completely screwed. Until we figure out how Mother is doing this, you need to be more careful."

"I know." Bryan sat down on the couch.

Lysander could see he was fretting about something. "What's bothering you?"

"Mother was wearing a strange pendant today. And it wasn't a style she would normally wear. There was something intriguing enough about it that it caught my attention, even in the middle of our fight."

Lysander smacked his forehead. "Damn it. I meant to tell you. It was during the battle at the mansion. She had a pendant around her neck then too. There was something odd about it. When I looked at it, it seemed to call to me, pulling my attention. I can't believe I forgot about it."

"That's okay. A lot was going on that day. I think Nico's birth erased everything else from your mind." Bryan smiled at Lysander. "Still, I think it would be a good idea to check into it. It sounds like we both noticed something peculiar about it. You say it called to you, to me it felt like it was winking at me."

"What?" Roman crossed the room to Bryan. "Tell me everything you can remember about it. You too, beloved."

Lysander's eyes widened, surprised by Roman's intensity. "Okay, I'll do my best. I think it was made of gold and had a round shape." He frowned, trying to recall more. "It also had a large jewel in the center. Maybe, red?" He looked at Bryan for confirmation.

"Yes, that's the same one," Bryan said. "It also has filigree around the edges."

"Hmm. I think I know how your mother is escaping your magic," Roman said.

"You do? Really? Just from that? How?"

"Come sit beloved, this may take a bit." Roman went behind his desk. Lysander followed, taking his customary place on Roman's lap.

"What you are describing sounds like a dragon mating talisman. A dragon makes his talisman, or amulet if you prefer, for his future mate. The stone holds part of his magical essence, which is probably what was calling to you. When given freely, the holder of the amulet is impervious to any magic. That includes magical attacks or bindings. It also allows the holder to use the dragon's magic offensively."

Lysander shook his head. "That doesn't make sense. I can't see any dragon giving an amulet to Mother."

"I agree. Which brings us to when the amulet is not given freely. I believe your mother is in possession of a mating amulet that has been stolen from a dragon. Use of these amulets carries a great price."

Bryan snorted. "Yeah, that sounds more like Mother. What's the price for using a stolen amulet?"

"The passive magic will still work, although at a slower rate."

"Passive. You mean if someone caught her with a binding spell or shielded her?"

"Exactly. The dragon's magic would counteract the magic holding her."

"That must have been what happened during the battle, Bryan. Her escaping wasn't your fault. There would have been nothing you could do against dragon magic."

"Which is a relief in one respect but terrifying in another. How do we stop her? Roman, what happens if she uses the amulet to attack?"

"This is where the penalty starts costing the wielder. If the holder of the amulet uses the magic in an offensive manner, the magic rebounds on the user threefold. But not immediately. The magic always rebounds on the holder the next time they use it to attack."

"Let's think this through. If Mother got the amulet and used it against us during the mansion battle," Bryan said,

"Like when she attacked us with air?" Lysander asked.

"Yes, just like that. If that was her first time using it, nothing would happen to her." Bryan's eyes widened. "But when she used it again, the rebound would have hit. Like that big gust of air that knocked her and the Elders over at the Council building. I've been trying to figure out where that came from."

"Yes. But you need to be aware. Her usage at the Council building reset the penalty since she wasn't able to actually attack you.".

"But she did attack me today, using air again. If she'd used anything more harmful, you're saying it would rebound on her with three times the effect."

"Precisely. Unless she was willing to give up the amulet after a lethal attack, the magic would rebound on her and kill her the next time she attempted to use it."

Lysander mused, "I wonder if we can use this knowledge to our advantage. We know the next time she tries to use it, the magic will rebound." He looked up. "Bryan, there has to be a way to control the time and place we meet her next. If we can use the amulet against her, we might be able to defeat them, because the amulet is giving the Elders an unfair advantage."

"If they even know she has it," Bryan said.

Which was a good point.

"There is more, beloved." Lysander turned to Roman. "After the first time the amulet is used offensively, the dragon magic starts working against the unsanctioned wielder. Each time it is used, the desire to draw on the dragon magic grows stronger, resulting in escalating degrees of the severity of their attacks. Ultimately, the user will be unable to resist the magic and will use the amulet offensively at a level where the rebound is certain to kill them. They won't be able to help themselves, even knowing they are doomed if they do so. The magic will give them no choice."

"Oh. That could be a problem," Lysander said. "What about the person the magic is directed toward?"

"It would depend on how lethal the attack was, but there is always the possibility that they too would perish."

"That means if we're going to use the amulet against Mother, we have to come up with a plan right away before the magic forces her to use a more dangerous attack."

"Then let's call in Max and see if we can come up with something," Bryan said.

"No need. I'm right here." Max came around the corner.

Lysander glared. "I wish you guys would stop sneaking around and spying on conversations. It's getting very annoying." He scowled when everyone laughed.

* * *

Arriving in Salt Lake...

Edgar got out of the SUV, grateful for a chance to stretch his legs. They'd arrived at the Salt Lake pack just as night had fallen, so Jackson had full vampire support behind him if this pack meeting went as sideways as the rest had. He met up with Jackson at the front of the vehicle, and they started toward the packhouse, Bill, Ted, and Eric, falling in behind them, leaving the rest of their escort waiting by the vehicles.

The sound of a gun cocking cut through the night air. "That's far enough, Alpha. Hands in the air." A man moved from the shadows on the porch, the gun's barrel pointed at them.

Edgar could see movement off to the side. A quick glance showed more men with guns trained on them.

"Jackson." Edgar whispered.

"I see them," Jackson whispered back.

"How do you want to handle this?"

"I thought I'd let you take lead. As an Alpha, they'll probably shoot first if I approach them."

"Me? Are you sure?"

"Yes. I trust you, Edgar."

"Okay," he said slowly. Edgar wasn't sure this was the sanest thing Jackson had ever done, but it pleased him to know his mate had that much faith in him. Before he could think about it further, a bullet hit the ground by his feet. He charged forward, enraged, stopping only when the man pointed the gun at Jackson's head.

"Better stop now. The next bullet won't miss."

"Are you out of your mind? That's Alpha Jackson you're aiming a gun at."

"I'm well aware he's an Alpha. That's why there's a gun pointing at his head. We've had a lot of trouble with Alphas around here lately."

Edgar snarled, startling a surprised grunt out of the man. "Get that gun off of him right now or I'll take your head off your shoulders. Alpha Jackson is fine. He hasn't been afflicted like the other Alphas."

"Are you sure about that blood-sucker? It doesn't take much to set off an Alpha these days and you don't get a second chance if you're wrong."

"We're name-calling now?" Edgar rolled his eyes. "Yes, I'm sure. If he wasn't fine, your head would already be separated from your body."

"And why is that?"

Edgar grinned evilly. "Because you have a weapon pointed at his mate." Edgar ignored the way the man jerked in surprise. "Now put that gun away before I get angry. I won't ask you again." He glared the man down, until he slowly lowered the weapon, pointing the muzzle to the ground. "Better. Tell us about the trouble you've been having."

"Are you the man in charge then? I'm surprised the Alpha would let a bloodsucker speak for him."

"No, I'm not the man in charge. But I am the vampire who's going to kick your ass if you don't stop being one." Edgar bared his fangs, hoping to get his point across before he had to follow through on his threat.

"It's okay, Edgar. There must be a good reason a Beta would be so disrespectful to an Alpha."

The man spat in the dirt. "Depends on what kind of Alpha you are. Lately, all we seem to have are abusive, murdering Alphas."

"Luckily for you, I'm not one of those." Jackson took a step forward, stopping when the man tensed and started to bring the gun back up. "You can relax. I won't come any closer. Tell me what you know. We're trying to figure out what's going on."

The man squinted, looking hard at Jackson for a long time. Finally coming to a decision, he nodded, walking over and holding out his hand, the gun at his side pointing to the ground. "Alpha. The name's Stuart."

Edgar kept a close eye on Stuart as Jackson shook his hand. He wasn't about to trust him blindly. He had, after all, held a gun on them.

"Jackson. This is my mate, Edgar."

Edgar smirked at the man's startled look. "Is that a problem for you Stuart?"

"No, sir. I'm just surprised. I thought it was one of the other men who was his mate. I didn't expect it to be a vampire." He paused. "Not that there's anything wrong with that."

Edgar snorted. "Of course not."

"Stuart, tell me what you know regarding the Alphas," Jackson said, drawing his attention back to him. "It sounds like you've been dealing with more than one."

"Yes, sir. The boys and I have run into a few of those murderous sons of bitches. We've had to put them all down."

"How many Alphas have you killed?"

"About five so far. We tried to give them a chance, but when they started going after the women, we had no choice but to take care of them."

"I understand. What can you tell me about them? When did they start going feral?"

"We first noticed it in our own Alpha about ten or so months ago." He scratched his head. "It may have even been before that. It's hard to pinpoint exactly when since it came on so gradually. At first, we tried reasoning with him. That was okay for a bit. Then after a few months, we had to start running interference between him and the pack to keep him away from them. But we could only keep that up for so long. Eventually, all of us Betas tried to work together and force him to listen, but—"

"But he was an Alpha," Jackson said.

"Exactly. We couldn't control him. In the end we had no choice but to shoot him. He went crazy mad; feral, just like you said. He wasn't the good Alpha he'd been for years. As much as it broke my heart, I had to take him out to protect the rest of the pack."

"I'm sorry you were put in that position," Jackson said quietly.

"Thank you, Alpha. Hank was a great man before he changed. If you find out what caused his madness, I'd like to know. I worry that there was more we could have done." He stopped, a distressed look crossing his face. "It eats at a man."

Jackson placed his hand on the Beta's shoulder, squeezing gently. "You had no choice. There was nothing else you could do. Hank wasn't the same Alpha anymore.

Whatever is making the wolves angry and crazy is not controllable." Jackson stepped back. "You did the right thing saving his pack. Other packs weren't as lucky. They didn't have strong Beta's like yourselves looking after them."

"Appreciate you saying so, Alpha."

Jackson nodded. "What else can you tell me?"

"After Hank was gone, the boys and I took a trip out to Grand Junction to check on the Alpha there, but we were too late to help. He'd already destroyed his pack. We got rid of the Alpha, then stayed long enough to bury everyone."

"That was you then." Jackson nodded. "Thank you for looking after the pack, Stuart. I'm sorry it was left to you, but I'm glad they were tended to."

Stuart spit again. "They didn't deserve what was done to them."

"No, they didn't. Which other Alphas have you had to deal with?"

"We traveled to all the packs within a few hours of here. It was the same at every one of them." Stuart paused. "Except...you might want to take another look at the Jackson pack. There should have been some pups there, but we couldn't find them."

"Pups?"

"Yeah, there were toys and bikes and stuff like that lying around."

"And you didn't see any little ones?"

"No, Alpha."

Jackson shook the man's hand again. "Thanks for the information. We need to get going if we're going to make it to Jackson before the sun rises."

"You're welcome. I sure hope you find those pups."

"Me too, Stuart. Me too." Jackson turned, striding quickly towards the vehicles.

Edgar waited long enough to exchange contact information with Stuart, "We'll let you know if we find them."

"Thank you, Alpha Mate. I'd appreciate that."

Edgar nodded, then raced after Jackson.

"You did good back there, Edgar."

Edgar smiled. "Thanks. For a moment, I thought you were crazy, but I guess it all worked out."

Jackson laughed. "I may be crazy, but I never doubted you could handle it."

Edgar turned to the window, his smile so big it hurt his face, and stared out into the night, holding tightly his mate's hand.

* * *

A few hours later, Edgar stirred. "There's something I don't understand. How are the wolves being affected over such a large area? Unless someone from the Council visited every pack, it shouldn't be possible for this affliction to be hitting all the Alpha wolves in the country."

Jackson grunted in surprise. "I never even thought to question that." He glanced at his mate, in awe of his analytical mind. "You amaze me sometimes."

Edgar blushed and cleared his throat, shifting restlessly. "Thanks."

Jackson felt a wave of tenderness sweep over him as he took in his mate's shy reaction to the compliment. It seemed he wasn't used to getting them. At least, not from anyone other than Roman. He reached over and grabbed Edgar's hand.

Gripping his fingers tightly, Edgar smiled at him before he began speaking again. "It could be my imagination, but it seems like the wolves are being affected much worse the further north we go than they were in Dallas and Denver?"

"No, I didn't." Jackson frowned. "What could cause that?"

"I'm not sure. I'll keep thinking about it. There has to be some explanation."

Jackson lifted his head when the vehicle slowed down as they arrived at the Jackson pack lands. The unnatural quiet as they drove to the main pack house hurt Jackson's heart.

After the vehicle came to a stop, Jackson got out and started calling out orders. "Everyone spread out. Look for any sign of the pups. If they managed to escape the Alpha, they will be hiding and wary of strangers. Find them, then call for me. Let's all pray this is a rescue mission and not a recovery one."

"Yes, Alpha Jackson." As instructed, everybody took different sections, searching for signs of the pups. The magic users stuck close to the buildings, relying on their mage lights, while the vampires used their nocturnal hunter's eyes and ranged further out.

Jackson started his own search around the packhouse, leaning heavily on his wolf's sense of smell. No matter how carefully he searched, he didn't see any fresh signs of the pups. All he could smell was death.

"Jackson, come here." Edgar's voice called out from an old shed. "I think I found something."

Jackson sprinted over to his mate. "What do you have?"

"Look here." Edgar pointed to the ground. "See the oil stain. There was a vehicle parked here not that long ago. And it looks like someone took the time to brush the ground, but they missed this." Edgar pointed to a spot on the floor of the shed. Jackson walked over, crouching to see better. There in the dirt, almost completely obscured, was a partial footprint of a small child.

"Great job Edgar. Whoever took the pups must be driving the vehicle that was parked here." He stood up, looking around. "Damn it. We need to know what it is."

"Let's look around the house. Maybe there are some pictures that show what was parked in the shed."

Jackson looked at Edgar, amazed again at his agile mind. He made a formidable partner. One Jackson was honored to have been blessed with. He grabbed his mate, pulling him close. "Thank the Goddess for your quick, logical mind. You are the balance to my aggressive, reactive nature. The Goddess knew what she was doing when she matched us. I have the feeling we will do great things together."

"I agree." Edgar's arms wrapped around him.

Jackson took a moment to enjoy the comfort of holding his mate. His wolf wanted them to get on with the mating, but there were too many problems they had to deal with first. When the opportunity came, Jackson wanted to be able to take his time and do it right. The wolf could wait a bit longer. After all, Edgar wasn't going anywhere, not if Jackson could prevent it.

He pressed a kiss to Edgar's hair. "Let's go check out the house and see what we can find."

"Hopefully, something's there. We need to find those children. I bet that's why the Consort sent us in this direction."

"You're probably right. Let's go see."

* * *

Edgar was on his phone the moment they got back into the SUV.

"Roman, we're looking for a light blue van, the last four digits three-one-nine-four. That's all the information we have right now. Is that enough for you to put the word out to your contacts so they can keep their eyes open for it? It's probably heading north since that's the direction the Consort wants us to go." Edgar nodded his head, even though Roman couldn't see him. "Has Bryan managed to find anything? No. Tell him to please keep looking. All the wolves are dying up here. We need answers soon." He nodded again. "Of course. We'll keep you posted. Thanks, Roman."

Edgar ended the call and put his phone in his pocket before leaning back in his seat with a huge yawn. The sun was going to be rising soon. He really needed a nap before they hit the next location. Looking over at his mate, who was watching him closely, Edgar smiled. Who would have thought that the ex-military Alpha wolf, who could tear someone's throat out without hesitation, would be so gentle and patient with him while he adjusted to the realities mating with him would bring to Edgar's life? Even though he knew he had to stay with Jackson and the pack, part of him was still struggling with it. Edgar didn't want to leave Roman. Being his assistant provided him with a sense of value and belonging that his family had never given him. If he left Roman's side, who would he be then?

Edgar sighed, knowing he couldn't leave Jackson hanging for much longer. Wolves were notoriously aggressive in pursuing their mates and always in a hurry to secure the bond after meeting. Jackson giving Edgar as much time as he had to come to terms with it said volumes about his strength.

But all of this thinking was making Edgar's head hurt. He slid over in his seat and laid his head against Jackson's chest. His heavy thoughts could wait until after he'd had a nap. He closed his eyes and was asleep in seconds, distantly aware of Jackson wrapping his arms around him, holding him tight and keeping him safe while he rested.

* * *

Casey bit down on his lip, eyes squeezed tightly shut, muscles locked, too terrified to even breathe.

"Where are you, you little shits? I know you're hiding in here."

The small bodies tucked in tight beside him shook with fear. He clamped his hands tighter over their mouths to stifle their sobs as the footsteps came closer. Blood ran down his chin from where his teeth cut into his lip.

"Casey," the voice growled, "I can smell you." The deep rumbling growl of an angry beast stopped on the other side of the wall. Three bodies jumped when the beast punched the thin barrier hiding them from him.

Tears ran freely down Casey's face, joining the streams of blood.

"Alpha," a new voice said.

"Who the fuck are you?" Footsteps moved away. "Get the hell off of my land before I rip your throat out."

"Stay back, Alpha."

A loud growl filled the air.

Boom. The blast of the shotgun stunned Casey's ears. He barely heard the sound of the body dropping to the ground.

"Alpha's dead, Stuart. I don't see anybody here. He must have killed them all."

"Good shooting, Will. Gather the men. We'll bury everyone then head back home."

"Yes, sir."

Casey gasped, bolting upright, sleep gone in an instant. Checking to make sure his charges were still sleeping, he pressed a hand to his racing heart. Taking deep breaths, he kept telling himself they were fine. They were safe. The

Alpha was dead. He couldn't hurt them anymore. He curled in on himself, face buried in his hands, praying to the Goddess the dreams would stop. They kept him up most nights and he had seven pups to look after. He was so tired. As each day passed, it became harder and harder to stay strong for the pups.

He blinked away his tears and told himself to toughen up. He might only be an Omega, but he was all the children had. He needed to keep going, no matter how difficult it was.

Rubbing his eyes, he decided to get started on the day's journey since there was no chance of him going back to sleep. He had only two more mountain packs to check on then he would head towards one of the cities to see if he could find someone to help them.

Climbing carefully over the sleeping bodies, he got behind the wheel and started the van, praying he wouldn't be too late if there were more pups in need of rescue.

* * *

Crouching, Jackson carefully moved broken stalks of dried weeds aside and breathed deep. A shifter had been here recently. He leaned closer to the ground. There. A faded impression in the dirt. Taking in another breath to be sure, Jackson stood and nodded at Edgar. "It's him. It looks like he was here fairly recently."

Edgar walked over. "Are you sure he's saving them? He could be gathering them up for trafficking. It's a huge problem. Shifter children would be in high demand."

Jackson shook his head. "He's an Omega. He wouldn't be able to harm him. His instincts are driving him to save them. But he's not like any Omega I've even heard of."

"What do you mean?"

"Omegas are nurturing, caring wolves. They bring peace to a pack through their very presence. They look after the old and teach the pups before their first shift. Essentially, they're the caretakers of a pack."

"That sounds like the perfect wolf to save the kids."

Jackson shook his head again. "It's really not. They're not built that way. Omegas are nurturers, but they're timid wolves. It goes against their very nature to be in charge. Leading a rescue mission would be exceptionally difficult for him. He'll be under a great deal of stress trying to push himself past his natural limitations."

Edgar frowned. "I didn't realize that."

"That doesn't even take into consideration what taking a life is costing him. The last two Alphas we found were shot by someone inexperienced with a weapon. Omega's have such tender hearts I can barely fathom the thought of one shooting anyone but I don't see another explanation."

"He must be an exceptional wolf."

"He is. But we need to find them soon. I fear what the strain of acting so far against his nature is doing to him."

"Alpha Jackson."

Jackson turned to the magic user coming down the packhouse steps, a light orb floating above his head. "Yes, Bill."

"There was nobody left alive in here. It looks like the Alpha got to them before he was shot. We did find small tracks leading out from the back door, but they stop part way to the trees. There are tire tracks where they end."

"Thanks, Bill. We found signs of the Omega near where the Alpha was shot. It looks like he got here too late to save the adults but managed to rescue at least one pup."

"After going through the house, it looks like only one kid lived here."

"Okay, good. Get everyone together. We've got some digging to do to get everyone buried before it gets light."

"Yes, Alpha."

* * *

The SUV slowed, coming to a stop at the roadside rest area. They were taking a break for everyone to stretch their legs and attend to any private business they needed to do. From the hollow ache in his stomach, Edgar knew he couldn't put it off any longer.

"Jackson, I need to feed soon."

Jackson nodded. "Okay. My wolf needs to run. Do you think you can keep up so we can run together?" He raised an eyebrow in question.

Run with his mate? Edgar had never done anything like that before. He tilted his head, thinking about it. The fact Jackson had asked him warmed his heart. And it sounded like fun. Besides, he was pretty sure he could run faster than a wolf. "Let's run and find out?"

Jackson started grinning wolfishly. "Alright then." He got out of the SUV, pulling off his clothes, then tossing them in the backseat. "Ready?"

Edgar whistled as he eyed him up and down, his blood heating as he took in his mate's amazing physique. Eric and Clancy snickered from the front seat. Edgar hissed at them. "Stop looking at my mate." Eric winked before rolling up the privacy screen. Edgar looked back at Jackson, who was posing in the moonlight, the sight causing his heart to speed up from excitement. He scrambled out of the vehicle, reaching his mate just as Jackson shifted into his wolf.

Edgar laughed. "You want to play, do you? Okay, Jackson. Let's run." The wolf yipped, then took off, Edgar right behind him.

Edgar had no idea how much fun it would be to run with Jackson. The wolf sprinted ahead, then pounced in the bushes, flushing out whatever animals were hiding there. When Edgar ran past, the wolf would bound ahead of him and terrorize the next colony of rabbits until Edgar caught up. They kept this up for a couple of hours, finally stopping at a creek so Jackson could drink. Edgar flopped down on the grass, smiling at the night sky, feeling better than he had in days. He had no idea running with his wolf would feel so amazing.

Jackson bounced over to him, pinning him with his front paws, and started licking his face. Laughing, Edgar twisted to the side, pushing his head away. "Gross. Stop that. You're getting drool all over me." The wolf sat back, tongue hanging out of his mouth. Edgar narrowed his eyes. "I can tell you're laughing at me. Now shift, so I can feed. I don't want a mouthful of fur."

Jackson shifted, then threw himself at Edgar, covering his body. He tucked his face into Edgar's neck and breathed deep, raising goosebumps all over his body.

Rising up on his forearms, Jackson stared down at him, the need in his eyes shining as bright as the moon in the sky. Edgar's heart thumped, realizing this was it. He was about to be bonded with his mate. Was he ready? Was he prepared for the changes this would bring? Staring into his mate's eyes as Jackson waited patiently for his decision, Edgar decided to follow his heart and nodded.

Jackson sat back and pulled his tie loose, lifting it over his head. Never losing eye contact, he undid Edgar's shirt, one button at a time. Reaching the last few buttons, he tugged his shirt from his pants, undoing them, before pulling the sleeves off his arms and tossing the shirt to the side. He cupped Edgar's neck with his warm hands, then ran them slowly down his bare torso, leaving a trail of tingling skin in their wake. Reaching his pants, Jackson released the top button, before carefully pulling down the zipper.

Edgar toed off his shoes so Jackson was able to slide his pants off his legs. Once Edgar was completed naked, Jackson moved over him, covering his smaller frame with his large, warm, muscular body. He bent down, nuzzling along Edgar's jaw, then whispered in his ear. "Feed, my mate. Sate your hunger."

Drowning in his mate's pheromones, Edgar bit down, eagerly drinking in his rich shifter blood.

Jackson threw his head back as he reached his climax, body shuddering as he filled his vampire with his essence. Edgar pulled him down, hands on his face, forcing his attention.

"Jackson, do you freely agree to become my True Bloodmate, forging our souls into one, as fated by the Goddess, bonded together through eternity?" Jackson nodded, his heart racing in anticipation. "Then bite me Jackson and forge our souls into one."

Jackson bent down, gently placing his teeth in the crook of Edgar's neck, savoring this moment of their bonding. Taking a deep breath, he bit down, joy suffusing his soul when he felt his mate's teeth strike home. Then lighting exploded, traveling along his nerves as his body climaxed again, the power of it rolling through him like an electrical current. He was helpless to do anything but hold tight to Edgar and ride it out as it went on and on.

Time seemed to still as they held each other close, wild energy raging through them, tying them together as sparks lit the air around them. Eventually, the aftershocks slowed, allowing them to catch their breath.

Jackson pulled his teeth free and carefully separated from Edgar before rolling off his mate. His Mate. Finally. It felt like he'd been waiting forever for this moment. Panting, he laid on his back, looking up at the full moon, limbs twitching every few seconds. He could feel Edgar's presence inside him, stronger than before, fitting easily alongside his wolf as though he'd always been there.

"Jackson, are you okay?"

He turned his head, surprised to see the worry on Edgar's face. He rolled to his side and cupped his cheek. "I'm very good, mate. Everything feels perfect, as though a missing part of me has finally come home." Edgar's smile was glorious to see. "How do you feel?"

Edgar hummed, then grinned. *"I can see your wolf. He's very strong and handsome."*

Jackson sat up, stunned. "Are you talking in my head?" Edgar's chuckles tickled his brain.

"Yes. We are True-bonded Bloodmates. We've gained the ability to speak without words."

Trying for himself, Jackson asked, *"Can you hear me?"*

"Loud and clear, mate."

"Do you feel any different?"

"Of course, I do. A great big wolf just ravaged my body."

Jackson laughed. *"That's not what I meant. Can you tell if you gained a special ability when we completed our bond?"*

Edgar frowned. *"There's something a bit different, but I'm not sure what. How about you?"*

"My wolf feels stronger. I don't know how much, but a stronger wolf means I can protect you and our son better."

"Our son?"

"Yes, Nico. Though we'll probably have to share him with the Prince and Consort."

Edgar snickered, *"We'll be lucky if we're even allowed to see him. The Consort will not easily let him go."*

Laughing out loud, Jackson stood, then reached a hand to help Edgar up. "I have a pretty good idea of how difficult it's going to be."

He led Edgar to the creek's bank and carefully washed him, stealing kisses frequently. Once his mate was clean, he waded out further and dunked himself, before climbing up the bank and sloughing the water from his skin. They got dressed in silence, Jackson taking joy in the feelings of satisfaction he could feel flowing through his link with Edgar. He pulled him close and kissed him gently. "Thank you for agreeing to mate with me."

Edgar rubbed noses with him. "Thank you for giving me time to adjust." Tugging his head down, Edgar kissed him deeply. Jackson thrust his tongue in his mouth, trying to capture as much of his taste as possible.

Finally running out of air, Jackson pulled back. Touching his forehead to Edgar's, he quietly said, "We need to get back to the others."

Edgar nodded, closing his eyes. "I know. I just want a few minutes more."

Jackson nodded. "Of course." Wrapping his arms around his mate, he looked at the moon shining down on them, listened to the sound of the trickling creek, felt the warmth of his mate's breath on his neck, and felt complete. He was finally home.

Sheri Eleese

Chapter Twelve

They were nearing Butte when Edgar spotted the van on a service road, partially tucked under the trees.

"Jackson, there. Did you see it?"

"Yes." Jackson leaned forward. "Eric, the first chance you get, turn around. We need to go back to the road we just passed. Clancy, can you call the other vehicle and let them know. Tell everyone to stay back, but fan out. We don't want to scare them, but we can't let them get away either."

"Sir, the magic users can put up a shield that will prevent them from running off. That way, we can all stay back and leave you and your mate to talk to them," Clancy said.

"Good idea. Please do that." Jackson leaned back, grabbing hold of Edgar's hand, anticipation filling him now that the long chase was almost over.

Eric stopped the SUV a short distance from the van. Jackson got out, then breathed deeply, his sensitive nose picking up all the scents in the air. His eyes widened when he counted ten individual scents coming from the van. Holding up all his fingers to Edgar to indicate how many there were, he motioned for him to go around to the other side of the van. Closing in on the driver's side door, he had just put his hand on the handle when the van started, its engine revving loudly.

"Stop." He yelled, pushing with his Alpha power. "Turn it off." He tore open the door and found himself facing the muzzle of a gun, held in the shaking hands of a panicked Omega.

"Let us go or I'll shoot."

"It's fine, Omega. We're not here to hurt you. Put down the gun."

"No. You're an Alpha. I won't let you have them." He raised the gun higher. The shaking got worse.

Jackson sighed, tipping his head to the side in case the Omega got off a lucky shot and quickly snatched the gun from his hand.

"No," he cried, his body trembling in terror. "Please don't hurt us."

"Hush, little wolf. It'll be okay." Jackson took a step back. "We're here to help you."

Gasping for breath it took a moment before the Omega could ask, "Who's we?"

Jackson smiled. "My mate. He's right behind you."

The Omega turned. Seeing Edgar sitting in the front passenger seat, he screamed, rearing back and falling out of the open door, landing on his back. Crying in terror, he rolled to his stomach and crawled away from Jackson, trying to get under the van. Obviously misjudging the distance, he cracked his head, and fell to the ground, knocked out cold.

Jackson winced as he looked down at the unconscious wolf, then up at Edgar, who was leaning out of the driver's side door. "That could have gone better."

* * *

Jackson chuckled at the expression on Edgar's face as he stared in amazement at the amount of pizza the nine little bodies were putting away.

"Seriously, when was the last time they ate anything?" His eyes drifted over to the bed Casey was tucked into, frowning at the still unconscious young Omega.

"Don't worry." Jackson's hands landed on Edgar's shoulders as he leaned against his back. "He'll be fine once he's had some rest. Being in charge of the rescue operation used all the resources he had. He probably hasn't had time to sleep since he first started running."

"Alpha, sir." Jackson looked down at the pup who was staring up at him with big, round eyes.

"What can I help you with, Robin?"

"Are you going to hurt us like Alpha George hurt my mommy?" The pup's lower lip trembled, his eyes watering as he waited for his answer.

Jackson pulled away from Edgar and crouched down. "No. Edgar and I are going to make sure you all get somewhere safe. A place where nobody can hurt you like that ever again."

The pup squinted at Jackson, as though judging the truth of his words, then suddenly rushed forward, throwing his arms around him. "Thank you, Alpha. I didn't want to die. Thank you for feeding us and taking care of Casey." He tilted his head back, eyes watery, and his small face scrunched up. "You're not going to hit him and make him sleep in the closet, are you?"

Jackson gently cupped the pup's shoulder. "Did your last Alpha do that?"

A small head nodded. "Whenever Casey tried to help us, the Alpha beat him and locked him up without any food. He shouldn't have done that. A stronger Alpha is supposed to protect those weaker than him. That's what my dad told me before he died. I tried my best to look after my mommy, but the Alpha hurt her real bad." His face pressed against Jackson's chest again. "Please, Alpha," he whispered, "please don't hurt Casey."

Jackson gritted his teeth, wishing Alpha George was still alive so he could deal with him personally. "I won't hurt Casey. I promise. He'll be going with the rest of you to the safe place I told you about."

Jackson looked up when a sharp gasp came from the bed. Casey was pressed up against the headboard, terror rolling off him in waves. "Robin, get away from him. Please, don't hurt him, Alpha. He's only a pup."

Jackson stood slowly, holding Robin's hand, the other one held in front of himself, trying to placate the frightened Omega. "It's alright, Casey. Nobody is going to hurt you or the pups. Everybody is fine. Look," he pointed, "they're all here, happy and having something to eat."

Casey looked to where the pups were.

"They've been worried about you. Why don't you go sit with them and let them know you're okay."

Casey nodded, then slid slowly off the bed, keeping his back pressed to the wall as he joined the pups. When they swarmed over him, it seemed to relieve his fears, though he kept casting anxious glances toward Jackson.

Crouching down, Jackson whispered to Robin. "Go over and let Casey know he's safe. I think he's still scared but he'll be relieved to have you near him."

"Yes, Alpha." The young pup rushed across the room, landing in Casey's lap, and wrapped his arms around his neck. He started speaking quickly into his ear. Whatever he was saying reassured the Omega, who still looked anxiously at Jackson, but with less fear in his eyes this time.

"What was that about?" Edgar came to stand by him.

"Young Robin will make a fine Alpha one day. He has great instincts for his age."

"An Alpha? Do you think he's in any danger from whatever's infecting them?"

"His wolf hasn't matured yet, so I think he should be fine. However, it might be best if we got them back to New Orleans as soon as possible."

Edgar nodded. "It'll be great to get back home. All this traveling through the mountains is getting tiring. I can't wait to see civilization again." Patting him on the shoulder, Edgar wandered over to sit near the pups and Casey, easing his way into their conversation.

Jackson stared after him, pain ripping through his chest. He tried not to let Edgar's words hurt, but it was difficult. Knowing that Edgar wasn't even aware of what he'd said somehow made it worse. Jackson had no choice but to live with the wolves. Traveling to check on the other packs was part of the responsibilities that came with being of the Alpha line. His shoulders slumped as he realized he would be making those journeys on his own, that Edgar wouldn't be with him. That he wouldn't be able to show him more of the beauty to be found in the wilderness. Because he didn't want any part of the shifter world, needing to be closer to civilization.

Screw it. Jackson straightened his back. It was time to face reality. A wolf and a vampire would never have worked out in the long run. Pushing his feelings down, he hardened his heart, hoping to protect himself from being hurt like that again and left the hotel room to call Roman. He needed to make arrangements for the pups and get them taken care of before the rest of them could travel south to check on the rest of the packs. Everyone except for his mate.

Edgar could go back with the pups to civilization.

Edgar's gut clenched as he watched Jackson leave the room. It wasn't until he'd sat with the kids that he realized what he'd said or how much it had hurt his mate. He needed to fix the damage he's caused with his careless words. His cheeks heated with shame. When would he remember that his mate should always come first in his thoughts? Jackson deserved so much better than what he'd been giving him.

Edgar turned back to the conversation when he heard Casey talking to Robin about Jackson.

"The Alpha said we were going somewhere safe? All of us?" Casey asked. Robin nodded. Casey's suspicious eyes landed on Edgar. "Who are you? Where do you think you're taking the pups?

Holding out his hand, he said, "I'm Edgar. Mate to Alpha Jackson." He waited until Casey tentatively reached over and shook his hand. "It's nice to meet you, Casey. I'm so glad the kids had you to look out for them." Edgar leaned in closer. "Can you tell me what happened?"

Casey looked at him for a long moment before nodding. "But not here. I don't want the pups to know all the details. They already know more than they should."

"Okay." Edgar stood up, holding out his hand for Casey. "We can go outside and…." Casey shook his head. Edgar paused, wondering what the problem was. Casey looked over at the kids, then back to Edgar. It took a moment before the lightbulb went off. "Or we can go over by the door and talk there. That way you'll be able to keep an eye on the kids." Casey smiled and followed him to the other side of the room.

Once they were out of earshot, Casey started his tale. "Robin, Emily, and I come from a pack just outside of Jackson. Our Alpha went crazy. I mean, more crazy than normal. He's always been mean and ornery, but it got really bad in the last few months." Casey paused, looking down at his feet. Edgar waited patiently as the Omega sniffed a few times before rubbing his wet cheek against his shoulder. "Anyway, one day he started killing everyone in the pack. I was out in the field working with the pups on their reading. When I heard the screams, I grabbed them and hid the van. Then the Alpha, then he, he…" He started gasping for breath.

Edgar gently rubbed his back. "It's alright, Casey. Remember. You're safe here. Nobody's going to hurt you again." Edgar waited until he settled down before asking, "What happened next?"

"The Alpha found us. He was going to kill us too. I could hear it in his voice. But someone came into the shed and shot him. We waited in the van all day until we couldn't hear them anymore. When we came out, they were gone and all of our pack was buried. We're all that's left." Tears trickled down the young Omega's face.

"You're doing really good. Do you think you could answer a few more questions?"

Casey nodded, shifting his feet, his glistening eyes watching Edgar warily.

"Thank you." Edgar pointed to where the children were watching the TV now. "You managed to rescue nine kids. Can you tell me how?"

"I found a gun in the house, so I grabbed it when I packed up our stuff. Then we left. Then I started worrying about what was happening to the pups in the other packs, so I began checking on each of them as I drove."

"That's a lot to take on by yourself."

Casey shrugged. "I was headed to a big city to find someone who could help us."

"Which is great thinking," Edgar said. "And a very brave thing to do."

Casey smiled shyly before his face went serious. "The first couple of packs I went to, the Alphas seemed fine. I hid and watched them for a bit to be sure. But both times something set them off and they started attacking everyone. The pups were told to run and hide, so when I got the chance, I snuck in and grabbed them. I got them away while the Alpha was busy doing, well, uhm, he—"

Edgar held up his hand. "I know what kept them occupied."

Taking a deep breath, Casey continued. "I did the same at the next few packs. I'd wait until I had a chance, then I'd grab the pups and run. If we got caught, I'd shoot the Alpha. They didn't expect it from an Omega. They'd just laugh at me when I told them to stop. They looked so surprised when I shot them." His shaking hands covered his face. After a few moments, he pressed his palms into his eyes, wiping away his tears. "I don't know if any of their parents survived. I just couldn't stick around to find out."

"We didn't find anyone, Casey," Edgar said gently. "We buried everyone we found, but it doesn't look like anybody other than the children got away." He pulled Casey into his arms, hugging him tightly. "Thank the Goddess you were there to keep the children safe. We're so proud of you. You did amazing for a man as young as you."

"Thank you." Casey was still upset, but Edgar could see a glimmer of pleasure in his eyes from his words. "Where are you taking us?"

Edgar released him, stepping back and smiling. "This is the exciting part. We're going to send you back to New Orleans, where my coven is. We live in a huge mansion, so there's room for all of you to stay together."

"Really? Who owns the house? Why would they let a bunch of strangers stay with them?" Casey started backing up, his voice rising with each question. "Who are these people?"

"My Prince and his Consort and the Consort's brother," Edgar answered, confused why Casey was suddenly afraid.

"And what do they want from us?" Casey kept backing up.

"Nobody wants anything from you. We just want all of you to be safe."

"Why should I believe you? I don't know you." He started moving toward the children. "Maybe we should just leave."

"Casey, stop. We're here to help you."

"No. I got us this far. I can take care of them by myself."

"Listen to me. You've done great up until now, but you don't have to handle it alone anymore. Alpha Jackson won't let anything bad happen to you."

Mentioning Jackson brought the panicked Omega to a stop. Eyes watering, Casey's breath started coming fast again. "I don't know what to do," he whispered.

"I know. First, I want you to take a deep breath. Good. Hold it for three seconds. Now breathe out. Excellent. Let's do that again. And again." Edgar waited while he calmed down. "Excellent Casey. Now, you have nothing to be afraid of. I'll answer any question you have. Okay?"

Casey nodded.

"Okay. As I was saying, Alpha Jackson and I are sending you to stay with my coven. Prince Roman, his Consort Lysander, and his brother Bryan want to help you."

"Why," Casey whispered. "They don't even know us. Why do they want us?"

"Because they're good people and know you're in trouble. There's lots of room at the mansion so you'll all be able to stay together, if that's worrying you. And I want to be clear. Nobody wants anything from you, Casey. They won't make you do anything that scares you. They just want to give you guys a safe place to stay and help you look after the pups."

"How will we get there? I'm too tired to drive that far." Casey bit at his lip. "And I don't think the van could make it anyway."

Edgar chuckled. "No, the van is done. We tried to get it running again, but yeah, it's not going anywhere. I don't know how you kept it running as long as you did."

A tentative smile crossed Casey's face. "I did a lot of praying to the Goddess."

"It seems like she answered your prayers. Nothing else can explain how that thing was still working."

Casey snorted, then covered his mouth.

"But you don't have to worry about the van," Edgar said. "We're going to fly all of you to New Orleans. We're just waiting for a call to tell us when we need to take you to the airport."

"We're going on a plane? I don't have money for that."

"You don't need money, Casey. It's Roman's plane. He's sending it here special just for you guys."

"No." Casey shook his head and started backing away again. "We're not going on a special plane."

When Edgar moved toward him, he held his hands out to stop him. "Stay back."

"Casey, I don't understand. Why are you so upset?"

"I know a plane costs a lot of money. I don't have any money and you can't make me pay for it the other way. Not anymore. I won't do that ever again." Keeping his eyes on Edgar, Casey called over his shoulder. "Robin, gather up the pups. We're leaving now."

Edgar stood there, stunned. What had just happened? "Casey, I don't know what you're saying. What's wrong?"

"Just leave us alone."

He rushed over to him. "Casey, please. Stop." He didn't even realize he'd raised his voice until Casey dropped to the floor and curled into a ball with his arms covering his head.

A small foot kicked him in the leg. "Alpha promised nobody would hurt him anymore. He lied."

Edgar shook his head at Robin. "Alpha Jackson didn't lie. I didn't hurt Casey, but I scared him somehow. Can you stand beside him and keep him safe? Be strong for him. Maybe he won't be afraid of me if you're there." At the boy's solemn nod, Edgar squatted next to Casey. His heart broke at the scared whimpers coming from the terrified young man.

The hotel door opening brought Edgar's head around. Jackson entered, took one look, and scowled at Edgar.

He glared back, gesturing for him to go back out. The last thing this situation needed was an angry Alpha.

Jackson didn't move.

"Get out of here and let me deal with this."

Jackson's eyes widened when Edgar yelled in his head. *"Looks like you could use some help. What happened?"*

"Nothing."

"It doesn't look like nothing."

"I know, but I didn't do anything. At least, I don't think I did. But something I said scared him."

"What did you say to him?"

"All I did was mention they would be flying on a plane and he started freaking out."

"Why? Is he afraid of flying?"

"I don't think so. He said he didn't have money for it."

"Didn't you tell him he didn't have to pay for it?"

"Yes, but he wouldn't listen. He just said he wouldn't pay for it that way."

"Oh. That poor Omega. I think I know what the problem is."

"Then explain it to me. I don't understand what's going on."

"Edgar, pretend you're young and scared and someone offered to fly you across the country. How do you think you would pay for your tickets if you had no money?"

"I don't understand what you're asking. Roman's paying for it."

"Casey doesn't know that. He thinks you're going to make him pay for it. But not with money."

Edgar gasped in horror as he realized what Jackson was saying. *"I would never do that."*

"You wouldn't. But it sounds like his previous Alpha did force him to do that kind of thing."

"That's revolting. Who would do that to a kid?"

"Unfortunately, a lot of people. Especially to Omegas. Too many Alphas don't treat them the way they should. Omegas are special and can make a pack stronger by being a part of it, but because they're physically weak and have delicate natures, Alphas don't think they bring any value to the pack so they usually abuse them or sell them. Since Omegas are unable to defend themselves, very few live to adulthood."

"You have to stop that from happening, Jackson. You need to protect any omegas who might still be out there."

"We can do that, Edgar. We can find them and offer them shelter."

Edgar could hear the challenge in his words and feel his resigned doubt through their link. He was thankful Jackson was giving him the opportunity to make up for his thoughtless words from earlier. *"You're right. Together, we will find all of the Omegas and keep them safe."*

Jackson's wide smile showed he understood what Edgar was saying.

"That's good to hear." He looked over Edgar's shoulder. *"We need to leave in thirty minutes, so see if you can get him settled. Call me if you need a hand."*

"I will."

"Okay. Good luck."

"Thanks." Edgar smiled at Jackson as he backed out of the room, then looked down at Casey, wondering how he was going to clear up the misunderstanding he'd accidentally caused.

"Robin, how's Casey doing?"

Robin's serious face looked up at him. "I think it's okay if you talk to him, but I need to stay with him."

"I agree." Edgar slowly shuffled over to sit near Casey's head. "Casey, I need you to listen to me for a second, okay?" He waited, relief filling him when he received a small nod. "I want to clear one detail up quickly since I know it's worrying you. The plane that's taking you and the kids to New Orleans won't cost you anything. Nothing, Casey. My Prince wants to bring you guys to his home because it's the right thing to do."

An eye peeked out from the arms Casey had wrapped around his head.

Edgar smiled at him. "Do you understand? Nobody has to pay for the ride. You're all safe. Nobody will make you do anything you don't want to do."

Casey lifted his head. "What about clothing and food for all of us? Who's going to pay for that?"

"That's a great question. Right now, Roman and his Consort Lysander will look after all of your needs. No strings attached. All you have to do is accept their help. Do you think you can do that?" Edgar raised his eyebrow.

Casey nodded.

"Once you're all safe and we've figured out what's happening to the rest of the Alphas, we'll sit down and discuss what you want to do with your future."

Casey sat up, frowning. "What do you mean, discuss my future. I have to do whatever the Alpha tells me."

"No, you don't," Edgar said, shaking his head. "It doesn't work like that anymore. Your life is changing. You can do whatever you dream of. If you want to go to school, we'll help you do that. If you want to stay living with Roman, you will. If you want to go live with the Alpha in Denver, you'll come live with us. From now on, you have a say in everything." As he spoke, Edgar could see the boy was becoming overwhelmed.

"I don't know what to do."

"That's okay. You don't have to decide anything today. But what I do need you to do is to get everyone's stuff together. It's time for us to take you to the plane and send you to safety."

"You're not coming?"

Edgar shook his head. "Alpha Jackson and I need to travel back to Denver and check in with his pack. We're trying to find out what's making the Alphas sick."

Casey hung his head. "I'm sorry I shot a few of them."

"I'm not." Casey's head whipped up. "You did the right thing, Casey. Those Alphas would have hurt you and the children. Alpha Jackson and I are so proud of your strength and courage. You truly are an amazing Omega."

Casey's shy smile was the best thing Edgar had seen that day.

* * *

Jackson and Edgar waived at Casey as he went up the stairs. He looked over his shoulder, waving back, then stepped onto the plane. Edgar was relieved the kids were finally on their way home where they'd be safe. That is, Roman's home. It wasn't his anymore, even though the thought hurt his heart. His home was now with Jackson and he needed to start putting his mate first and the coven and Roman second.

They stood quietly watching as the plane taxied down the runway and took its place in line, waiting to depart. Only once it was safely in the air and did Edgar relax, leaning against Jackson, who wrapped his arm around his shoulder.

"We did a good thing. Those kids will all have a better chance for a good life now," Edgar said.

"Pups, Edgar. If you're going to be a wolf's mate, the term is pups, not kids."

Edgar looked up. "What do you mean, if? I am a wolf's mate?"

Sober eyes regarded him. "Are you?"

"Of course, I am. You know that."

"Do I?" Jackson shrugged. "Sometimes I wonder where your heart lies."

Edgar looked away and stared at the night sky. "In many ways, I wish I could stay with the coven, but I know my home is with you. I just need a bit more time to fully come to terms with that."

"I understand, Edgar. I just hope it's soon. It's hard knowing I'm not your first choice."

"I don't know if this will help or make it worse but I do like and respect you. I admire both the man and the wolf. But I don't love you. At least, I don't think I do. Not yet anyway. But I know that will come as we spend more time together."

"And Roman?"

"I'm not sure what you mean. If you're asking if I love him, then yes, I do." Edgar elbowed Jackson in the stomach. "Stop growling. I love him as an older brother, not a lover. I've been with Roman a long time and I've admired him since the beginning. I always will. But that doesn't mean I won't learn to love both you and my new home."

"That's good to know. It's just…my wolf is jealous and wants you all to himself. He doesn't like sharing with a vampire."

Edgar smirked. "Just the wolf?"

Jackson rolled his eyes. "Perhaps I'm jealous too." He grabbed Edgar's hand. "Let's go. It's time for us to head back to Denver, and maybe find some answers."

They climbed into the SUV. Clancy, who was driving for this leg of the trip, started off once they were buckled in.

Edgar turned to Jackson. "I've been thinking about it and keep getting stuck on how the Alphas are the only wolves affected. I asked Casey if anyone from the Council had visited their pack in the last year, but he said they hadn't. So, how could the Elders be doing this without any contact?"

"I don't know. But it seems to be worse in the more isolated spots. The Alphas in Jackson and further north completely lost themselves to the madness, but my brother was aware enough of what was happening to him to take steps to keep our pack safe. Part of that could be because of how strong he is, but something else could be at play."

Edgar nodded. "I think you're right."

"But what's so different between the southern Alphas and the rural Alphas further north? Their wolves are the same, they have the same instincts, they eat the same food. If anything, the rural Alphas would eat better as they survive more off the land than the shifters closer to the city."

"Could the Council have poisoned their food source?" Edgar asked.

"I don't see how. They would have to infect every mammal across the country to ensure the sickness spread. Someone would have noticed that."

"True," Edgar said slowly. "But the shifters in the urban regions probably eat a lot of food that's been processed by humans; whereas, the mountain ones live solely off the land. If the Elders did infect their food source, that might explain why they were affected more."

Jackson hummed, then shook his head. "It seems a little far-fetched to think they infected every animal."

Edgar thought about it a bit more, then nodded. "You're right. That doesn't sound like a very efficient way to infect everyone. But I think I'll mention it to Roman anyway. They might be able to come up with something we've overlooked."

"Okay. While you do that I'm going to sit here and relax. It's been hectic the last few days. My wolf's feeling a bit agitated."

"Are you feeling okay?"

"Yes. He's just a bit wound up. It's probably leftover worry from chasing after the pups. It was stressful knowing how much danger they were in."

"Okay, if you're sure."

"I just said I was," Jackson snapped.

Edgar reared back. "Jackson?"

"Just leave it."

Edgar watched Jackson worriedly as he took a few deep breaths.

After a few moments, Jackson looked at him. "Sorry about that. My wolf is still very angry about the danger the pups were in. I'm so thankful Casey was able to overcome his Omega instincts. His courage saved them all."

"I know. I told Casey we were both proud of him."

"You did? That's what a good Alpha Mate would have done."

"There you go. I'm already fulfilling my new role." He smiled at Jackson, even though his stomach clenched with fear for his mate. "Rest and I'll wake you before we arrive at the next pack."

Jackson nodded and closed his eyes. His soft snores filled the vehicle within minutes.

Once he was sure Jackson was asleep, Edgar dialed Roman. He needed some options in case Jackson turned out to be the next casualty of the Council.

Chapter Thirteen

Lysander waited with Roman on the stairs as the SUV pulled to a stop in front of the house. When Jamie got out of the front passenger seat and went to open the rear door, he started bouncing excitedly on his toes, impatient to see the children. Hearing the mansion door open behind him, Lysander turned, smiling at Mrs. Davies as she joined them.

"I see the young ones are finally here."

"Yes. Do you have everything ready for them?"

"I do, Consort. The cook has put together a quick lunch in the small dining room. If I know anything about little boys, it's that feeding their stomachs is the best way to make them feel at home." She grinned. "For little girls too."

Lysander laughed. "Let's hope so, Mrs. Davies. These kids have been through horrors we can't even imagine."

"We'll do our best to replace those memories with better ones, Consort. Oh, here they come. Look how precious they are."

Small bodies scrambled out of the rear door, squealing in delight as they raced around the car. Jamie helped a timid young man climb out of the back seat. That must be Casey, the Omega. He could see the poor kid trembling as he looked around nervously. Lysander was about to go to him when Mrs. Davies rushed past him down the stairs and gathered Casey into her arms.

"Oh, you poor thing. You've had such a rough go of it lately. Haven't you, lovey?"

Casey's head nodded, even as he held his hands out to his sides, his fingers twitching, as though not sure whether to grab onto her or not.

Mrs. Davies loosened her hold and smiled down at him. "We're so very proud of you, Casey. Your Alpha told us how brave and strong you were. How smart and resourceful you were to keep everyone safe. The Prince and Consort are very much looking forward to meeting you and all the pups."

Casey's face crumpled as she spoke.

Mrs. Davies grabbed him up tight again, speaking in a soft voice. "You just cry it out, love. You don't have to be strong anymore. We'll look after you and the pups, keep you all safe. You're home now." Casey's arms wrapped around her waist, his hands clutching the back of her shirt as he cried.

Lysander looked on in wonder at how easily Mrs. Davies had earned Casey's trust. A small noise alerted him to the presence of the child standing before him. He'd been so wrapped up in watching Mrs. Davies work her magic, he hadn't noticed the little boy come over.

"Hey there, young man. What's your name?"

"Robin. Is it true we're going to live in this big house?"

Lysander squatted and smiled at him. "Yes. You're all going to live here, where we can keep you safe."

Distrustful eyes narrowed. "Casey too?"

Lysander nodded. "Casey too."

"Will you be nice to him, or are you going to yell at him and hit him? Cause we won't stay if you're going to be mean."

"We're going to be very nice to Casey. In fact, we're going to be good to all of you. But if it makes you feel better, I can put you in the room next to his so you can watch over him and make sure everyone's treating him good. How does that sound?"

The boy thought it over before nodding. "Okay. But if anyone is mean to him, we're going to leave."

Lysander stood. "If anyone is mean to him, I expect you to come and tell me and I'll make them leave. This is your home now and no one is allowed to be mean to any of you." He held out his hand. "Why don't you introduce me to everyone else while Casey finishes saying hello to Mrs. Davies."

Robin frowned. "He's crying, not saying hello."

Lysander chuckled. "Sometimes adults look like they're doing one thing when they're actually doing another."

The boy rolled his eyes at him. "Whatever." He grabbed Lysander's hand. "Come and meet Emily."

Smiling at Roman over his shoulder, Lysander went to meet the newest members of their growing family.

* * *

Jackson gritted his teeth in frustration as Bill looked around the house for the third time. They'd already buried the broken bodies and followed the tracks until they'd found the Alpha, who'd been halfway up the mountain when he'd run into a bear, coming out on the losing end of that fight. The vampire enforcers were burying his remains while the magic users looked over the area. Again.

Jackson emitted a small growl, tired of the time being wasted. There was nothing new to be discovered here. He was ready to move on. He paced jerkily, rubbing his itchy arms, growling intermittently as he waited for everyone to finish and get back in the vehicles.

Realizing his growling was getting louder, he stopped his restless walking and looked up at the moon. He breathed deep, trying to center himself, but gave up after a few moments when it didn't work and resumed his pacing. As more minutes passed, he was starting to really regret his decision to drive straight south from Helena instead of backtracking through the mountains along the same route they'd taken while chasing after Casey. They'd be making faster time if they didn't keep having to make all these stops that were serving no purpose.

He wiped a hand over his brow, trying to calm down and be patient. He needed to remember that Bill was being diligent in searching for clues on how to stop this infection. They needed answers and were running out of time. Besides, if he didn't get himself under control, Edgar would start badgering him again. His mate was driving him crazy with all of his fussing the last few days.

"Jackson, are you feeling okay?" Edgar asked, walking over to him as he wiped his hands off on the jeans he'd finally agreed to wear. "You're looking a little flushed."

"I'm fine," Jackson gritted out, any pleasure he'd felt at seeing Edgar dressed more suitably erased by the annoyance of him being all up in his face again.

"Are you sure? You seem a bit tense. Maybe you should relax in the vehicle while we finish up. I think we're about done here anyway."

"You don't need to send me off for rest like I'm a child."

"That's not what I'm doing."

Of course, it wasn't. He glared at Edgar, who seemed to forget Jackson was an Alpha. The strongest Alpha of them all. He was getting tired of being constantly watched and having to worry about what he said so Edgar didn't get that look on his face. That look. The one he was giving Jackson right now.

"I'm sorry. I'm just worried about you." He reached for Jackson, but he ducked away from his hand.

"I said I was fine. Why don't you ever listen to me?"

"You need to calm down."

"I am calm," Jackson yelled. He was so done with the conversation. Ignoring the hurt look on Edgar's face, he said, "I'm going for a run. By myself. I need to get away from the stink of death around this place."

"But Jackson—"

He held up his hand and backed away from his mate, fighting against the urge to hit him though it was getting harder to resist every time Edgar gave him that look. "I'll be back later."

Not giving him time to respond, Jackson rushed through his shift, not caring about destroying his clothing, then took off up the hillside. He sped past the tree line, praying that Edgar would leave him to run in peace. Crackling pine needles and the rushing sound of his mate chasing after him killed that hope before it had fully formed.

They raced through the trees, Jackson jumping over obstacles and running under low hanging branches, trying to shake his pursuer. He charged down a short drop off and raced through a small creek before shooting out the other side. Splashing sounds behind him proved his mate was undaunted by his efforts to get rid of him.

When the terrain leveled out, Edgar rushed past him, trying to cut him off. Jackson pulled out of his run, sliding in the loose soil before he was able to get his legs under him, then cut sharply to the side and sped away from him again.

"Damn it, Jackson. Get back here. You need to stop running from me." Noise from behind him told him his mate hadn't given up on his pursuit.

Putting on more speed in hopes of outrunning the annoying vampire, Jackson barely stopped in time to avoid plunging into the deep gorge that suddenly appeared in front of him. His hind legs slid in the dirt as he threw his body sideways, fighting for every bit of traction he could get. Yelping when he felt his left back leg slip over the emptiness, he dug in with his front claws and slowed his momentum enough to complete his turn, then raced along the edge, not giving a thought to the mate chasing after him.

"What the hell? I almost went over the edge. Stop running away before one of us gets killed."

Jackson didn't want to hear it, so he pushed himself harder, digging deeper for more power and speed. He raced along the edge, his wolf howling joyfully as he finally felt his pursuer fall behind. He ran for miles, exulting in his freedom as the wind rushed past him, stopping periodically to howl his joy to the moon, before picking up his furious pace again.

Sweat coating his fur, legs moving so fast they were a blur, Jackson felt like he could run for days. He jumped over a large boulder in his path, his left paw hitting loose soil when he landed on the other side. Suddenly he was flying through the air, then bouncing off rocks that jutted from the sides of the gorge. He pawed frantically at the air, howling in fear as the river rose to meet him. Plunging into its icy depths, he was swept away by the strong current.

He pawed frantically at the water, rising then going under, rising again, then sinking, bouncing off rocks and trees before finally smashing into a large boulder buried in the rapids.

He yelped in pain when his ribs cracked. The unrelenting current swept him along, heedless of his struggles. He was dragged helplessly through the water into another rock. His head slammed against its unforgiving hardness. Darkness descended.

Edgar scoured the riverbanks frantically searching for Jackson, knowing he had to be here somewhere. He'd followed the turns of the river, checking the banks on both sides, finally coming upon a large bend where the waters slowed as they became shallower. He was praying to the Goddess that the current that had carried Jackson's body away had left it here and that he hadn't been lost to the rapids. His breath caught, lodging in his throat when he saw the body of a wolf gently bumping against a half-submerged log, rising and falling in time with the slow-moving current.

Racing through the water to Jackson's side, the first thing he did was check to make sure he was still breathing. When he felt soft puffs of air against his face, Edgar rested his head against Jackson's cold, wet shoulder, allowing himself a moment to sob in relief. But only for a minute. He needed to get Jackson out of the water as quickly as possible.

Standing, he grabbed his mate's front legs and pulled, using most of his strength to drag him further up the bank. Jackson's gigantic wolf form had to weigh at least three hundred pounds, a weight almost too much for even his great vampire strength to manage.

Finally, after considerable effort, he'd managed to pull Jackson's body mostly out of the water. Gasping from exertion, Edgar dropped to his knees and started checking his mate over to see what injuries he'd sustained. Carefully running his hands along the wolf's body, he heard a soft whimper when his hands moved over his ribs. Pressing around the area gently, he decided they were only cracked and not something to worry about, Jackson's shifter healing could easily take care of those. Edgar didn't find any other injuries until he got to his head. Lifting it gently to have a look at the side laying on the ground, he winced when he saw the large gash that had opened Jackson's fur down to his skull, but that injury too had already started to heal.

Edgar hung his head, his fists clenched tightly in Jackson's fur, taking his first full breath since his mate had plunged into the river. He'd had no idea how much he cared about Jackson until he'd seen him fly off the edge of the ravine. His overwhelming relief that Jackson wasn't seriously injured or worse, brought tears to his eyes. Raising his head, Edgar sat back in the muddy water, shivering as the cold water soaked the jeans he was wearing. Glancing down at the muddy, torn denim, he chuckled, grateful Jackson had pushed him into jeans and boots after he'd ruined his last suit. His normal attire would never have survived the race through the woods or his diving run down the side of the ravine.

Thunder crashed overhead.

Great. He now had a storm to contend with in addition to everything else, unless it was moving away from him. A couple of minutes later, a bolt of lightning cut through the air, striking further down the ravine. The resulting thunderclap reverberated through Edgar's ears. The skies overhead broke open. Icy rain pelted his skin, causing him to shiver until his whole body was trembling. He pushed himself up, knowing he needed to get them out of the water and under cover as quickly as possible.

He grabbed Jackson's front paws again and strained mightily, dragging him inches at a time further up the riverbank. After what seemed like hours, he finally had them tucked away under the nearby trees. Not the safest place to wait out a lightning storm, but better than sitting in the open in the water.

But now that he had nothing to do but wait out the storm, Edgar's mind started to work. He stared at Jackson's trembling form, terror freezing his insides worse than the icy rain the wind kept blowing into their shelter, as he came face to face with the realization that Jackson was infected with the Alpha's madness. He'd had his suspicions, but today's race through the mountains had proved Jackson was no longer in control.

Shivering in the cold, Edgar racked his brain trying to figure out how it had happened. They'd had no interactions with anyone other than the wolves. Jackson had washed thoroughly after every encounter in case the infection was spread through contact. They'd all eaten the same food, they drank at the same places. They'd seen no sign of any of the Elders or their pet magic users. How could he possibly have become infected?

A gust of wind caused a change in the direction of the rain, pushing it down the back of his collar. Gasping at the icy coldness, his eyes opened wide as a thought crossed his mind. Breathing quickly as panic started to set in, he ruthlessly pushed it to the side and forced himself to calm down. He needed to use the brain he prided himself on. Once his heartbeat leveled out, he tried to piece it together. He stared blankly at the river flowing in front of him and went over everything they'd learned.

Fact number one; only the Alphas seemed to be affected. Except, he remembered Clint's note saying the strongest Betas felt anger too. He shook his head. No. That was wrong. The Betas felt the anger until they remembered they were Betas, then the feelings disappeared.

Fact number two; wolves closer to the city were less affected than their mountain counterparts. What differences in their lifestyles were great enough to lessen the impact on the urban wolves?

Edgar looked through the pelting rain at the river. The thought he'd had earlier solidified. But the idea of it was so horrible he almost pushed it away, but it was the only thing that made sense. It was the only solution that fit everything they knew. Edgar turned it around in his head, looking for flaws in his logic, trying to come at it from different angles, but it all slotted neatly together.

He had no idea how they'd managed it, but the Elders must have poisoned the water. The rural and mountain wolves relied solely on streams, creeks, and wells for water so had no way to avoid being infected, whereas the urban wolves had access to water that had been run through the humans' purification systems, which probably reduced the effectiveness of the contamination. That could explain why they hadn't succumbed to the madness as quickly.

The question was how? The country was huge. How did you contaminate water across that huge landmass without having to poison every lake and stream? Did you send out hordes of acolytes to poison all the water sources? Or perhaps they'd just infected the higher altitude water, hoping it would be carried down from the mountains and enter the water table and then spread everywhere else. No. That would take too long. Their plan for the Alphas was too successful for them to have left that to chance. The Council would have come up with a fool-proof method.

Edgar struggled to think of other options but kept getting stuck on the water table being the key. Unless…could they possibly have poisoned the Alphas at some large pack gathering? Maybe the infection was transmissible between Alphas. Feeling lost, Edgar looked at Jackson, wishing he could ask him if the wolves even had an annual gathering. There was just so much he didn't know about the shifter community.

Lightning shot from the sky, striking closer to where they were sitting. Edgar looked up at the roiling clouds, trying to determine which direction they were headed, hoping they were heading away from him. He was more than ready to get out of this storm.

He did a double take when the solution came to him. The clouds. Holy shit. They were seeding the clouds. He squeezed his eyes shut, trying to think his way through it. How would it work? The clouds traveled across the entire US, dropping rain everywhere, but mostly in the mountains. If they used the clouds to carry their poison, they could sit back and let nature do all their work. The infected waters would flow down from the mountains, running through every creek and stream, and travel through to the water table. The cloud system in the Central US would rain poison down, soaking the ground, and draining through to the water table. Once the water was traveling underground, the contamination would spread, able to reach the wolves wherever they lived. Wet zones or arid zones, everyone depended on the water they could get from the ground.

He shivered as the full scope of the Council's malevolent plan unfolded in his mind, the evilness of it freezing him colder than the frigid rain soaking his clothing.

He pulled his jacket around him tighter. Something pressed against his side. Edgar felt like smacking himself as he reached into the inside pocket and pulled out the satellite phone the Consort had insisted everyone carry with them. Quickly checking it over, it looked like it had made it through all the obstacles and water he'd exposed it to in his frantic search and rescue of Jackson.

Hunching over, he dialed, exhaling in relief when his call was answered. Before Roman could say a word, Edgar started talking, telling him what he'd figured out. He prayed the information would help Bryan find a way to cure the affliction killing the wolves. Jackson's life depended on it.

"Edgar, Lysander sent your coordinates to Bill. They should be reaching you soon and can help you get Jackson out of the mountains. Bryan is headed back to the Council building. He recalls seeing something about clouds that didn't have any relevance at the time, so he disregarded it. He will call as soon as he finds something." Roman stopped talking as Lysander said something in the background too low for Edgar to make out.

"Lysander says you need to keep Jackson calm. You might be able to hold off the worst of the effects if you can keep his wolf from getting agitated. That should allow you time to make it back to Denver. He says to lean on your mate bond to help."

"Okay. I can do that."

"Congratulations on your mating Edgar. I am sorry it is happening under such stressful conditions, but your bond may end up being the very thing that saves Jackson."

"Thanks, Roman. He's a good man, a good wolf. He makes me happy."

"That is good to hear."

"You know this is going to change everything, don't you?"

"As any mating should."

"I really appreciate everything you've done for me over the years."

"Do not talk as though we will never see each other again. We will always be family."

"I know. Still, thank you."

"No need for that. Now keep your eyes open. Help should be arriving shortly. We will do everything we can to save him. You must have faith that Jackson will be fine."

"I do," Edgar lied. Whatever Roman said, Edgar didn't think whatever they did would be enough. He ended the call, doubt and fear for Jackson the only thoughts filling his mind.

* * *

Sitting in the back of the SUV, both Jackson and himself safely out of the mountains, warm again and dressed in dry clothing, Edgar should have been feeling more optimistic about their chances. Unfortunately, all he could focus on was how worried he was about his mate. Edgar gripped his hand tighter. "Jackson, you're growling again. You need to try to stay calm."

"I know. I'm doing my best but my wolf is very angry. He's getting harder to control." Jackson turned to look at him, regret written all over his face. "I'm sorry, Edgar. I'm trying so hard, but I don't know if I can beat this."

Edgar refused to give his mate up without a fight. It was time to give Jackson's wolf something else to focus on. Edgar unlatched his seat belt, then straddled Jackson's lap. "You will make it. I know how strong you are. Link with me. I will help your wolf keep calm."

Jackson frowned. "How do I link? We've never done that before."

Edgar smirked. "We definitely have. Let me refresh your mind." He bent over, whispering in Jackson's ear. "We start with our bodies. Our minds and souls will follow." He settled back and pressed his lips to Jackson's, vaguely aware of Eric raising the privacy shield. Good idea. He smiled against Jackson's lips. This could get very loud because he was planning on using every trick he'd learned over the centuries to distract Jackson's wolf.

Except, his mate was holding back. Edgar couldn't have that. "Kiss me, Jackson. Give your wolf a different emotion to feel." Edgar bit his lip, hoping to goad his mate with his small display of dominance.

Jackson growled and grabbed hold of his hips as he thrust his tongue past Edgar's lips. Edgar groaned, quickly falling under the spell of his dominant mate, who took advantage of his surrender licking deep into his mouth. His fangs dropped, nicking Jackson's lip and scraping along the sides of his tongue. Moaning, he swallowed the small drops, the power in Jackson's blood raced through him as pleasure rolled through his body.

Reaching down, he pulled on Jackson's tee-shirt, yanking it over his head. Jackson's hands slid around his sides, slipping under his Henley and pushing his shirt up to his armpits. Edgar moaned again, loving the feel of his mate's hands on his skin. Refocusing on his efforts to drive his mate wild, he sucked hard on Jackson's collarbone, pulling the blood to the surface, intent on leaving a dark mark. Jackson grunted, his body jerking beneath Edgar. Grinning, he ran his tongue along his mate's skin, nibbling as he went until he reached the juncture of his neck. Placing his teeth on Jackson's skin, he bit down and sucked hard, swallowing the blood that filled his mouth.

Without realizing how it happened, Edgar found himself flat on his back, his shredded jeans in tatters around him. Jackson grabbed his hips, lifting him into position. Edgar looked into his eyes and saw the wildness of the wolf staring back at him. Licking his fingers, he reached down and quickly gave himself minimal preparation, knowing his mate was too far gone to look after it.

"I'm sorry." Jackson's voice was barely recognizable, buried as it was beneath the rumbling growl of the wolf. "I can't be gentle. Not tonight. The wolf's need is too strong."

Nodding his acceptance, Edgar forced himself to relax as Jackson thrust forward, burying himself to the hilt. He flung his head back and reached overhead, bracing himself against the door as Jackson proceeded to unleash all of his furious passion into Edgar's willing body.

Jackson's pounding motion got jerky as he neared the end. He lowered his head, teeth burying into Edgar's neck. Edgar struck back, fire burning down his veins as they consumed each other. He pressed forward with his mind, searching down the link for Jackson. Finding his shifter spirit, he wrapped himself around the angry beast, soothing the raging wolf, even as his body provided a haven for the man.

Jackson's chuckles brought him back to awareness. "Edgar, are you okay? Did I break you?"

Somebody sounded very pleased with themselves. And in control. Edgar breathed a sigh of relief, thankful that Jackson's anger had been driven back. He opened his eyes to see his mate grinning at him. He closed his eyes again. "I see you're feeling more like yourself. That's great. Now get off of me and let me rest. You wore me out with your wolfish appetite."

Jackson laughed. "As much as it thrills me to hear that, I can't do as you ask. You need to wake up. We're getting close to Denver. And I have something important to show you."

Edgar opened his eyes again, took one look at Jackson's face, then sat up. "What is it? What's wrong now?"

Jackson smiled softly. "Everything's okay. Really okay."

"Are you sure?"

Jackson nodded and took his hand. "Thank you for giving yourself so freely to me. You have no idea how much it means to me that you would do that."

"It meant everything to me as well," Edgar said seriously, "more than I think you realize."

"I think I know what you're talking about." Jackson looked down, uncharacteristically shy, then glanced at Edgar through his lashes. "It's possible the wolf and I care about you a lot." He paused, biting his lip, then gasped out. "We might even love you."

"Jackson," Edgar whispered, "you have no idea how scared I was for you. How scared I still am. Almost losing you made me realize I might love you too."

Jackson blew out a breath and smiled.

Before he could say anything, Edgar cut him off. "But don't let it go to your Alpha head. You're still not the boss of me."

Snorting out a laugh, Jackson said, "Understood. But it's a good thing we both care about each other. Look." He pointed to his chest, just under his collarbone.

Edgar's eyes went wide. Raising a shaky hand, he brushed his fingertips over a symbol of a wolf print, encasing three drops of blood.

"Where did this come from?"

Smiling, Jackson said, "I think it came from the Goddess. You have one too."

Edgar looked down at his chest and saw a matching mark. He touched it gently, blinking away dampness from his eyes. They truly had been blessed by the Goddess. Grinning up at his mate, he suddenly felt much better about the possibilities for Jackson's survival.

He pulled Jackson down on top of him, kissing him passionately in thankfulness and relief. Denver would have to wait. They had some more celebrating to do.

Chapter Fourteen

The sun had set an hour before they arrived at the Denver pack lands. Jackson looked at the window, frowning, as Eric brought the SUV to a stop. A growl rose in his throat. He quickly throttled his wolf back, relieved when it settled.

"Jackson, shouldn't there someone be here to greet us? We told Mary we were arriving tonight."

"Something's wrong." Jackson put his hand on the door handle. "Please stay in the vehicle while I check it out."

Edgar snorted. "I don't think so. You can't tuck me safely in the corner whenever there's danger. I told you before, it may not look like it, but I can hold my own in a fight. Don't let my pretty face fool you." He batted his eyelashes at Jackson.

Jackson rolled his eyes. He hadn't thought it would be that easy, but it had been worth a try. "Just try to stay safe. I don't like the thought of you being in danger."

"As long as you promise to keep yourself safe as well."

Jackson nodded. "Clancy, alert the others. Everyone is to proceed with extreme caution. Be ready for anything. There's something in the air I don't like."

"Yes, sir. I'm calling the other vehicle now though I suspect they're already aware something is wrong."

Climbing out of the vehicle, Jackson raised his face to the sky and breathed deep. "I can smell blood. There's been fighting recently." He pulled more air into his lungs, letting his wolf rise to heighten his senses. "Edgar, there's another vampire nearby. I can't tell if it's friend or foe."

"I can feel them too. There's something familiar about them." Edgar looked at Jackson. "It feels like family, but I don't know why they'd be here." He frowned, looking out into the darkness. "As they haven't come to greet us yet, I'm going to assume they're not here as a friend."

"Agreed." Jackson looked behind to the men standing around the vehicles. "Eric, keep your eyes peeled. I also sense something familiar, and nothing about it feels good."

"Yes, Alpha. I'll take Clancy and do some recon of the area. The others can pair up and do the same."

"Good thinking. Report back to me at the packhouse when you've finished. Hopefully, by then, we'll know what we're dealing with."

"Yes, sir."

As the men spread out, Jackson headed for the front porch, constantly scanning the area. The dark, silent houses troubled him. Somebody should have come out to meet them by now. That they hadn't meant they weren't able to. His anger grew at the thought of someone harming his pack.

"Steady Jackson," Edgar said, laying a hand on his shoulder. "Don't let the anger overwhelm you. You must stay in control of your wolf so we can deal with whatever we find."

Gritting his teeth, Jackson began the arduous process of trying to rein in his wolf. It was getting more difficult every time he had to wrestle him down. Now, when both the man and the wolf were angry, it was next to impossible. Jackson knew he was going to lose the battle today.

"I don't think I can control him. Promise me you won't come too close. I don't want there to be any chance of my wolf hurting you. That would send him over the edge. I'd never recover from that." Sweat began beading on his forehead as he struggled to remain in control. "Edgar," he said through gritted teeth, "promise me."

"I promise. I'm moving away now."

Edgar's hand slipped off his shoulder. Jackson heard his footsteps as he backed up.

"I'll keep my distance, Jackson, but you need to keep fighting. I believe in you. I expect you to win this battle."

Jackson wasn't so sure he could. A red haze was slowly covering his vision as his wolf's anger took over, no matter how hard he fought to push it back. A loud growl rumbled up his chest when the front door of the packhouse opened and Russel stepped out with his arm locked around Mary's neck. The corner of Jackson's mouth lifted in a snarl, foam flecking his lips as his eyes traveled over her. Her face was bruised and swollen, and both of her eyes had been blackened. Streaks of dried blood tracked down her neck from a fresh bite and bruises and bites mottled both of her arms.

Seeing the marks of her abuse was the last link in the chain that was holding the wolf's anger at bay. Jackson sank to the background when it snapped, no longer in control. The fury of the wolf was driving them now.

"What have you done to my pack?" The words barely sounded human, filled as they were with the wolf's rage.

"You're not the only one with friends in high places," Russel sneered. He motioned behind him to the packhouse. "I think you'll like what I've done with the place. But before you can see it, you'll have to make it past the welcoming committee." He looked over Jackson's head. "Boys, come on out now. It's time to play Kill the Alpha. The winner gets to have the delectable Mary. I can personally attest to her charms, can't I, sweetie?"

Tears may have been running down her face, but she hadn't lost her fighting spirit. Mary raised her leg high, then kicked back at Russel's knee. Once her foot connected and Russel relaxed his hold, she bent forward then flung her head back and smashed him in his face, while at the same time driving her elbow into his ribs. His cry of pain was sweet music to Jackson's ears. He watched in satisfaction as Mary was able to pull free. Unfortunately, she only made it two steps before Russel was able to recover. He fisted his hand in her hair, holding her immobile while he wrapped his arm around her neck and lifted her off the ground in a chokehold.

Jackson snarled, his rage hitting its peak as he watched Mary clutching at the arm around her neck, digging in with her nails as she tried to get enough air to breathe. The wolf began to shift. The time for talking was over. It was time to fight.

"You stupid bitch. You'll pay for that." Russel's head jerked up when Jackson growled, finished with his shift. Tossing Mary carelessly to the side, he called out, "It's time boys, let's show this Alpha who's really in charge around here." He dropped to his knees to begin his transformation from man to wolf.

Jackson spun around when he heard movement behind him, unsurprised to find himself facing six wolves. Russel's gang of bullies. Jackson growled, foam dripping from his muzzle as he challenged them to come at him. Two of the stupidest ones rushed in first. Bracing his rear legs, he shot up when the first attacker reached him and clamped his jaws around his neck. Shaking his head vigorously, he flung the wolf to the side, ripping out his adversary's throat.

The wolf flew through the air, landing and skidding along the dusty ground before crashing to a stop against one of the cars. It didn't get back up.

Jackson yipped when he felt teeth sink into his hindquarters. The second wolf had come in for a sneak attack while he'd been distracted. Jackson whipped around, yanking his leg free, but losing a chunk of his flesh in doing so.

With his attention pulled away from them, the other wolves mounted a joint attack led by Russel. Jackson fell under the weight of the six wolves, biting anything he could get his teeth into and clawing with his back legs as he tried to fend them off. He felt the flesh of his vulnerable stomach being ripped open. Knowing his time was running out to finish the fight, Jackson increased his efforts against the superior numbers.

"Jackson!" Hearing his mate screaming his name, fearing he needed help, the wolf went wild. Jackson lost himself to the feral rage that overtook his shifter spirit. Deep red clouded his vision. His body was racked with pain as power burned through his veins. He howled in rage when his joints forcefully shifted, then realigned into new configurations. His flesh burned where it felt like he was being sliced by a thousand razors, then dipped in a sea of salt.

When the pain receded, Jackson's body overflowing with energy, his Alpha power magnified beyond anything he'd felt before.

Roaring his fury to the universe, Jackson lumbered to his feet, his huge hands tearing the wolves off of him and throwing them to the ground. When they barked and snapped at him, he raised his head and howled, before reaching out and grabbing a wolf in each and bashing their heads together. Bones snapped as their skulls were caved in.

Dropping their lifeless bodies, his black-tipped clawed feet dug into the ground as he jumped over his attackers, landing behind them. He grabbed the next wolf in reach, took hold of it with both hands and yanked, tearing its body in half with one pull. He bared his teeth when he smelled Russel's fear, his muzzle quivering with his long-sustained growl as he dropped the pieces of the dismembered wolf to the ground and stalked his enemy.

As one, Russel and his remaining wolves turned tail and raced away from him. Howling in victory, Jackson pursued the mangy wolves who thought they could escape his wrath, but there was nowhere they could run to avoid death that day.

Holy Goddess. What in the hell had Jackson turned into? Edgar blinked, still not believing he had just seen him tear a wolf in half without effort. And now his mate, who moments before had been close to death, was chasing after his attackers on two feet. Two very large hairy feet.

Edgar completely understood why the wolves were running instead of staying to fight. They couldn't hope to stand against the raging beast Jackson had turned into. His mate had transformed into a gigantic half wolf half man creature over seven feet tall and covered in fur. His body had expanded and filled out in proportion to his height, but it had drastically changed. His hands and feet were huge with black-tipped claws and his head was eerily man-shaped but sported a wolflike muzzle and pointed ears. Edgar's body thrummed from the force of Jackson's Alpha power that radiated off him, the overwhelming energy perfectly matched to his immense size and strength.

His eyes widened when Jackson caught up to another hapless wolf, first tearing him into bits and then throwing the pieces at the remaining two fleeing wolves. He wrinkled his nose. That was kind of gross.

In another moment, Jackson was only a speck in the distance. Edgar turned to go find Eric and the others, then froze when he saw the man standing behind him.

"Uncle Armand?"

"Hello, nephew." He nodded in the direction Jackson had gone. "I haven't seen a Dire Wolf in centuries."

"Is that what he is? I've never heard of one."

"That doesn't surprise me. They are extremely rare. And really, as a young vampire, you didn't get out much."

No thanks to his family. "What are you doing here, Uncle Armand?"

"You have something of mine and I want them back."

As Edgar looked at him in confusion, he missed the sound of someone coming up behind him. A prick in his neck alerted him to his danger. But by then, it was too late. He shivered at the hate he saw in his uncle's eyes as everything faded to black.

Eric stood with Clancy, watching Jackson's form grow smaller as he pursued the remaining wolves into the distance. "Holy shit. What was that?"

"I don't know," Clancy said. "I don't think I have enough power to stop it, whatever it is."

"That, my friends, is a Dire Wolf." Bill joined them, staring off into the distance where Jackson had disappeared. "And no, you do not have enough magic to stop it. None of us do. The Dire is filled with so much Alpha power, I doubt there is much on Earth that could stop him. Especially now in his battle rage."

"What do we do if we can't use magic to stop him? He's crazy mad. He could destroy us all."

Eric piped up. "I might have just the thing. Give me a minute."

He walked past Clancy, Bill, and the ever-silent Ted, and opened the rear of the SUV. He grabbed the duffel of special equipment he'd brought and rummaged through it, pulling out what he needed. He joined the others a few minutes later with a gun strapped over his shoulder and a big grin on his face.

Bill's eyebrows rose. "Is that a tranquilizer gun?"

"It sure is."

"Why on earth do you have a tranquilizer gun? Clancy asked. "Especially one that big."

Eric snorted. "The Consort said to load up on weapons. Since we were supposed to be checking on Alpha wolves, I thought it might come in handy. I bet you're glad now that I thought to bring it." He patted the barrel. "I just hope the darts are strong enough to put him out. I'd hate to get him angry at me."

"Ted and I should be able to hold him long enough for you to tranq him. Once he's sedated, we'll need to find a safe place to store him until he regains his human form."

Eric stared at Bill, his eyebrow cocked.

"What?"

"By safe place to store him, you mean someplace we can lock him up. I don't think Edgar will like us doing that to his mate."

"Do you have a better idea? We can hardly leave an angry Dire wolf to run around free. You have no idea of the power we're dealing with here." Bill stopped and looked around. "His mate is probably our best bet to control him. Has anyone seen him?"

"He's just over by the packhouse." Eric pointed, his hand dropping when he realized Edgar wasn't there. He frowned. "He was there a few minutes ago. Did anyone see where he went?"

When everyone shook their heads, Eric started to worry. Edgar wouldn't have just taken off. Especially not with Jackson running around out there in his Dire form. He walked quickly toward the packhouse, then, spotting something on the ground, flashed the rest of the way there. He picked up a dart laying in the dirt and brought it to his nose. "Oh fuck. We're so screwed."

"What is it?" Bill shouted out as the rest of the men raced over.

"We weren't the only ones with a tranquilizer. Edgar's been taken."

* * *

"Yes, Prince Roman, he's still unconscious." Eric glanced over at Jackson. They'd tranquilized the Alpha when he came back to the packhouse looking for his mate. Eric really hoped Jackson didn't remember it had been him who'd shot him. Three times. That wouldn't bode well for his continued survival.

Once Jackson had been knocked out, they'd handcuffed him, wrapped him with magical bindings, and carted him off to the airplane, making him as comfortable as possible on the couch in the main cabin of the private jet.

"Thank you for sending the plane so quickly. I don't think we could have gotten him back if we'd driven. Especially with how angry he's going to be once he finds out his mate has been taken." Eric winced at the furious growl that came over the phone. "I'm sorry, my Prince. I failed in my duty."

"Never mind that. Did you find any clues as to who took him?"

"No, Prince. There were no signs of anyone where Edgar was taken, other than the dart."

"Which was deliberately left for you to find. Did the wolves have anything to say?"

"No. The wolves who were still alive had all been knocked out, so they weren't any help. Mary was the only one conscious at the time, and she didn't see who took him. However, she did say she smelled another vampire." Eric snapped his fingers. "Sorry, Prince. I just remembered. Alpha Jackson said the same thing when we first arrived."

"That there was another vampire nearby?"

"Yes, Prince."

"Then we will work under the assumption this strange vampire took him. I suspect I will hear from the kidnapper shortly. Grabbing Edgar was most likely meant to get my attention. It is unfortunate for them that they now have it. I do not take it well when someone hurts my family."

Eric swallowed hard. "No, Prince."

"Bryan will meet you at the airport to help transport Jackson to the Council dungeons. Report to me immediately when you are finished."

Eric whispered, "Yes, Prince."

Roman's sigh was loud over the phone. *"Do try to relax, Eric. You are not to blame for what happened to Edgar"*

"But I was supposed to keep everyone safe."

"As were the others with you. Whoever took Edgar had access to great power to have gone unnoticed by all of you. Report to me when you return so we can determine our next steps. We need to come up with a plan to get him back."

"I'll be there as soon as we have the Alpha secured."

"Very good." Roman ended the call.

Eric turned off his phone, smiling with relief that he got to keep his head. It had been a huge concern.

Chapter Fifteen

Edgar groaned as awareness slowly came back, pushing past the cobwebs fogging his mind. He let his eyes drift lazily open, blinking to clear the spots blurring his vision. When his Uncle Armand's face came into focus, he closed his eyes again, intending to escape back into the dark.

"Uh, uh, uh, nephew. I know you're awake. It's time to pay attention. We have things to discuss."

Edgar opened his eyes again, blinking furiously, which helped fully restore his vision. Ignoring his uncle—and the pounding in his head—he scanned his surroundings, not understanding at first where he was. When he tipped his head back he saw he was chained to a wall. He pulled on his cuffed hands to make sure it wasn't just his imagination. Unfortunately, the rattle of the chains told him he really was chained to the wall. He shivered, only then realizing he was completely naked. His bare toes were freezing where they made contact with the cement floor. As he became more alert, he noticed a frigid heaviness to the air, making him think they were underground. Squinting at the metal walls, he figured he was being held in some kind of bunker.

"Did you hear me?"

Continuing to ignore his uncle, Edgar looked for a way to get free. He looked again at the metal walls. They held some promise. If they were steel he'd be out of here in a flash since his vampire strength was greater than what any steel binding could hold. He gave a hard yank on the metal cuffs fastened to the wall, waiting expectantly for them to pull free. But they held firm. Frowning, he pulled harder, using all of his strength, even pushing his back against the wall for extra leverage.

His uncle's laughter finally brought his unsuccessful efforts to a halt. He dangled from the cuffs, still securely fastened to him and the wall, his heart sinking as he realized how much trouble he was in.

"Did you really think you could get free that easily? The walls and bindings are all made of titanium infused with magic. There will be no escape for you, I'm afraid."

"What's going on, uncle?" Edgar glared at him, his chest heaving from his exertions. "Why did you bring me here?"

"I'm glad you asked." Armand pushed off the wall he'd been leaning against and came over to stand in front of Edgar. "I'm disappointed in you. Cavorting around the countryside looking like a thug, keeping company with wolves and humans." He spat on the floor. "I thought we taught you better than that. We certainly tried hard enough. I'll have to do a better job showing you the proper way to behave this time." His smile promised a world of pain coming Edgar's way.

Edgar worked up some saliva in his mouth and spat on the floor as well, returning the vulgarity of the gesture back to his uncle. Unfortunately, the angle was all wrong, and instead of landing harmlessly on the floor, his spittle hit his uncle on his cheek, where it ever so slowly slid down his face, curving under his jaw, before finally landing on his collar. Edgar flinched at the anger that flared in his uncle's eyes, not noticing when his other hand moved to strike. His head snapped to the side when the blow landed.

Turning back, Edgar ignored his stinging cheek to sneer at his uncle. "Don't act like you're any better than me. That was you working with a lowly Gamma, was it not? I, at least, have enough breeding to deal with Princes and not third-ranked mongrels."

"You'll be wanting to watch your mouth. You're not exactly in a position to defend yourself." Armand chuckled harshly, "Not that being free would help a puny, little weakling like yourself anyway."

Edgar rolled his eyes, about done with the posturing. "Just tell me what you want."

"What I want are my vampires. Where has that pretender to the throne hidden them?"

Edgar frowned. "What are you talking about?"

"Don't play dumb with me. I know you hid them somewhere. I want them back."

His eyes widened. "Those were your vampires? You're the one who helped the Elders attack us? Why would you do that?"

"Why does anyone ever do anything? For power, of course. The Elders promised I could take over your Prince's coven if I assisted them." He spat on the floor again. "Since I hate that traitorous coward you ran off with, I was more than happy to assist."

"Roman is no traitor. Or a coward. He was your Prince."

"He left us!" Armand yelled in Edgar's face, flecks of spittle hitting his cheeks. "He was our Prince, and he turned tail and ran away like a cowardly piece of crap. He left a useless, spineless fool on the throne. The Court was in shambles, with vampires fighting vampires. Nobody followed the rules of our society. It was complete anarchy, and it's all your Prince's fault. When the opportunity came to take his world away from him, many of us leaped at the chance." He smiled, the madness in his eyes frightening Edgar. "I was the only one to survive." He pressed his forehead to Edgar's, crushing Edgar's skull between his head and the wall. "My reward is finally at hand, and you will help me defeat him. Tell me where my vampires are."

"No." Edgar's head snapped sideways from the punch to his face.

"No? Did you forget what a weakling you are? You're only a fourth son with no value. How dare you say no to me." He punched Edgar on the other side of his head.

Edgar worked his jaw and slowly turned his head back, his eyes watering from the pain throbbing in both sides of his face. He was pretty sure his uncle had broken his cheekbones. A few seconds later, the fragments shifted back into place and fused together.

"You are nothing," his uncle spat out, seemingly on a roll. "You're like a maggot under my feet. I'll crush you. I'll chop you into little bits and send you back to your Prince one piece at a time for every day he keeps me from my vampires."

Edgar watched as the madness in his uncle's eyes grew. It was frighteningly similar to the Alphas they'd found. A punch to the gut distracted him from the line of thought.

"Tell me what I want to know. We both know how weak and useless you are, worried only about your fancy suits and kissing the feet of your pretty vampire Prince. You don't have the strength to stand up to me. You know it and I know it." Another punch was delivered to his stomach. "Even your Prince knows it." Next was an uppercut to his chin that had Edgar seeing stars. "I'll give you a few minutes to think about what I've said." An elbow to his face cracked his head against the wall, momentarily dimming his vision. "Maybe that will help jog your memory."

Armand leaned in and patted Edgar on the cheek, which was fractured again. "I suggest you use your time wisely and really think about your situation. I won't be so gentle on you next time." Chuckling, his uncle walked out of the room, slamming the door behind him. The click of the lock sealed Edgar's fate.

Gasping for breath, Edgar finally allowed himself to groan from the throbbing pain in his abdomen and head and the fire burning in his face. He blinked the wetness from his eyes, wincing as he tried to stretch out his abused muscles. Then he glared at the door. His uncle was wrong about him. He'd never betray his coven or Roman. He wasn't weak and useless. And at one point he may have relied on his expensive clothing and Roman's pride in him for validation. But Jackson had shown him he had worth of his own. That he didn't need to impress people with how he looked, or who he worked for. If Jackson thought he, alone, was enough, then Edgar didn't have to prove anything to anyone. He could believe in himself the way Jackson believed in him.

So yes, his uncle was very wrong about him. And the best way to prove it was to get himself out of this mess.

Edgar tugged futilely against the manacles around his wrists, looking for any weakness in the metal. He took another look around the cell he was in, desperately searching for anything to help him escape. Jackson's life, never mind his own, depended on him getting free. His heart sank when he realized that except for him, the room was completely empty. There was nothing that would help him.

Pain sliced through his chest, knowing he was going to be responsible for his mate's death. His amazing, beautiful, patient mate, who'd survived against overwhelming odds time and time again, was going to be struck down because Edgar had been careless enough to get himself captured. The thought of Jackson not being a part of the world anymore broke his heart.

Damn it. He couldn't just give up. He had to get free and find his way back to Jackson. He looked up at his chained wrists and pulled on them again, desperately wishing he had some of that Alpha strength right now. Edgar froze. Could he tap into that through his link with Jackson? Was something like that even possible? It had worked for Roman and Lysander. Maybe it would work for him. He had nothing to lose by trying.

Edgar reached for the mating bond connecting him to Jackson, growing a bit worried when he was barely able to feel it, the line between them stretched so very, very thin. How far away was his mate? He'd never be able to reach him from here. He shook his head. No. No defeatist talk. He had to give this his best effort. Edgar closed his eyes and concentrated on their bond. Please, Goddess, let this work.

* * *

In the Council dungeons…

"How's he doing?" Bryan stepped up beside Eric.

"Not good, sir. I wish we didn't have to cage him up."

"I don't like it either." Bryan looked at the seven-foot-tall ravening beast who was currently destroying his cell. "But we don't have much choice. Not as long as he's like this." Bryan winced when Jackson ran full tilt into the wall, bouncing back and landing on his butt. A moment later, he shifted to his human form. Bryan blinked, sure he was seeing things, but no, Jackson, as a man, was sitting on the ground, rubbing the large bump on his head.

"Huh. Who knew smashing his head would cause him to change? We'll have to remember that."

Eric shot him a look. "I don't think that's the reason it happened, sir."

"Perhaps not, but let's keep it in mind. Jackson, how are you feeling?"

The shifter looked over, the wolf's wildness showing in his eyes. "Edgar," he said, his voice deep with a throaty growl. Pressing a hand to his chest, Jackson threw his head back and howled.

* * *

Well that had been a colossal waste of effort. Edgar let his head fall back against the wall, the hopelessness of his situation draining his belief that he would ever get free. For one incredible moment, he thought he'd felt Jackson, connected with him. But it had been so fleeting that he knew it had only been wishful thinking.

Sounds on the other side of the door alerted him to the fact his time was up. Closing his eyes, he had a moment's regret that he hadn't had a chance to tell Jackson he loved him again. The feeling was so new and tender, that he'd wanted to hold it close, cherish it. He didn't realize he'd never have another chance to say it. Jackson would also never know about the changes he'd made in Edgar, how he'd helped him to believe in himself.

"I'm so sorry, Jackson. I tried, but it wasn't enough. I love you, my fierce mate. Come find me. I'll be waiting for you on the other side." He sent his thoughts out to the universe, pushing them along their bond, hoping Jackson would somehow hear and know he'd been loved.

A key turned in the lock. At the sound of the door opening, Edgar panicked, realizing he wasn't ready to die. He pushed his back into the wall, praying to the Goddess to please help him. It took a moment to realize that he was actually pushing himself through the wall. Landing on his butt on the cement floor on the other side, he sat there a moment, stunned. What had just happened. Standing up, pressed against the wall but it was completely solid. He ran his hands over the entire surface looking for a weak spot, but it was solid as rock. How the hell had he fallen through?

"He's gone." His uncle said from the other room. "Search every room. I want him found."

Crap. They were going to catch him again if he didn't get out of here. Running to the wall on the far side of the room, Edgar put his hands against the wall and tried pushing through it but all he managed to do was bang his nose when his hand slipped. Turning and putting his back to the wall, he pushed against the floor with his feet but the wall stayed solid, without the slightest amount of give. He was trapped with no way out.

The door behind him crashed open. "There you are, you little shit. How'd you get in here?" His uncle stalked across the room, Edgar's death a promise in his eyes. Reaching him, Armand grabbed him by his throat and pulled him forward. "I asked you a question. How. Did. You. Get. Free?" Every word was punctuated by him slamming Edgar's head into the wall.

His head dizzy and throbbing, Edgar whispered, "I don't know." He didn't see the punch, but it felt like his face exploded. Closing his eyes, knowing further resistance was futile, he finally gave up, relaxing in his uncle's grip and letting the wall support his weight.

His uncle's yell and the sudden feeling of weightlessness told Edgar he'd done it again. Moving slowly away from Armand, he moved back through the wall like it was made of gelatin. His uncle's shocked expression when his hand passed through Edgar's neck was the last thing he saw before he was on the other side of the way. Looking around, he realized he was in a hallway. He immediately took off running. Later, he could figure out what had just happened. For now, he needed to find a place to hide. And some clothes. And maybe a phone so he could call for a ride.

* * *

Crawling quietly through the air duct, Edgar stopped when he heard his uncle's voice.

"I'm telling you, Ruth. One moment I had my hand around his neck, the next it was like he was phasing through the wall."

Phasing. Was that what he'd done?

"Did he manage to bond with that wolf after all? This is why these types of bonds are forbidden. We cannot control them if they run amok and start giving each other unique powers. They must be stopped."

"You never have to worry about me. The very thought of joining with a wolf turns my stomach. Nothing could make me want to get that close to one, even for the possibility of gaining special powers."

"We are aware of this. That is the reason you were chosen, Armand."

"What do we do now? If he can phase through solid objects, how do we stop him?"

"I will make enquiries and let you know. There is always a way to control these things. It only takes figuring it out."

"Okay. I'll keep looking for him. He has to be here somewhere. It's not like he's invisible or anything. Someone will eventually spot him. Then we can test your idea to see if it will work."

"Very good. Now be on your way. I have important matters to attend to."

As his uncle walked away, Edgar heard him mutter stupid bitch under his breath. He wondered if Ruth could hear him as well. That would be unfortunate for his uncle. Edgar waited until he heard Ruth leave before continuing through the air duct.

* * *

Edgar crept silently down the hall, turned left at the next corner, then stopped. Another dead end. He bit back his frustrated curse. This place was like a maze. None of the passages made any sense. It shouldn't be this difficult to find an outside wall so that he could follow it to the entrance. He'd thought of phasing through the walls and trying to escape that way, but if the place was built underground like he suspected, he didn't want to phase out at the wrong place and get lost in the middle of a hill. Or worse. Unfortunately, the more he tried to reach a perimeter wall, the more twisted around he got. He was never going to find a way out of here at this rate.

Hearing a noise behind him, he quickly phased through the wall in front of him, grinning at how much easier it was to do. Most likely because of all the practice he'd been getting. Coming out on the other side of the wall, he found himself in a closet. Edgar pushed through the wall of clothes to reach the door, spitting out a mouthful of lace when he breathed in at the wrong time. He had his hand on the doorknob to exit when he realized there was someone in the room beyond.

"Elder Zachary, not so hard."

"It's your fault I'm under so much stress." Strange thumps sounded, then a loud groan. "This is the only thing you're good at, so just lay there and be quiet while I work it off."

Edgar's eyes widened as he listened to the bumping noises and grunts, realizing how Elder Zachary was destressing himself. As much as they all hated Jillian, Edgar felt queasy at what the Elder was doing to her.

"But Elder Zachary," Jillian sobbed, "I did exactly as you asked. I seduced the wolf for you." She gasped, her words stopping as the banging against the wall sped up for a few seconds before slowing down again. "You were happy I got pregnant. Why are you punishing me for it now?" she cried out.

More groaning and banging before he answered. "I was pleased until you turned the brat over to the Galways. So stupid."

"But Elder…."

"Enough." Edgar winced when Jillian cried out. The sounds the Elder was making were harsher and more vigorous. "No more talking while I finish. Your whining is ruining my pleasure."

Hoping the hall was clear, Edgar turned and pushed his way back through the closet, having heard more than he could stomach.

* * *

Edgar was back to crawling through the air ducts. While it was slower and more awkward, it was a lot safer than creeping along the hallways and ducking into rooms.

Especially after Zachary and Jillian. He shuddered. He'd never scrub that memory from his brain.

He was moving over a vent in the floor of the air duct when the door to the room below him opened. He froze. Shit. What did he do now? Should he move forward and hope they didn't hear him, or just lean to the side as much as the space allowed and hope they didn't look up?

Elder Ruth stopping directly beneath the grating made his decision for him. Holding his breath, he carefully edged back as much as he could, hoping the angle was enough to block him from view.

"You reek of that girl, Zachary. Why must you always dally with your playthings when we have situations that need our attention?"

"Ruth, you need to chill. A good romp in the sack takes the edge off. You should try it. It might make you more bearable to be around."

"Zachary!"

"What? You're getting more rigid every day. Much more and you'll snap in half."

"You would dare speak to me this way?" Ice dripped from her words.

"I would. You forget we're in this together. You have as much to lose as I do."

"It would behoove you to remember that I do rank you. One day your insolence will go too far."

"Whatever, Ruth. What did you want me for?"

"The vampire has escaped."

"Did he now? That was very careless of you."

"It had nothing to do with any oversight of mine. It appears he has gained the ability to phase."

"Damn it to hell. Those fuckers bonded. Do we know what the Alpha gained?"

"Not as of yet."

"You'd better find out. We'll need to take care of him. I didn't kill John so that his sons could team up with the Alpha line and mess with our plans. I did my part. You seem to be screwing up yours."

"John's death was necessary. His conscience kept interfering with our work."

"Yes, it was a shame he wouldn't fall in line. His powers would be very helpful right now, in particular against his sons since you can't seem to handle them."

"His sons will be taken care of soon."

"If you say so. As far as I can tell, they're doing whatever they want. Their mother is no better at controlling them than you. You better hope she never finds out you ordered her husband's death."

"Leave Charlotte to me. You concentrate on finding that runaway vampire. I have come up with a way to prevent him from phasing."

"Let's hope so. And you might want to watch your back around Charlotte. She's not as stupid as you think. I don't know if you could actually take her if it came down to a fight."

"She will not be a problem."

"Well at least try to find out how she's evading magical traps before you kill her."

"I'll get your whore to find out. She thinks she's so smart playing both sides, so she can get the information for us before we get rid of her as well."

"Don't kill her yet. She does have her uses."

"You'll be too busy taking care of the vampire to require her services."

"I can make time for both."

"Zachary."

"I'm telling you, Ruth, a good, hard pounding would do you, and everyone else, the world of good." He laughed as he left the room.

Hardly daring to breathe, Edgar watched as Elder Ruth stood ramrod straight, staring after Elder Zachary. Her hands fisted at her sides, opening and closing, opening and closing. Edgar jerked when a ball of fire burst from her fists and exploded against the wall.

"One day, Zachary, you'll regret your insolence. Your time will come. It might be sooner than you realize." A sweeping motion of her hand put out the fire, leaving scorch marks as the only evidence of her anger. A moment later, she, too, was gone.

Edgar let out a long breath. Dear Goddess, that had been tense. He shifted, ready to crawl over the vent when another sound from the room halted his movement. Peering through the grate, he was shocked to see Charlotte step out from behind a hidden panel. But not as shocked as she was, judging by the size of her eyes and the pallor of her skin.

She walked over to the burnt wall and delicately ran her fingers over the blackness, staring at the surface for a long time. Eventually, Charlotte stirred and moved her hand across the scorch marks, leaving silvery, unblemished wall behind.

Suddenly, she looked over her shoulder directly at him, pinning him with her gaze.

He froze, afraid to move, caught in the trap of her eyes for an excruciatingly long moment. Finally, Charlotte turned her head, breaking the connection, and left the room.

Edgar took his first gasping breath when the door closed behind her. He put a hand over his racing heart wondering why she'd let him go? Then realized the why didn't matter. Only that she had. He needed to get out of here before she changed her mind.

Edgar started crawling as fast as he could while still being quiet. It was time for him to get the hell out of this place.

* * *

The final turn…

This was it. He knew it.

After hours of crawling through this cursed place, Edgar was so close he could almost smell the air of freedom. One more room to get past and he could finally get out of here. Curbing his excitement, he kept to his slow crawl, not wanting to make a mistake and get caught this close to escaping. He was approaching the last air vent before the tunnel went left, which should take him to the exit, when he heard voices. A lot of voices.

Oh. Come. On. This couldn't be happening. Not when he was this close. Edgar hung his head, praying this wouldn't take long. As he listened to the sound of chairs moving as people sat, he knew he was going to be stuck there a while.

Sighing, he dropped to his stomach and settled in to listen.

"Sit down and be quiet. We have much to discuss."

"Ruth, what is so important we had to drop everything and rush here? I don't know about the rest, but I'm getting tired of you always ordering us around."

Edgar perked up. He had no idea who was speaking, but the Elders were clearly not as united as they'd thought.

"Olivia, I told you to be quiet and sit down."

"You're not the boss of me."

"With Thomas dead, I am. Do as I say and sit down."

229

"Fine." A chair scraped back. "This better be worth it. I was working on one of my projects."

"We know all about your special projects. They'll keep until we're done."

A harsh cackle raised the hair on the back of Edgar's neck.

"They're not going to keep that long. Try not to go on and on this time. I want to enjoy them a bit more before they expire."

There was a long silence. Edgar could almost feel Ruth's anger from where he was listening.

"You forget your place, Olivia. No," Ruth snapped. "I don't wish to hear it. Keep quiet so I can let everyone know why they have been brought here."

"Could you get on with it, Ruth. Olivia's not the only one who was in the middle of something."

"Your pet will keep as well, Zachary."

"At least I have one," Zachary muttered.

"If everyone could refrain from further unproductive interruptions, I could begin."

"Go ahead, Ruth. We're listening."

"Thank you, Peter. First off, I wanted to make everyone aware that the vampire has escaped and is running loose somewhere in the building."

"What? How did it get away?" Olivia asked.

"The wolf and vampire bonded. He gained the power to phase," Zachary drawled.

"Phase? How are we supposed to stop him from doing that?"

"I have an idea of how we can secure him; however, he first needs to be apprehended. Zachary is heading the search. If you see or hear anything, report it to him."

"Are the vampires searching as well?" Olivia asked.

"Yes. Though they are proving to be quite inept. It will soon be time to cut all ties with them."

"Both Carlos and Armand?"

"Yes. All the vampires will be disposed of."

Poor Armand. He was going to regret working with Ruth. Edgar almost felt sorry for him. Almost.

"I'll need a couple more before you get rid of them."

"Take them quickly, Olivia. They won't be around longer than it takes to capture the rodent in our walls."

Edgar flinched. Did she know how he was getting around or was that just a figure of speech?

"Peter, how are the efforts to break into the Council building coming along?"

"We still can't get through Galway's shield. The only one who's come close is Charlotte, but she won't share how she managed it," Peter said.

"Then make her. It's time she learned who answers to whom. Use whatever means short of killing her you need to. At least for now. We must get back inside."

"Are you worried about them digging through the files and finding our plans for the shifters and vampires?"

Vampires? What was this about the vampires?

"You give them too much credit, Olivia. They'll never think to look in the records of Gaea."

Edgar felt sick. The thought of hiding plans for the genocide of the shifter race with documents for the Earth Mother was abhorrent. Their evil truly had no limits.

"If they can't find the plans, then why the urgency to get in the Council building? Don't we have everything we need here?" Olivia asked.

"Unfortunately, we do not. There is one vital piece of information missing, which is preventing us from moving on with the next phase of our plan. We also need to destroy records of the prophecy before the wrong person stumbles across it. It has the potential to ruin everything if they manage to decipher it."

"What piece of information? And what about the prophecy? Did you figure it out and not share it? When were you going to tell us?"

"Calm yourself. I have everything—"

"And the Alpha pup," Zachary interrupted to ask. "When are we going after him?"

"Once Peter gains access to the Council building, we'll get the information we need to begin moving against the vampires. While everyone is distracted with that, we will capture the wolf brat."

"I still want to know what this information is. Why don't we have it with us? We took everything else. You're keeping secrets, Ruth, and I don't like it."

"Olivia, you are testing my limits."

"And you're testing mine."

"Girls, please. You sound like you belong in the schoolyard. Next thing we know, you'll be pulling each other's braids."

"You dare?" Ruth hissed.

"I always dare, Ruth. You should know this by now," Zachary said. "Please answer Olivia's question. I'm growing bored with this conversation."

"If you must know," Ruth gritted out, "I neglected to bring the notes on the stabilization experiments. The test subject is devolving as expected; however, the poison had to be administered directly as it was unstable through the planned delivery method. To move forward with our plans, we need to ensure it will remain viable until it can reach the vampires. The method for doing so is contained in those notes."

That didn't sound good. Bryan needed to find those notes before Ruth did.

"Are you sure the campaign against the vampires will work? They've proven fairly resilient so far."

"I am confident it will work as desired, as proven by the test subject's imminent madness."

"I'm not sure your idea for spreading the poison is the best option," Zachary said.

"To the contrary, the campaign is ingenious. It follows the same principle as what we used for the shifters, which has been far more successful than anticipated. Why waste our time, which could be better used preparing for the next phase, coming up with a new method when the current one has proven to be so effective? They will not be prepared for what we are about to unleash on them."

Okay, that really didn't sound good. Bryan had to find those notes first.

"And what about the Galway boys?" Peter asked. "They are proving more formidable than anticipated. When are we going after them?"

"They will have to wait. Once the shifters and the vampires have been removed from the field, we will take care of them. To move any sooner would be foolhardy."

"Fine. But let's not wait too long. From the reports I've been getting, their powers are growing daily."

Reports? Who was sending reports?

"Once we come to the final stages of our plan, they will be attended to. Do not concern yourself further"

"Have you located the artifact then?" Olivia asked.

Artifact? Since when was there an artifact?

"Not yet. Peter and I are closing in on it, so I anticipate it will be in our hands soon."

"I thought we needed it for the last phase. How can you take care of the brothers if you don't have it?"

"Enough, Olivia. Leave the Galway brothers to me. They are not the threat you are making them out to be.

They are no more than young, untried, arrogant boys who have no hope of succeeding against us. We have had years to perfect our strategies. I insist you all stay calm and follow my instructions. Everything will go according to our plans."

"Ruth, you're beginning to sound like you're more important than the rest of us. I would remind you that we're all in this together. Without us, you will fail in what we are all trying to achieve," Zachary said.

"And without me, we wouldn't be this far along. You would do well to remember that, Zachary." A brief moment of tension-filled silence followed. "Unless there are further questions, you all have things that require your attention. Dismissed."

Edgar used the noise from the squealing chairs being pushed back and the grumbling complaints of the Elders to cover the sound of him moving past the vent above the meeting room. He needed to get out of here. These people, with all of their plots, intrigues, and bickering, made him disgusted. This place was more of a cesspool than the vampire court had ever been.

Chapter Sixteen

Lysander's eyes opened wide as he processed what Edgar was saying. He looked over his shoulder at Roman to see if he was hearing the same thing. His grim expression confirmed he was, and the dismay on the faces of everyone gathered around Roman's desk showed they had as well.

Edgar continued speaking over the speakerphone. *"The plans for seeding the clouds to poison the shifters is filed with the records on Gaea. Tell Bryan to keep his eyes open for something similar that can be used against vampires. We're the next target."*

"Edgar, it's Bryan. I'll head to the Council building as soon as we're done talking to you."

"Good." There was a pause, then Edgar asked quietly, *"How's Jackson?"*

Lysander exchanged a worried look with Bryan, before speaking. "He shifted back to his human form…"

"But? I hear a but in your voice."

"He's not Jackson right now. He's fully under the influence of the affliction."

"Damn it. Bryan, you have to save him."

"He'll be the first one I cure once I figure out how. I promise you, Edgar. I won't let him suffer a moment longer than necessary."

"Thank you."

Roman spoke up. "Edgar, are you safe to stay on the line for a few more minutes? We almost have your location narrowed down."

"I think so. I used my phase abilities to steal a phone and get out of the bunker, but I had to revert back to a solid state to use it. Apparently, cell phones don't work if they're phased. I don't think anybody saw me leave, but I'd like to get off the line as quickly as possible just in case."

Lysander piped up. "Why don't you put the phone on speaker and then phase. We should still be able to hear your voice and then you'd be safe."

"Great idea. I don't know why I didn't think of that. Ouch."

"What happened?"

"Something just bit my neck. Oh shit. I think they found me."

Lysander tensed when he heard a noise that sounded like Edgar falling. Yelling and pounding footsteps came through the phone's speaker.

"Edgar. Edgar. Can you hear me?" Roman's voice rose with every word.

"I'm sorry. Edgar can't come to the phone right now."

"Who am I speaking with?"

"Ahh. Do I have the pleasure of speaking with Prince Roman?"

"Yes. Who are you?"

"I'm about to become your greatest nightmare. Pick him up, boys. We have work to do. Roman, are you still there?"

"I am."

"I'll have to get back to you. I have a vampire to deliver. Someone is quite eager to be reunited with him." They heard the phone hit the ground, then a loud crunching sound before the line went dead.

They look at each other in horror.

Bryan's phone chirped. Pulling it out, he cried. "They got a lock. Let's go get him."

"Not so fast, Bryan," Lysander said, regret in his voice. "You need to stay here."

"What? No. You need me with you."

"No. You need to go to the Council building and find a way to reverse the spell or poison, whichever it is. Saving Jackson is your priority."

"Damn it. You're right. But once he's cured, I'm coming after you."

"Absolutely. And bring Jackson with you. Edgar will need his blood when we find him." Lysander got off of Roman's lap and walked over to Bryan, and pushed him gently toward the door. "Bryan, hurry. You have to go now. I can feel it."

"I'm going. No need to push." Bryan turned to leave, then paused, frowning at Lysander. "Your Consort powers are growing strong, little brother. I think I liked you better when you weren't so bossy."

"He's always been bossy." Max said. "I have no idea how you missed that."

Bryan snorted as he walked out the door. Eyeing Max and Roman who were snickering, Lysander figured it was more from relief at having a location for Edgar than because Max was humorous. Which he wasn't. There was nothing at all amusing about his comment. Unless he meant it for real. Lysander narrowed his eyes, scowling at both men. Max winked. As he'd thought; it was only a joke. Unlike what he was about to say.

Bracing himself, Lysander spoke. "Max. I'm sorry, you can't go either."

All sounds of joy stopped.

"Consort, you can't be serious."

"I am. I need you to stay here and look after Nico and the rest of the children. We already know that he's a target.

The pups could be in danger as well. You're the only one we trust to keep them all safe."

"Thank you for saying that, but I have to go."

Lysander shook his head. "Not this time. I need to be there and Roman won't let me walk into danger without him. That leaves you being the only one we can count on to keep everyone safe."

"Roman, you can't mean to leave me behind."

"I am sorry, Max. Lysander is correct. As my Second, you will be in charge of ensuring the safety of both Nico and the coven."

Max stared at Roman. Lysander could see him thinking of and discarding arguments before finally admitting defeat. "Yes, Prince. I will do as you say."

Roman walked over and gripped his shoulder. "Thank you, Max. I know I can count on you."

"Yes. You can." Max looked over at Lysander. "You both can. Please excuse me." Tilting his head, he left the room.

Lysander looked helplessly at his mate. "I'm sorry. You know he has to stay here."

"I do, beloved. Max knows that as well. Now, let us discuss who we are going to take and make preparations. We will need to leave soon if we are going to save Edgar."

"We could really use Max's input."

"He will be back shortly. Of that, I am certain. Once he has a moment to think, Max will realize his staying behind is the only logical choice. I expect we will see him before Bryan has time to get to the Council building."

"I sure hope so. You saw what happened the last time Bryan and I planned a battle." He shook his head, grimacing.

Roman snorted, before breaking into laughter. Lysander glared at him before he too started chuckling.

What else could he do? After the fiasco of the mansion battle, they'd pretty much proven that planning warfare strategies was not something the Galway boys were any good at. Not even the slightest bit.

* * *

Bryan spoke toward the phone lying on the desk, which was set on speaker so he could keep looking through the records while he talked. "It's all here, just like Edgar said. He was right about how they did it, too. They were seeding the clouds with a nasty hybrid spell that combined magic with a variant on wolfsbane so it wouldn't affect the humans. It was targeted specifically to the Alphas. The stronger the wolf, the harder they were hit. We're lucky Jackson was able to hold on as long as he did."

"Can you heal him?" Roman asked.

"Yes. It's fairly simple now that I know what they used. I'm getting the counter-spell ready as we speak. Once it's administered, it should take effect almost immediately.

"That's wonderful. Edgar would be happy to know that."

"What's even better is that we can deliver the cure the same way the Elders poisoned the wolves in the first place. But we can do it much faster if we send out as many magic users as we can field to seed the clouds in every state. It would exponentially speed up the process and prevent further deaths."

"That's fantastic, Bryan. Great job" Lysander paused before asking, *"Did you see anything about the vampires?"*

"No, but I didn't look very hard. Let's save Jackson and Edgar first. I'll see what I can find afterward."

"Sounds good. When will you be back?"

"I should be done here in an hour or so. Is everyone ready to go?"

"Yes. Since you finished so quickly, we'll wait for you and Jackson."

"Okay. Do we know where we're going?"

"The bunker is by the Denver airport."

Bryan blinked. "Uhm, Sandi. I hate to burst your bubble, but the bunkers under the Denver International Airport aren't real. They're only conspiracy theories."

Lysander laughed. *"I know. I think that's why they built one there. To hide it in plain sight, since everyone knows the rumors of bunkers are false. The GPS coordinates show the bunker is actually near the airport, not underneath which will make it easier for us to break in. Max is getting satellite photos of the area so we can plan how we're going to infiltrate it."*

"Excellent. Let me take care of Jackson. We should be there shortly."

"Okay. Roman has a plane waiting for us. We'll leave as soon as you get here." The call ended.

Bryan shook his head. Bunkers at the airport. Who would have guessed? At least they could fly to the location, which meant getting to Edgar quicker. Focusing, he got back to work on finishing the cure. He had a wolf to save.

* * *

Lysander picked up Roman's phone off the kitchen island and handed it to him. "Let me grab a bottle of water, then we can get everybody assembled. I want everyone ready to leave as soon as Bryan gets back with Eric and Jackson."

"Of course, beloved." Roman came over and wrapped him in a hug. "I know you are worried but Edgar is strong. He will hold out until we get there."

"I know he is. I just have a feeling something is going to go horribly wrong."

"One of those feelings?"

"Yes."

"Do you have anything more specific to go on?"

"No. Just that there will be a problem."

"I see. We will have to stay vigilant then. Come, let us gather the troops. It is time to storm the castle."

Lysander snickered. Roman had come such a long way from the stuffy vampire he'd first met. And he was taking full credit for the change too.

Grabbing his water from the refrigerator, Lysander took a last look around, feeling like he was forgetting something. When nothing came to him, he shrugged, and linked his arm with Roman's. "I'm ready. Let's go."

A moment later they left the kitchen headed toward Roman's office.

Behind them, the door to the pantry swung slowly open, revealing Jamie standing there, a bag of pretzels dangling from his fingers.

* * *

Edgar opened his eyes, groaning when he saw his uncle's sneering face.

"Welcome back, Nephew. I missed you while you were gone."

"Go to hell."

"The only one going to hell is you. Now, let me think," Armand said, tapping his lips. "What were we discussing the last time we were together?"

Edgar ignored him and studied his surroundings. He was in another room in the bunker. However, instead of being cuffed to the wall, this time he was strapped to a chair with his arms and legs tied down. He could feel a collar or band around his neck and there was something wrapped around his head. None of which should be a problem. He'd been in a worse situation the last time he'd been captured. And now it was time for him to go.

Smirking at uncle, Edgar relaxed his body and prepared to sink through the chair. As the phase took hold, he started screaming. Bolts of lightning shot through his body and fire ran along his nerves before exploding in his brain. Black rolled across his vision as he passed out, the pain following him into the dark.

The next time Edgar opened his eyes, his uncle was standing in front of him, pouring water over his head. Flipping his wet bangs out of his eyes, he glared at him.

Armand smiled. "Did I forget to mention a little something Ruth came up with? Every time you try to phase, this little device," he patted something off to Edgar's left, "will register the change in your brain wave activity and send a hundred and fifty volts of electricity through your body. It's not enough to kill you, but certainly enough to get your attention."

"Couldn't you have just told me that before?"

"I probably could have but I believe in the power of a good object lesson. I wanted to be sure you fully understood your situation." He walked a few steps away and dragged a chair back, placing it in front of Edgar. Sitting down, he crossed his legs and folded his hands in his lap. "Now, where were we?"

"She's going to kill you, you know.'

His uncle laughed. "It's not me who's going to die."

"I wouldn't be so sure about that," Edgar muttered.

Armand tilted his head, then shook it. "You have no idea what you're talking about. But enough about me. I believe you were about to tell me where I could find my vampires."

He placed his hand on the device beside Edgar and smiled.

* * *

Jackson growled and grabbed the bars keeping him away from the man on the other side and pulled, trying to tear them out. Roaring his fury when the bars stayed firmly in place, Jackson reached through them, swiping at the man with his claws, but missed. He threw himself at the bars, again and again, sure he could get through them if he tried hard enough.

The man stood just out of reach, tormenting him with his nearness. Jackson tipped his head back and howled. When he got free, he'd tear the man to pieces and anyone else who got in his way. He was the Alpha. The strongest of them all.

Too late, he saw the weapon pointed at him.

"Sorry, Jackson, it's the only way." The man fired, hitting Jackson in the chest and knocking him back several steps. He grabbed at his chest, growling at the man, then fell to his knees when sudden weakness overtook him. He toppled to his side, groaning as pain spread through his body.

The pink haze clouding his mind abruptly disappeared. Jackson sat up, surprised to see he was in a cell with Bryan standing on the other side of bars. Why had he been locked up? He put his hand to his forehead, trying to think. Images flashed through his brain, discordant bits and pieces that made no sense. Definitely nothing to explain how he got here. Turning his head, he winced when he saw the destruction of the cell. Uh oh, this was bad.

He opened his mouth to ask, but his throat felt like he'd been swallowing razors. It took a couple of tries. When the words finally came, they were filled with the wildness of his wolf. Oh yeah, this was really bad.

"What did I do?" Jackson finally managed to get out.

Bryan moved closer. "It's nice to have you back with us."

"Is Edgar okay? Did I hurt him?"

"You didn't hurt him."

"Good. Why am I locked up?"

"To keep everyone safe."

Oh, yeah. Bad didn't even cover it. Jackson stared back at Bryan, not sure he wanted to know what had happened.

Bryan narrowed his eyes, obviously looking for something. "How you feel?"

"Fine. Confused." Jackson rubbed the back of his neck. "Are you sure I didn't hurt anyone?"

"Nobody who didn't deserve it."

"Then I did hurt someone."

Bryan waved his hand dismissively in the air. "Don't worry about it. I'll tell you everything later. Right now I need to know about you. Do you feel angry? How about your wolf? Does he seem normal?"

Jackson took a moment to do an internal check. Like he'd told Bryan, he felt fine. He was just confused about why he was in a cage. Even his wolf was sleeping peacefully. He frowned. His wolf should be awake. He never slept unless he needed to replenish his energy. Jackson's eyes widened. Oh shit. The only reason his wolf would need to recharge was if he'd used a great deal of energy in a challenge fight or a prolonged battle. A vision flashed into his head. Or went on a rampage.

He grabbed the bars, frantic with worry. "My wolf's asleep. Shit, Bryan. Who did we kill? It's bad, isn't it? That's why I'm locked up, right?"

"It worked," Bryan cried, looking relieved. "It actually worked."

"What worked?"

"The antidote. Here." Bryan passed Jackson some clothes through the bars. "Get dressed. I'll tell you everything on our way."

"Where's Edgar? Why isn't he with you?"

Bryan winced. "That's one of the things I need to talk to you about. We have to go rescue your mate."

Jackson growled. "Where is he?"

"Get dressed, Jackson. We're on a tight schedule. I'll explain on the way."

Glaring one last time at the uncooperative magic user who wouldn't answer any of his questions, Jackson got dressed as it looked like that was the only way he'd find anything out.

Sitting in the back of the SUV with Bryan and Eric, Jackson's head was spinning with everything he'd heard.

"I turned into a Dire Wolf? I don't know what to think about that." He couldn't recall the last time there had been a Dire wolf. It had to have been a few hundred years. "Then I destroyed Russel and his gang before I was tranquilized and locked in a cell." He glared at Eric in the rear-view mirror, who just grinned back, "While all this was happening, Edgar was kidnapped and is probably being tortured. Why are you only going to rescue him now?"

"Steady Jackson. You might want to control your anger in case there's any lingering effects of the Elders' spell. You don't want to turn into a Dire again."

Ignoring him, Jackson yelled. "Damn it, Bryan. Why has nobody gone after my mate? You're a powerful magic user. Couldn't you wiggle your fingers and find him? He's been on his own this whole time."

"I'm sorry, Jackson. We tried searching for him but couldn't find any trace. And I couldn't use my magic because it doesn't work that way. You need to have an affinity for location magic, which I don't have."

"Then what the hell good is having magic?"

"Sometimes none," Bryan said quietly. "When Lysander was kidnapped, my magic couldn't help then either. Roman had to follow the mate bond linking them to find him."

Jackson blinked, then reached for his bond with Edgar. It felt thin and his sense of Edgar was faint, but it was there. His mate was alive. At least for now. "How did he sound when you talked to him? Was he hurt?"

"He sounded great. Your mate is amazing. He escaped using the phase power he gained when you bonded then ran around the bunker, spying on everyone and finding out all the Elders' secrets. He's uncovered most of their plots." He sobered. "But it sounded like they have a way to compensate for his power, which is why we need to hurry. We were lucky enough to get a lock on him before our call got cut off."

"Thank the Goddess."

Bryan gave him a look. "You better wake up your wolf, Jackson. You both have a mate to rescue."

Jackson nodded and stared out the window, not seeing the landscape flash by as they sped down the road. His mate was out there, possibly hurt, more than likely being tortured, and he wasn't there to help him. Which is when it occurred to him he hadn't even asked how his pack was. Some Alpha he was.

Turning away from the window, he tapped Eric on the shoulder, meeting his eyes in the rear-view mirror. "What happened to my pack?"

Eric looked at him sorrowfully. "I'm sorry, Alpha. By the time we got there, Russel and his buddies had taken over. I'm not sure how much you remember after we arrived."

Jackson grimaced. "To be honest, not that much. Tell me everything."

"All right. From what we were able to determine, Russel's guys snuck in, shot everyone with tranquilizer darts, and tied them up. Then they broke into the packhouse. It sounded like one of the Elders was with them." Eric opened his mouth, then closed it.

"All of it, Eric. I need to know everything."

"Yes, sir. They took the Betas you left in charge and slaughtered them in the packhouse. And Mary, well, Russel, he uhm—"

Jackson held up his hand. "I know what he did to Mary." That particular memory was clear in his mind.

"The rest of the pack was pretty much left alone tied up in their houses."

Something to be thankful for at least. Jackson closed his eyes, his wolf mourning the loss of two of his Betas. And Mary. Poor Mary, who should never have been in a position to be treated like she'd been. Her brother, Simon, was going to kick his ass. "Who's looking after the pack now?"

Eric chuckled, surprising Jackson. There was nothing humorous in anything that had been said. "I'm sorry, Alpha. I'm not being disrespectful. Truly, I'm not. After you finished killing Russel and I tranqed you…" Eric stopped, shooting him a quick look.

"Don't worry about it. Continue what you were saying," Jackson said.

Eric nodded. "After I shot you, Mary took charge of everything. She ordered the magic users to clean up the packhouse, then sent the vampires out to make sure the rest of the pack was unharmed. Once everything had been looked after to her satisfaction, she sent us on our way. Nobody dared to disagree with her. Except Ted." Eric snickered. "He said he was staying to provide magical assistance if it was needed."

"What's so funny about that?"

"Nothing really. It's just, well, Mary and Ted have some strange connection."

Jackson frowned. "Ted, as in Bill's partner? The one who never says anything. What kind of connection are you talking about? Should I be worried about Mary?"

"No. If anything, you should be worried about Ted." Eric laughed again. "Mary just gives him a look, and he's off and running to do her bidding without a word spoken between them. It was the strangest thing."

"Huh. I wonder if they're mates."

"I wouldn't dare to speculate. Mary is formidable. You might want to consider her for your inner circle, Alpha. She'd make a great Beta." Eric smiled at him. "Rest assured, your pack is in good hands."

Jackson nodded, relieved to know the pack was okay. "Thanks for the update. And I'll think about your suggestion for Beta. It'll be interesting to see how accepting the pack is to having a female Beta. I can't recall there ever being one."

"Then maybe it's time to change that."

"Maybe." It was actually a great suggestion. He knew Edgar would approve. Edgar. His heart hurt thinking about his missing mate.

"Just so you know, the Consort has daily check-ins with Mary, so he might have more to tell you."

"I'm surprised the Consort is involved."

Eric smiled. "You're mated to Edgar, Alpha. You're family now."

Jackson leaned back in his seat. Family with vampires and magic users. His brother would laugh himself silly when he found out. Shit. Clint. "Bryan, what's being done to cure the Alphas? My brother's still out there somewhere."

"I've got the cure with me. Once we get back to the mansion, I'm sending out a group of magic users. They're going to spread across the country and seed as many clouds as they can."

"Seed the clouds? Why?"

"That's how the Elder's spread the poison in the first place. Your brilliant mate figured it out while he was rescuing you in the mountains. The Elders poisoned the clouds and let nature do the work of spreading it across the countryside. We'll be speeding up the process by administering it to the cloud network in as many places as possible, as well as heading up into the mountains to add it to every high-altitude water supply we can find. Based on how you responded, the effects of the spell are reversed almost immediately once the antidote is administered. If your brother's still alive, the water will find him and cure him."

Jackson sighed in relief. "Thank you. I know he's out there. He's a strong wolf. He'll fight until it becomes impossible to continue. I have no doubt he'll be back."

His world coming to order, Jackson relaxed into his seat, saving his energy to unleash on those stupid enough to take his vampire. Nobody could touch a mate of the Alpha line and expect to live.

Chapter Seventeen

Lysander fastened his final strap as he waited with the vampires and magic users gathered around Jackson. They'd departed for the airport the minute Bryan, Jackson, and Eric had arrived from the Council building. While Jackson worked out their infiltration strategy, everyone else was putting on their Kevlar vests and the communications devices Max had managed to procure.

In the short amount of time they'd had to prepare, in addition to the equipment, Max had also obtained numerous satellite maps of the bunker and surrounding area. He'd even managed to get a blueprint of the bunker itself, though he'd been cagey about his source. Not that Lysander cared. Anything that could help save Edgar was worth it. But he was impressed with the extent of Max's military connections.

Finished with his vest, Lysander waited, impatient to get started as Jackson went back and forth over the maps, using his penlight to focus on certain points. Finally, Jackson stood up. "Who's reporting for the reconnaissance teams?"

A vampire enforcer stepped forward. "That would be me, sir."

"Name."

"Dylan, sir."

"Did you find any indication of physical perimeter alarms or guards?"

"No, sir. The only cameras we could find are the ones located at the entrances. There was nobody on patrol and there were no guards around the facility."

"Idiots," Jackson muttered. Nodding at Dylan, he said, "Thanks." Jackson looked at Bryan and Lysander. "I'm assuming there are magical alarms."

"Yes," Bryan answered, with Lysander nodding in agreement.

"Are they around the perimeter, as well, or just the building?"

Bryan turned to the building, sweeping his focus to the far left and right. "It looks like the shields are only on the building." He shook his head. "Idiots is right."

Jackson nodded. "Yes. But that makes things easier for us. Can you take them down without alerting them to our presence?"

"No. They'll know the minute we breach them."

"Okay. Then we'll have to get everyone in place and hit them hard and fast." He shined his light on the map, indicating an area to the north. "Bryan, send one of your men to take out this power transformer. It'll take out their cameras so they won't be able to see how many of us there are as we get into position and they'll be blind when we access the building."

Nodding, Bryan pointed at Clancy. "Do as the Alpha says."

"Yes, sir." Clancy took off running, a vampire enforcer at his side.

"Look here." Jackson shined the light on three spots on the printout. "These are our points of entry. When I give the word, we'll rush simultaneously. Two men from each of your assigned groups are to stay back to prevent anyone from escaping."

"Yes, Alpha."

"Roman, it's time to send your enforcers to stand guard around the perimeter. If anybody manages to get out during the confusion, have your men take care of them."

Roman tipped his head to a group of vampires, half of whom immediately scattered to cover their assigned areas.

Jackson looked at Eric. "You'll need to take over command when I shift. I'll hold off as long as possible, but I have no doubt it's going to happen. Can you handle that?"

"Yes, Alpha."

"Good. The rest of you, listen for directions from either myself or Eric. Get into your groups and be ready to move. Do not use any lights. Let the vampires lead you through the dark. We go silently and quickly until we're in position. Be ready to breach the building in fifteen minutes."

Lysander exchanged looks with Roman, and smiled. Now this was how you ran a battle campaign. It was good to work with a professional.

"One final thing. Whatever happens, nobody is to be left behind. Do you understand?"

"Yes, Alpha."

"Good. We go on my command. Move out."

They all ran.

* * *

Lysander and Roman crouched in the dark, waiting for the signal. Every group had a magic user to blow up the door and provide shielding once inside. The vampire enforcers would be responsible for any close-quarter fighting as they started moving through the hallways and encountered resistance. Lysander wanted to get his group as far into the building as possible before shielding them became impossible.

"Magic users, on my mark."

Lysander prepared his fireball and waited for Jackson's signal. *"Now."* He released the ball of flame, ducking as it went streaking through the air and crashed into the door. Fragments of burning metal exploded around them, bouncing harmlessly off their shield.

"Go, go, go." Jackson's voice screamed through their earpieces. They rushed the building, vampire enforcers taking point, Lysander shielding them as they moved down the hallway.

The facility's emergency lighting came on making it possible for Lysander to see as they quickly made their way down the passage. They ran into their first resistance three hallways later when the Elders' acolytes and enemy vampires swarmed out of the doorways in front of and behind them, trapping them in the middle. Lysander held tight to his shield, preventing any of the attackers from reaching them, which also prevented the enforcers from utilizing their greater speed and strength against their attackers. They stood behind the barrier, facing their enemies and hissing at them, but unable to reach them through the shield. Lysander could see the frustrated looks they kept throwing at Roman, but he didn't have time to worry about them, focused as he was on picking off the magic users facing them.

Lysander, as the only one able to launch an attack past the shielding, used fire to take down only the closest enemies, afraid to send fireballs down the length of the corridor to incinerate all of their attackers in case Edgar was in one of the rooms nearby. But it was tedious work. The acolytes who were not actively engaged in battle with him were putting their efforts toward breaking through his shield, splitting his focus.

Lysander clenched his jaw as he tightened his shield and readied himself for the next attack.

"You have to let the enforcers out so they can fight, beloved."

"I don't want them hurt. I can deal with these guys."

"I know you can but you disrespect our vampires by holding them back. You must let them be the fighters they were born to be."

"Roman—"

"All will be well, beloved. Please allow them their freedom."

"Fine. I'm lowering the shield now." Lysander let their protection drop, allowing the vampires to engage. He watched in amazement as they moved through the attackers so quickly they were a blur, almost too fast for his eyes to follow. He winced when one of the enforcers took a slash across the chest. His partner ripped the head off the offending vampire, throwing it at one of the acolytes, who immediately started screaming, "get it off, get it off." Another enforcer took care of the acolyte, ending his cries. Within moments, the way was clear.

Lysander blinked. "Okay, then. Great job, everyone."

Roman chuckled. "Put your shield back up but give them room to spread out, front and back. You can let them move past it as needed."

"Okay. You heard your Prince," Lysander shouted. "Take your positions, the shield is going back up now." They pressed on down the hallway.

* * *

Jackson checked his watch as the time counted down.

"I'm glad Nick said I could stay with you guys for a while," Bill said. "Nothing exciting ever happens in our clan in Denver. You boys have been non-stop action since I met you."

Jackson grunted. He'd happily trade all of this action for a few quiet moments with his mate. His watch finished counting down. He called his signal to the teams, ducking as Bill blew down their door. Rushing the entrance, he searched for Edgar's location using their mate-bond as a guide. Feeling a tug, he gestured to the right at the next hallway crossing. Bill nodded, putting up a barricade to cover their backs. He was using a mobile barrier that traveled in front of them, filling the space from ceiling to floor and wall to wall. He was also putting up immoveable walls in the passage behind them once they'd cleared an area so no one could sneak up behind them. Eric was opening doors and searching rooms as they made their way to their target with the rest of the enforcers fanning out to cover all angles. They were completely in sync as they advanced through the building.

Jackson smiled. It was almost as good as working with his old team.

* * *

Bryan turned to the two enforcers next to him. "Stefan and Drew, right?"

The blond vampire on the left nodded. "Yes."

"Okay, you two lead. I'll provide what coverage I can, but you know best how vampires fight. Let me know if I can do anything to help you."

"Just keep yourself safe, sir. Max will have our heads if anything happens to you."

Bryan frowned at his back. He'd thought he'd blocked any connection between Max and himself, but it sounded like something had slipped through. Jerking to attention when he heard Jackson's signal, he targeted the door with his fireball, grinning in satisfaction when it was completely obliterated, not leaving any residual debris to rain down on them.

Stefan whistled. "Nice one, sir."

Hearing Jackson's order of *"Go, go, go,"* they ran through the opening.

* * *

"Carlos." Roman roared as he rushed down the hallway.

"Shit." Lysander followed Roman as he chased after Carlos and his vampires. They raced through the halls, occasionally slamming into walls when they took corners too fast. Or at least, Lysander was hitting the walls. Roman and the vampires seemed able to navigate the sharp turns just fine.

Carlos looked over his shoulder and gave them a huge grin before following his vampires through a doorway. Lysander was left behind as Roman put on a burst of speed, disappearing through the same opening. Panting, Lysander dug deep, trying to catch up, not wanting Roman to face a room full of vampires without him. Too bad he wasn't a runner. Panting, unable to catch his breath, he motioned for the enforcers to go without him. Two stayed behind with him while the rest flew past him and rushed through the doorway after Roman.

Lysander finally reached the room, tripping across the threshold on shaky legs. Bent over, lungs burning, gasping for breath, it took a moment to realize Roman was stalking around the room, growling, and hissing. The vampires who'd followed after him were inspecting different sections of the wall, pushing against it in places. "What's wrong," he gasped, forcing himself into an upright position.

Roman stomped over to a wall, pushing against the immobile surface. "They got away."

Lysander stood up. "They got away? How? You were right behind them."

"They were gone by the time I got in the room."

Lysander looked over the walls, up to the ceiling, then down at the floor. "How'd they get out? There aren't any exits."

"I don't know. I can't find any sign of them. All traces end at the doorway. It's like they never made it into the room, even though we saw them do so."

"Oh. That's not good."

"No. my beloved, not good at all."

"I wonder how they managed it."

Eric's voice came through their earpieces. "Everyone, Jackson has shifted. I repeat, the Alpha has turned into a Dire."

Lysander looked at Roman. "What do you think happened?"

"I don't know. Let's gather our men and go find out."

Lysander nodded. Giving one last look around the room, he followed his mate out the door.

* * *

A few minutes earlier…

Jackson stopped before the door and sniffed. Glancing behind him at Eric and Bill, he nodded in confirmation that Edgar was in the room. Taking two steps back, Jackson charged, crashing through the door with his shoulder, then skidded to a stop when he saw his mate. Shock froze him in place when he saw the condition Edgar was in. He quickly shook it off and moved closer, his eyes roaming over his mate's body taking in all of the horrific details.

Edgar was strapped to a chair, bands wrapped around his neck and forehead. He was drenched with sweat, his eyes red-streaked with broken blood vessels. Bruises covered every inch of skin Jackson could see. Considering Edgar healed almost instantly from simple cuts and bruises, someone had gone to a great deal of effort to injure him for signs of his abuse to still be visible. He stalked toward Edgar, intent on freeing him from his bonds.

"Ah, ah, ah, wolf. Not one step closer. You wouldn't want to turn the poor boy's mind to mush."

Jackson stopped, realizing for the first time there was someone else in the room. Lips curling as a growl worked up his throat, he turned to the vampire who had spoken. He took one step in his direction but stopped when the vampire raised a hand holding a black box with his thumb resting on a red button. Jackson saw Edgar flinch from the corner of his eye. Holding his position, he looked the soon to be dead vampire in the eye and allowed his wolf to rise.

The vampire jerked back, caught himself, then forced a smile to his face. "You're a little late to the party, wolf, but I'm glad you've finally made it."

"What do you want?" Jackson's voice was more growl than words, his humanity overshadowed by the wolf's rage.

"I'd watch my tone. Your mate will pay the price for your insolence."

Jackson scowled, but held his silence.

"Better. My nephew here is being most uncooperative. I'm sure you'll be happy to give me the information I'm looking for. If only to spare him further pain."

"What do you want to know?"

"Where are my vampires?"

Jackson frowned, not sure what he was asking. "I don't know."

"Wrong answer. That's strike number one." The vampire pressed the red button. Edgar screamed, his body convulsing as electricity sparked, running along the bands strapped around his head and neck.

"Stop," Jackson roared, taking a step forward before catching himself when the vampire held the black box higher. "Please stop."

The vampire stared into his eyes as he counted to three, then lifted his thumb, halting the current. Edgar collapsed back into his seat, his sweat-covered body trembling uncontrollably. The vampire kept his eyes on Jackson as he turned a dial on the little black box. "In case you were wondering, I've just upped the voltage. The next wrong answer may cause permanent damage, though I'm not completely sure. I'm learning as we go. Shall we try that again? Where are my vampires?"

Jackson turned from him to his mate and looked into Edgar's eyes, seeing his determination to not give in to his torturer. His mate had been so strong for so long and was prepared to keep on fighting. Whatever the cost.

It would be so easy to answer the vampire—having finally realized what vampires he was looking for—but Jackson couldn't invalidate Edgar's efforts by giving in to his tormentor. Though it would kill Jackson, he would keep his silence so as not to make Edgar's sacrifice, his amazing demonstration of loyalty, meaningless. Smiling at his mate, Jackson hoped Edgar could see the pride and love he had for him. When Edgar raised an eyebrow, Jackson tipped his head in agreement. The wobbly smile he got in return warmed him to the depths of his soul.

"Are you fucking kidding me? You would actually let me fry his brain? And for what? Some grand delusion of honor. Don't be stupid, wolf. Tell me what I want to know. Don't make the mistake of thinking I won't kill him if you don't." The vampire held up the black box. The thumb resting on the button twitched slightly.

Jackson ignored him, holding Edgar's gaze. His mate wouldn't go through this alone. Jackson would be with him every step of the way and would be right behind him when they met again in the arms of the Goddess.

"Alpha. If I might make a suggestion."

Jackson tilted his head, keeping his eyes locked on Edgar's. "Go ahead, Bill."

The magic user snapped his fingers. The black box vanished from the vampire's hand, reappearing in his. He held it up to Jackson. "I thought this way might be faster and a lot less painful for your mate. Though I am impressed with how devoted you are to each other."

Jackson directed his attention to Edgar's uncle, who was staring at his empty hand in shock, which turned to terror when he looked at Jackson, . "Thank you. If you'll excuse me, I have a vampire to kill."

Jackson shifted, turning into his Dire Wolf form. He leaped across the room and grabbed the terrified vampire around the throat. He grabbed a handful of hair with his other hand, prepared to yank his head off when he heard Edgar telling him to stop.

"Why?" Jackson growled, his voice harsh with the wildness of the Dire. "Why are you stopping me? He deserves to die for touching you." Jackson gave his attention to his mate, taking no notice of the vampire clawing at the hand he was choking him with.

Coughing to clear his throat, Edgar's raspy, broken voice almost changed Jackson's mind about tearing his uncle's head off. "He wants to know where his vampires are. We should show him."

Jackson slowly turned to the vampire hanging in his hand and bared his teeth. The vampire quailed at whatever he saw. "An excellent idea, mate." Jackson brought his large fist up and slammed it into the vampire's head, rendering him unconscious. Jackson looked over to Bill. "Can you keep him under control until we're done?"

"It would be my pleasure, Alpha. Just leave him with me."

Nodding, Jackson opened his fist, dropping the vampire to the ground. He paused when his head bounced off the cement floor, thinking he'd killed him anyway, but when he saw his chest move, Jackson hurried over to his mate.

Standing in front of Edgar with his hands out, he wasn't sure where to start. His mate was so badly injured he was afraid to touch him in case he hurt him some more. But when the lingering smell of ozone hit his sensitive nostrils, he knew the electrical bands had to go. He carefully dragged a black-tipped claw down the band encircling Edgar's throat, slicing cleanly through the metal. He then made short work of the rest of the straps tying him down.

Once he was freed, Edgar yanked the last band off his head and threw himself into Jackson's arms, completely disregarding the fact he was a Dire Wolf, a creature of nightmares.

"You have no idea how happy I am to see you. Thank you for trusting me and not giving in to that crazy asshole." He squeezed Jackson around the neck, then leaned back. "I love you so much."

"I love you too." Jackson looked down at him. "I'm so proud of you. You are a worthy mate for the Dire Wolf of the Alpha line. I could not ask for a stronger or more loyal

Alpha mate to lead the pack by my side. Thank you for surviving until I could get here."

Edgar choked out a watery laugh. "Of course. I'm glad I survived too."

Jackson held his mate, his heart full, his wolf howling joyfully in his head. Once he found his brother, he would have everything he wanted. He carefully placed his large hand on his mate's back, pressing him closer, giving thanks to the Goddess that they'd made it here on time to save him.

A throat cleared behind them.

They both turned to Bill.

"I don't mean to interrupt, but we're on somewhat of a schedule here."

Eric choked back a laugh.

Jackson growled at both of them.

"Or we can give you another couple of minutes. Come on, Eric. Let's take this idiot out of here. We'll be waiting outside, Alpha."

Edgar snorted his amusement into Jackson's neck. A few more minutes sounded like a great idea.

They held each other as Eric scooped up the comatose vampire and followed Bill from the room.

* * *

Bryan and his enforcers sprinted down the long hall. Two fireballs arced around the corner, heading directly at them and splashed harmlessly against their protective barrier. Bryan skidded to a stop as Ruth and Zachary stepped into view.

"Galway, you're becoming quite the nuisance these days," Zachary said.

"I do my best."

"I would not be too confident," Ruth said, her ancient eyes cold. "You are here only because we chose to let you live."

Bryan tilted his head. "Really? I kind of remember you being completely at our mercy until my mother got you free."

Ruth's lips tightened.

"As lovely as it's been chatting with you, Galway, we have places to go," Zachary said. "Come on, Ruth, it's time for us to leave."

"You two are going anywhere." Bryan raised his hand, but before he could release his spell, Zachary laughed.

"Wrong again, Galway." Zachary made a gesture, filling the hall with smoke. When the air cleared, Zachary and Ruth were gone.

"Damn it." Bryan kicked the wall.

"Sir, please don't light me on fire for saying this, but maybe next time do more attacking and less talking."

Bryan nodded at Stefan. "You're absolutely right. I shouldn't have let them distract me." He looked down the empty hallway. "They're pretty ole. Let's see if we can catch them."

Grinning at each other, they took off down the hall.

They were sprinting down the hall after Zachary and Ruth, who were proving to be most elusive, when Elder Olivia walked out of a room ahead of them, blood running in streaks down her chin and dripping off her hands.

"What is all this racket? Stop it at once. Hey. How did you get in here?" Her hands came up.

Learning from his last encounter, Bryan reacted immediately, letting go with a whip of lightning before she could finish her gesture. It struck Olivia's torso, cleaving her in half. Bryan froze, his eyes wide in shock as he exchanged a look with Stefan. "Uhm, that shouldn't have happened. I thought she'd be shielded."

Stefan stared down at her body. "At least this one won't be able to run away."

Gagging pulled their attention to Drew, who was backing out of the room the Elder had come from, his face completely drained of color.

Bryan started forward to check out what was in there when Drew blocked his path, shaking his head.

"No, sir. You don't want to see what's inside. Just know that you did the world a favor in killing that woman." When Bryan went to step around him, the vampire pulled the door closed. "Please don't. Just seal the door so nobody else can get in."

Bryan gave him a long look, which the vampire returned, unblinking. "Trust me on this."

Nodding his agreement, Bryan waited until Drew moved out of the way, then used his magic to melt the door and surrounding wall into a flat impenetrable surface.

"Thank you, sir."

"No problem. Let's find the others and end this."

"Yes, sir."

Stepping over Olivia's body, Bryan headed down the corridor, the vampires falling in behind.

* * *

Jamie gave a sigh of relief as he neared the bunker. It had taken ages to catch up to the others. After Roman and the rest of the team had left the airport, he'd waited until the coast was clear before he snuck off the plane. As Edgar's assistant. he should have been included in the group rescuing him. Knowing Roman would have disagreed, Jamie decided it would be better to ask for forgiveness later when Edgar was safely back home.

Catching a glimpse of movement from the corner of his eye, Jamie dropped to the ground. Poking his head up, he saw a vampire sentry looking in the other direction. He quickly scooted behind some bushes. Crouching, he looked through the branches, studying the entrance to the bunker and he tried to determine the best way to get past the guards.

An arm wrapped around his neck.

"Well, well, well. Who do we have here? It looks like a lost little vampire."

"Carlos?" Jamie asked, voice quavering.

"I think I'll take you with me. You'll come in handy to keep Roman off my back."

Jamie felt a prick in his arm, then the world turned dark.

* * *

"Who's that you're holding?"

Turning, Eric saw Bryan and his vampire escort walking up the hall toward him and Bill.

"This is Edgar's uncle."

"You found Edgar?"

Eric nodded and pointed to the room behind him. "The Alpha's with him right now. They needed a few minutes to reconnect."

"I'm sure they did. Has anybody seen Roman and Lysander?"

"We're right here, big brother. Hey, who's that?"

"Armand." Roman hissed when he saw Eric's captive. "Why is he still alive?"

"Whoa, Roman. Who is this guy?" Lysander blocked Roman when he reached for Eric's captive with his claws extended.

Jackson and Edgar stepped out of the room with Jackson noticeably supporting most of his weight.

"That's my uncle, Armand." He looked at Roman. "Do you mind if I tell them?"

"It is your story as well."

"Okay." Edgar turned to Lysander. "When I told you what happened to King Nico, I didn't tell you this part of the story. Armand's sister, my aunt, was the vampire responsible for killing King Nico's mate."

"She was? His sister? Why is he still alive?"

Bryan snorted. "You're sounding more like your mate every day."

The vampires' muffled chuckles filled the area.

"Laugh all you want. I want to know why we're keeping him and not sending him to join his sister?"

Edgar grinned. "Because he was very adamant about wanting to know what we did with his vampires. I thought it would be fitting to show him personally."

"Ahh. And by show him, you mean lock him up and throw away the key."

"Exactly."

"It will be as you wish, Edgar," Roman said. "If you could grant me one small favor, I would like to be the one to advise your grandmother of Armand's fate."

Edgar snickered, "Of course, Prince. I'm sure she'll be happy to hear from you."

"Undoubtedly."

All of a sudden, Lysander started to laugh. "I can't believe you hesitated to mate with Jackson over these people. What were you thinking, Edgar?"

"To be honest, Consort. I'm not really sure."

"I'm glad you decided to choose me." Jackson leaned down and kissed him. "If this is an example of your family, you're better off without them."

"Very true." Edgar leaned into Jackson. "Can we go now?"

Lysander nodded. "Unless any of you've seen Carlos. He managed to get away from us."

"Ruth and Zachary got away from us as well. I checked in with the vampires stationed around the building but they didn't see them leave."

"Did anybody check for secret underground passages?" Edgar asked.

Everyone froze, eyes wide. They looked at each other before turning to Jackson, who shrugged. "If you think about it, this whole place is an underground passage. There may have been other tunnels that weren't noted on the blueprint but it's hard to know for sure. Those kinds of things are always added later."

Bryan smacked his forehead. "I can't believe this?" He turned to Lysander, pointing his finger. "Next time, that is the first thing we check. They continue to do this to us and we keep letting them get away with it."

"You know it, big brother. Now what?" Lysander looked around for options.

"I think we should blow the place up to keep it out of their hands, Consort," Eric piped up, adjusting Armand's body on his shoulder.

"But what if there's information in here that could help us stop them?" Bryan asked.

"It might not be worth the risk," Edgar said. "Anything that could help up will also help the Elders. We can't take the chance of giving them access to it."

"Edgar's correct. We also don't want some innocent stumbling on anything that could harm them." Bill waved his hand around him. "This place is a warren of tunnels and secret passages. Anything you could imagine might be hidden in here."

"You have no idea," whispered one of the vampires.

Lysander nodded. "All valid points. Edgar's given us enough information to work with anyway. Besides, this place gives me the chills. I say we blow it sky high."

Bryan laughed. "You would, baby brother. That's your go-to these days."

Lysander blew on his fingers then brushed his nails over his chest. "When you have a talent, you need to play to your strengths."

Everyone broke into laughter, their happiness a punctuation mark to their successful mission.

Jackson smiled. He was sure going to miss these guys when he went back to Denver. Holding Edgar tight to him, he headed for the nearest exit. It was time to go home.

* * *

After an hour of walking, Charlotte and Jillian were finally nearing the end of the hidden passageway. It had been a close call when her sons had attacked the facility, but she'd managed to get out of the central complex with Jillian before they'd been spotted. Charlotte had kept a close eye on her as they made their escape. Jillian readily agreed to join with her and break from the Elders. Too readily, truth be told. She'd have to find out what part the girl was playing and turn the game around on them.

Charlotte quickened her pace when the exit came in sight.

Something shifting in the shadows was her only warning before Peter stepped into the middle of the passage, blocking their way out. "Going somewhere, ladies?"

Red flashed in his eyes, chilling Charlotte to her core.

Chapter Eighteen

Living at the Denver pack…

Mary stopped next to the couch. "Are you sure I can't get you anything, Alpha Mate?"

"I'm fine, Mary. Thank you."

Looking him over as though verifying the truth in his words, she finally nodded and continued to the kitchen. Edgar bit back his groan as he leaned his head back. The constant worrying over him was more tiresome than the healing had been.

"Have you fed enough, Edgar?" Jackson's voice asked from behind him as hands landed on his shoulders

"I'm fine."

"Are you sure? It's only been a few days."

"Jackson, I was fine the day after you rescued me. You need to stop worrying. It's kind of driving me crazy."

Jackson sighed, flopping down on the couch beside Edgar. "I know it is. But I can't seem to help myself. The memory of you strapped to that chair is stuck in my mind."

"You can't keep carrying it with you or soon it will be the only thing you think about when you see me." Edgar grabbed his hand, holding tight. "Do you know what I remember the most about that time?"

Jackson shook his head. "I can only imagine the nightmares you must be having."

"That's just it. I'm not."

"I don't understand. That whole thing with Armand must have been terrifying for you."

"It was. But Jackson," Edgar smiled at his mate, "my strongest memory of that day is how my mate stood up for me. Even though it went against every Alpha and mating instinct you have, you were prepared to let me be tortured so that everything I'd gone through up to that point wouldn't have been in vain."

"Which sounds really stupid when you put it like that."

Edgar snorted. "It kind of was. But my point is, that's what I remember. I remember you showing how much you respected and loved me. That's the moment I realized how much I loved you too." He brought Jackson's hand to his lips and kissed his knuckles. "That's the only memory I'm carrying from that day and the only memory I want you to carry."

"Edgar," Jackson whispered. "Your strength humbles me."

"Your belief in me allowed me to believe in myself. It gave me the strength to survive. I want you to promise you'll remember that moment, when we stood up for each other, and let the other memories die."

"I'll try. I promise I will. But it won't be today."

Edgar chuckled. "I know. But one day you'll only remember how we stood united." He dropped Jackson's hand, turning to face him, with his bent knee pressing into Jackson's hip. "But now that we've got that covered, what's really bothering you?"

Jackson's eyes went wide. "How did you know?"

"Because you're my mate. I can feel it in here." Edgar rested a hand over his heart.

Jackson shook his head. "I should have known I couldn't hide it from you."

Edgar waited expectantly.

Jackson sighed. "You know I have to stay with the pack."

"I do."

"And I need you to stay too. My wolf and I can't survive without our mate."

"I know that too." Edgar frowned, not sure what the problem was. Hadn't they already talked about this?

"But you need your coven and your pretty suits too and I know you want to look after Roman."

Oh. Now he understood where this was going. Edgar covered Jackson's mouth with his hand. "I have an idea of what we can do."

Jackson blew out a huge breath, misting Edgar's palm. He chuckled, pulling his hand away and wiping it off.

"That's good. Because I don't know how to blend our separate lives."

"Actually, that's kind of my idea."

Jackson frowned. "I don't understand."

Edgar climbed over Jackson's lap, straddling him. It worked for the Consort, so he was willing to give it a try. "Before I tell you, I need to know a couple of things. At what age do wolf pups have their first shift?"

Jackson just looked at him.

"Jackson, how old?"

"Sorry, but why are you sitting on me?"

"Because you're my mate and I want your undivided attention."

"I don't feel like talking when you're sitting on me. You're confusing my brain."

Edgar snickered. "I don't think it's your brain that's confused. Let's finish our conversation, then we can go unconfuse you."

Jackson grinned. "Deal."

Edgar squinted, realizing he'd just been played. Damn Alpha.

Snorting, Jackson said, "Pups usually mature anywhere between six and nine years old."

"Do you have special wolf training then or does it start earlier?"

"Special wolf training?"

"Yes, like how to catch rabbits and stuff."

Jackson laughed. "The wolf knows what to do when it comes to hunting. Part of a pup's play is practicing his stalking skills, but there's no special training for that. Any training is mostly for the human side. It's what any typical child would learn, reading, writing, pack laws, stuff like that."

"Okay. Good. Here's what I'm thinking. As long as the Elders are alive, all of us are at risk, especially the innocents."

"Like Nico."

Edgar nodded. "Yes. Exactly like Nico. I think it would be safest for him to stay with the Consort and Roman, protected in the mansion until the Elders have been dealt with."

"But that could take years."

"I know. But since his first shift won't happen for a few years, we have time."

"But I want him to be with me."

"I understand that. But Nico's safety had to come first and right now, he's safer with Roman and the Consort."

"But…you're right."

Edgar's heart broke seeing Jackson's shoulders slump.

He draped his arms over Jackson's shoulders, pressing their foreheads together. Taking a deep breath, he said, "And I still want to work for Roman."

"But, you said—"

"Don't get upset yet. Most of my work can be done remotely. I can set things up to work from here easily."

Jackson frowned. "Would you be happy doing that?"

"I'd be with you, so yes. But I was thinking we could time-share."

"You just lost me again."

Edgar sat up straight again. "Here's what I'm thinking. What if we spent three months here, letting you do Alpha things, then we could spend the next three months at the mansion? That lets me be with the coven and do the work I can't do from here. You'll get the chance to be with your son, and show him who his daddy is."

Jackson didn't say anything for a long time. Long enough that Edgar's heart started to sink. He'd been so sure this was a good plan. But perhaps Jackson didn't want to spend that much time with the coven. It hurt to think that, but what else could it be? Edgar was surprised when Jackson started grinning.

"I think I like being called daddy."

"What?" Edgar raised his voice. "That's what you were thinking about?"

"Of course. What else would it be? That's a great plan. You always have the best ideas. I just never thought about being a dad before. I knew I had a son, but being daddy is different somehow."

Edgar just stared at him, shocked by his easy acceptance. He threw his arms around Jackson's neck again, squeezing tight. "I love you so damn much."

"Enough for this conversation to be over?"

Edgar snickered. "Yes. Enough for this conversation to be over."

"Excellent." Jackson stood up, easily lifting Edgar's weight. "We've talked. Now it's my turn."

"Alpha Jackson, Alpha Jackson. Come quick." Mary rushed into the room, looking flustered. Ted followed right behind her. Even he looked more animated than usual.

Edgar exchanged looks with Jackson, who set him down on his feet, before following Mary out the front door. Running after him, Edgar crashed into his back when Jackson stopped dead.

"Clint," Jackson whispered, his body starting to shake.

Edgar peeked around him. He saw an older and rougher example of his Jackson. With him were four other men, all looking quite shaggy, like they'd been living in the woods.

"Clint," Jackson yelled, running for the man. Jumping into the air, he tackled his brother to the ground, both of them laughing as they wrestled and rolled around in the dirt.

"Oh," said Mary, tears in her voice. "It's so good to see those boys together again."

Edgar couldn't agree more.

"Mary." One of the men called hoarsely.

"Simon? Is that really you?"

"Don't I deserve a hug, little sister?"

"Simon," Mary yelled, running and jumping into the man's arms. He laughed, spinning her around and around.

Edgar smiled. Yes, it was good to see all of them back together again.

* * *

Back at the Galway mansion…

"I think that's a wonderful idea, splitting your time evenly between pack and coven." Roman thought for a moment, then said, "Jackson, with your brother back, the Denver pack now has an Alpha. Perhaps you and Edgar should spend your time visiting all the packs. After the last year, they would benefit from having someone checking on them, offering guidance, and making sure whoever is in charge is an Alpha who will properly care for their pack."

"Since I come from the Alpha line, that's already a part of my responsibilities. Clint has been doing most of it so far, but it's time for me to step up now that I'm not in the military anymore."

Edgar spoke up. "There might be another problem. Jackson also needs to look after the Dallas pack. They've been without an Alpha for too long already."

"How would the packs take to having a roving Alpha? There are not enough Alphas to go around for every pack to have their own. And I don't imagine the shifters want to give up their territories to join with another."

"No. The packs will want to stay in their own territories," Jackson said.

"Then I see no other option than for you to cover as Alpha for all the packs that do not have one. It will take years before everything is back on track. In the meantime, the hardest hit pack will require a great deal of assistance to recover from the Council's attempted annihilation of the shifter communities."

"We need to stop referring to them as the Council."

Roman looked down at his mate. "What was that, beloved?"

"They are not the Council. They are evil magic users who are trying to destroy the paranormal world. They are lawbreakers who will be executed when we finally catch up with them. We cannot keep calling them the Council."

Bryan snorted and walked over from the window where he'd been standing. "You sound like you're putting yourself in charge. You can't just do that."

Lysander looked at him, completely serious. "Why not? The current Council is abolished. If that's the case, we need to stop referring to them as the Council and set up a new Council. And we need to do it soon. There is a lot of damage to repair and the Elders are still moving forward with their plans. We need to make sure the paranormal communities are united if we're going to have any hope of defeating them."

Bryan nodded slowly. "You're absolutely right. What are you thinking?"

"The new Council needs to have representation from all paranormal groups, just like you told Ruth. I think we should have two from each group, with everyone having an equal voice in making decisions." He tapped his lip, humming. "In fact, it should have a new name too, so everyone will be able to tell the difference."

"How do we determine who is on this new Council? Do we put it to a vote?"

Lysander shook his head. "No. That would take too long. We need to get the Council put in place right now."

"So, what? You're putting yourself in charge, just like that?"

"Yes. As well as you, Roman, and Jackson."

"What?" Bryan exclaimed, throwing his hands in the air. "You can't just do that."

"Beloved, you cannot be serious."

Lysander looked at Jackson when he didn't say anything. Jackson shrugged. "It makes sense to me."

Bryan turned to him. "It does? We can't appoint ourselves to be in charge and expect everyone else to follow along."

"I don't see why not," Jackson said. "Who else could do it? We are the strongest among our kind. Our motives are pure. We only want what's in the best interests of everyone. We're also the only ones who know what the Elders are doing and are strong enough to stand up to them." He held out his hands, indicating everyone. "We're already doing the job. Especially if I follow Roman's suggestion and begin overseeing the packs. My having a place on the new Council would be of immediate benefit to the packs harmed the most."

Bryan sat down beside Jackson with a thump. "I didn't want to be in charge. Don't get me wrong. I wanted to take my place on the old Council, as Father's spot was rightfully mine, but I didn't want this."

"That's why you need to let me do your thinking for you, big brother." Lysander laughed at his scowling face. "Who better, Bryan, than someone who doesn't want to take over the world? None of us want power, we only want what's best for everyone. We have no choice but to become the new Council. In fact, we should call ourselves the Paranormal Council, since all three groups will be represented?"

"But the old Council was called the Council. Won't that confuse everyone?"

"Maybe in the beginning. But the previous Council was made up of only magic users, which is probably how the power corruption started. The Paranormal Council will be equally balanced between all three groups, so the name should signify that."

"Okay. I can see the logic. You and I represent the magic users. Roman, the vampires. Who would be the second vampire? Max?"

"No, I do not think he would be the best choice," Roman said. "It should be someone who is a respected coven leader. I could talk to Marcus about it. He might be willing to join us."

Bryan nodded. "That's a good suggestion. He'd fit in well with us." He turned to Jackson. "What about the shifters? Do you want to ask your brother?"

"No." Jackson shook his head. "He needs to focus on the Denver pack and being a father and mate first. I don't know who should fill the other shifter position, but it's not something that needs to be decided at this moment."

Lysander clapped his hands. "Okay, good. Then it's agreed. There's only one thing left to work out."

Roman smiled at his mate. "What is next in your plan of world domination, beloved?"

Lysander snorted. "I was thinking more about planning Nico's future."

"Ah, yes." Roman looked hard at Jackson. "I hope you understand that Nico will have four parents, all of us with equal rights."

Edgar squeaked, "Four?"

Jackson looked at him, his brow furrowed. "Of course, it's four. Don't you want to be his father?"

Edgar looked over at the baby, sleeping soundly in the crib by Roman's desk, with Jinx standing guard. He'd never even considered being a father. But now that the idea had been suggested, he wanted that. Badly.

"Edgar, don't you want our son?" Jackson asked him, worry in his voice.

He turned to Jackson, tears in his eyes. "I do. You have no idea how much."

Jackson pulled him into a tight hug. "You scared me for a moment there. I thought you didn't want him."

"I'm sorry. I just never thought of it before. But I do want him. I want both of you and any of the pups who want to stay with us. And all the Omegas we find. I want them all, Jackson. We can bring them all home and keep them safe."

Lysander wiped a tear from under his eye. "Look, Roman, our little vampire is all grown up."

Edgar flipped him the bird. The Consort laughed.

Bryan whistled. "I'm impressed, Edgar. You're going to make a fine Alpha Mate. Nico is a very lucky boy to have so many strong role models in his life."

"He is," Jackson said. "I'm very pleased to be raising him with such a strong Alpha Mate." He pressed a kiss to Edgar's head.

Edgar flushed, all this praise something he wasn't used to. He cleared his throat, "So if that's everything—"

"Prince, you need to see this." Max rushed into the room, a tablet in his hand.

Damn it, Edgar thought. They'd been so close to a happy ending.

"What is it, Max?"

"The security team at the airport noticed something peculiar. It's taken a couple days to obtain all of the video recordings and splice them together."

Lysander snorted. "By obtain, I assume you mean hack."

"Precisely." Max started the video. "Watch."

They all crowded around the desk, eyes on the small screen. At first, there wasn't anything to see other than their plane sitting on the Denver airfield. Then the video showed the rescue team disembarking, getting into the waiting vehicles, and driving away. After that, the video just showed the airplane, with no further activity.

"Max, what are we looking at?" Roman asked.

"Just keep watching."

A few minutes later, the passenger exit door opened and Jamie snuck down the stairs and walked away. A new video feed showed him walking, then running down a service road.

Edgar began to get a really bad feeling.

Several more video clips showed Jamie running until he reached the bunker where Edgar had been held captive. They saw Jamie suddenly drop, then crawl over to crouch behind a bush, not realizing he was surrounded. Horrified, they watched as he was grabbed and taken away by Carlos and his vampires. The video stopped.

"Holy crap. We have to save him." Lysander cried, turning to his mate. "Roman, we can't let him stay there. You know what Carlos will do to him."

"I am quite familiar with how Carlos treats his captives. We will find him, beloved. And this time, Carlos will die."

"I'm sorry, but I can't allow that to happen."

Everyone swung around to stare at the man who walked boldly into Roman's office.

"Who are you?" Bryan shouted. "Better yet, how did you get in here? The entire property is shielded."

The man smirked at Bryan as he continued over to Roman's desk. Once there, he leaned his hip against it and crossed his arms over his chest.

Jinx jumped down from Nico's crib and made a beeline for the man, weaving in and out of his legs, his purrs loud enough to wake the dead.

Lysander looked over at a grunt from Roman, who was watching the cat with the most irritated look he'd ever soon on the vampire. He started laughing before he choked on a breath, eyes widening in realization.

"Don't ignore me. Answer my question. How did you get in here?" Bryan got right up in the stranger's face. The man smiled at Bryan, still not saying a word, before bending over and picking up Jinx, who settled in his arms like he never wanted to leave.

"Bryan, stop for a minute. Look at him."

"I am looking at him. Soon I'll be looking at his back when I kick him off the estate."

"No. Look at him with your magic. Does he seem familiar to you?"

Lysander could tell the moment Bryan figured it out. "Holy shit. You're a dragon. That's how you got past the boundary."

"Yes. Gideon Carmichael, III, from New York. Red dragon from Clan Taren."

"I think our mother has your mating talisman," Lysander said.

"I believe so. I followed its signature but lost track of it in Denver."

Roman strode over to the man, his status as the Vampire Prince clearly evident in his regal bearing. Stopping in front of Gideon, he frowned at the purring cat before looking at the dragon, a considering look in his eye. "It is a pleasure to meet you, Gideon. Prince Roman Greystone."

"A pleasure to meet you as well, Prince. It's unfortunate it can't be under better circumstances."

"Indeed. About that. I'm not sure I understand your concerns regarding our rescue of young Jamie."

Gideon looked him dead in the eye, any signs of civility completely wiped from his face. "The vampire you want to kill. Carlos. I will not allow you to do that. He's my fated mate."

Sheri Eleese

Epilogue

This was the final step. The last piece. Then he'd have closure for the horrors he'd undergone and could put it away. Nodding to his escort to stay behind, Edgar continued down the row to the last cell. Once there, he grabbed hold of the bars, standing silently for a moment before speaking.

"Hello, Uncle."

"Come to gloat, have you then?"

Edgar looked over the sorry excuse for a vampire his uncle had become. Gone was the powerful tyrant, who'd taken such pleasure in having Edgar under his control. Now, such a short time after his capture, he cowered in the corner of his cell, his body frail and withered, hissing and flashing his teeth at the guards when they brought him his daily serving of blood.

"No, I didn't come here to gloat. I came to say goodbye."

"Why goodbye? Are you going somewhere?"

"No," Edgar said sadly, "you are."

"I am? Are you sending me home?"

"No. Mother and Grandmother want nothing to do with you."

"What? Why not?"

Edgar looked at him, pity in his eyes. "Because you failed. If you'd succeeded, they may have forgiven you for consorting with magic users. You know what they're like. But you didn't succeed, so you've been banished."

"No. They can't do that to me."

"Don't worry, Uncle. You won't have to suffer for long."

Armand made his way slowly over to the bars, gripping them weakly. "What are you saying?"

"The Elders did something to you. You've been infected with their latest spell and we don't know how to counteract it. You're dying and there's nothing we can do to save you."

"No," Armand whispered. "You're lying. Ruth said I was the Chosen One."

Edgar nodded, speaking softly. "You were. You were their chosen test subject. They learned everything they needed from you." Edgar stepped back from the bars. "You are only the first. I pray to the Goddess every day that you'll be the last, but I fear my prayers will go unanswered. Goodbye, Uncle." Edgar turned and walked back down the long hallway, a lone tear trickling down his face. His heart breaking for the things he couldn't change and for the lives he knew would soon be lost.

Armand's weak cries faded in the distance.

To be continued in Treasured Bonds….

If you enjoyed this book, it would be awesome if you could take a minute and leave a review on Goodreads or your place of purchase. Reviews really do help authors attract new readers.

Thank you for your support.

About the Author

Sheri is an MM Romance writer who believes that love should have no boundaries, in happily-ever-afters, that dragons are real…oh, and bacon; there's always room for bacon.

Her stories are romance with low angst, high action, fade to black or minimal sex, and characters who know how to kick butt.

You can visit her website @ https://www.sherieleese.com

Friend her on Facebook: sherieleesewrites

Or you can email her directly at sheri.eleese@shaw.ca

288

Other Books by This Author

Please visit your favorite ebook retailer to discover other books by Sheri Eleese:

Reforming the Paranormal Council:

Forbidden Bonds - Book One
Feral Bonds - Book Two
A Paranormal Family Christmas - Book 2.5
Treasured Bonds - Book Three
Hidden Bonds - Book Four
Fearless Bonds - Book 4.5

Paranormal Council – Legacy

A Dragon's Healing – Book One
A Dragon's Promise – Book Two
A Dragon's Faith – Book Three...*coming soon.*

9 781777 321734